Her Heart, His Home

Home to Collingsworth
Book 5

by

Kimberly Rae Jordan

THREE**STRAND**
P R E S S

A CORD OF THREE STRANDS IS NOT EASILY BROKEN.

A man, a woman & their God.
Three Strand Press publishes Christian Romance stories
that intertwine love, faith and family.
Always clean. Always heartwarming. Always uplifting.

✌ Prologue ✌

AMELIA Moyer knocked lightly on the door of her soon-to-be sister-in-law's room. As she waited for Cami to answer, she glanced up and down the deserted hallway of the second floor of Collingsworth Manor. She loved this place as much now as she had on her first visit over a year ago. And it went without saying how much she loved the Collingsworth family as well.

In the year since she'd last seen them, there had been a few changes to the family, the biggest one being the newest baby. Since she loved children, Amy held Violet's baby, Danielle, every chance she got. Benjamin, however, was a different story. Laurel and Matt's little guy was constantly on the move. Amelia didn't get much chance to hold him, and Rose was usually the one chasing him around anyway. It didn't matter though, as long as there were kids around, Amy was happy. As the baby of her family, she hadn't had any younger siblings to help her mom with, but she happily volunteered to work in the church nursery and babysat whenever she could.

They'd been at the manor for almost a week now, and she had loved every minute of it. Well, except for the cold. Being the middle of February in northern Minnesota, there was still snow on the ground and frosty temperatures. She kind of wished Cami and Josh had waited to get married when it was warmer, but she also found it super romantic that they were tying the knot on Valentine's Day, not even two months after they got engaged.

"Hey, Amy," Cami said when she answered the door. "What's up?"

"Can I come in?"

"Sure." Cami stepped back with a smile. "Something on your mind?"

She led the way to the window seat where it was apparent the bride-to-be had been sitting when Amy had knocked. Cami settled on one side, tucking her legs up under her on the cushioned seat. Amy mirrored her position as she sat down.

"Are you excited?" Amy asked, though she couldn't understand how anyone could possibly *not* be excited about their wedding.

Cami smiled. "Yes, I am."

"Did you always dream about having a wedding like this?"

"No," Cami said. "To be honest, I never dreamed of getting married at all."

"Really?" Amy could hardly believe that. For the past year, she'd spent even more time than ever dreaming about the wedding she hoped to have one day.

"I didn't have any good examples of marriage growing up, so I wasn't all that keen to try it out for myself."

Amy tilted her head. "But Josh changed your mind?"

Cami's gaze softened, and a dreamy smile curved her lips. "Yes, he certainly did."

"I'm so excited to have you as my sister-in-law." Amy could hardly keep from bouncing up and down. "And the dress you chose for me is so beautiful."

"I knew you'd like it. I think the color and style suit you perfectly."

Amy looked out the window to the darkness beyond. She wanted to ask Cami something important, but was worried how she might react. She looked back at the pretty blonde woman and blurted out, "Can you keep a secret?"

Cami arched a brow. "A secret? Well, as long as I'm not going to get in trouble for keeping it, I think I can."

Amy bit her lip and clasped her hands together. She'd kept everything inside since the last time she'd been at Collingsworth, afraid if she said anything, it would be ruined. "Is Will coming for your wedding?"

"Will? " Cami asked. "As in my brother, Will?"

Amy nodded. "He hasn't arrived yet. I just wondered if you knew if he was planning to be here tomorrow."

"Last I heard that was the plan. I'm not sure what the delay is though." Cami paused then said, "Why do you want to know?"

Amy was reluctant to answer. She didn't want Cami to laugh at her because, even at sixteen, she knew how crazy what she felt would sound to others. She looked away.

"Hey," Cami said.

Amy felt a touch on her knee and looked down to see Cami's hand with its sparkling diamond resting there.

"Talk to me. What's going on in that head of yours?"

Sighing, Amy met Cami's gaze again. "I think Will is the man God wants me to marry."

Cami's eyes widened. "Um. Okay... Why do you think that?"

Amy shrugged. How did she put into words the strong feeling she'd had the first time she'd met Will Collingsworth? How did she explain that when she looked at him, she saw a future with him in it? "It's just how I...feel. Ever since I met him that Christmas we all came here, I've just felt like he is the one God has for me."

"I'm sorry, but I don't understand that," Cami said, her tone gentle. "I didn't even feel confident that Josh was the one God had for me until we'd known each other quite a while. But of course, that doesn't mean your feelings aren't real." She paused. "You do realize, right, that Will is quite a few years older than you?"

Amy plucked at the fabric of her leggings. "Yes, but not too many. I know it wouldn't work now, because I'm not old enough, but I believe God will keep him for me."

"Have you told anyone else about your feelings?"

Amy shook her head vigorously. "My parents have always told us to pray for the person God might have us marry, but I don't think they'd quite understand this." She looked at Cami again, needing her to understand. "He's everything I prayed that my husband would be. And I know I'm young. I know it doesn't make sense."

"So you love Will?" Cami asked. "Even though you hardly know him?"

Put that way, it sounded a little ridiculous even to Amy. "Don't you believe in love at first sight?"

Cami gave a little laugh. "Sweetie, until I went through everything with Josh, I didn't believe in love at all. Have you prayed about it?"

"Every day. Every single day," Amy told her. "I pray for Will, and I pray that if it's not God's will that He would take away what I feel for him."

"You know more about praying than I do," Cami said. "Who am I to argue with God? If He's given you this love for Will, there must be a reason."

"You won't tell anyone, will you?" Amy asked.

Cami shook her head. "It will stay between us. And I'll pray for each of you, too. I want everyone to be as happy as Josh and I are."

Amy leaned forward and wrapped her arms around Cami. "Thank you." As she settled back on the seat, she said, "I hope Will comes to love me as much as Josh loves you."

"I am very blessed," Cami agreed. "And I love Josh more than I ever thought I could love another person."

"I can hardly wait for tomorrow," Amy said with a shiver of excitement. She slid off the window seat. "I'll let you get some sleep. If you can. I'm not sure I'll be able to."

Cami stood and hugged her tightly. "See you in the morning, sweetie."

Amy left Cami's room with even more excitement zipping through her body than earlier. Will was going to be there tomorrow. She could hardly wait. It felt good to share how she felt with someone else, even though she knew Cami probably dismissed her feelings as teenage puppy love. She just knew that somehow, some way, she and Will were going to be together in the future.

The next evening Amy stood in the bridal room with Cami and Lily. The other Collingsworth sisters had left a couple of minutes earlier, so it was just the two of them. Amy had been thrilled when Cami had asked her to be her maid of honor. She'd been worried about what Cami's sisters would think, but they had assured her they were fine with her standing up with Cami as maid of honor. Lily was the other bridesmaid, while Colin was a groomsman. Lance was Josh's best man. It was going to be a small intimate wedding with only a handful of non-family members present. Unfortunately, last she'd heard, the one person Amy wanted to be there still hadn't arrived.

Amy looked over to where Cami stood, her bouquet clutched in one hand. She wore a mermaid style dress that skimmed her curves without being too tight and had a softly flared skirt. The sweetheart neckline framed the beautiful necklace Josh had given Cami the night before, and the elbow length lace sleeves were perfect for their winter wedding. Amy thought Cami looked beautiful in her dress, but she also felt beautiful in her bridesmaid dress.

She turned to look at herself in the full-length mirror. The dusty rose color Cami had chosen suited her as did the fit of it. Chiffon fabric flowed from an empire waist band in a long handkerchief-style skirt. The layers were different lengths and swirled as she walked. The bodice was gathered from the empire waist to a band halter-style neckline that left her shoulders bare and had tiny sparkles of bling along it. The dress wasn't bare in the back like a regular halter, which was the only reason her mom had let her wear it.

Amy didn't argue much with her mom, but she would have fought over the right to wear this dress if she'd said no. Her hair hung in long loose waves down her back, and her shoes were silver strappy heels that added a few inches to her height. She felt like a fairy princess, and she hoped that Will thought she was pretty when he saw her.

There was a quick knock on the door before it opened to reveal Lance standing there. "Ready to go?"

Because Cami didn't have a father or mother to walk her down the aisle, she'd asked Lance to do fill in before he joined Will at the front as his best man. Amy wondered if any of the Collingsworth siblings had ever tried to find their biological fathers. She couldn't imagine getting married without her dad there.

"I'm as ready as I'll ever be," Cami said. "Is Will here?"

Cami didn't look at her, but Amy was pretty sure that she asked the question for her benefit.

"Sorry. Haven't seen him yet." Lance's brow furrowed. "Did you want to wait for him?"

"Nope." Cami grinned. "I have a man to marry. I'm sure he'll understand."

"No doubt." Lance stuck his elbow out. "Let's get you hitched."

Amy followed Lily out the door, a bit disappointed that

Will wasn't there yet, but still very excited for her brother and Cami. As she walked down the aisle, she smiled at her brothers. Colin grinned in return, but Josh's expression was tight with nerves, and he barely looked at her, his gaze going to the rear of the chapel. Her heart swelled with the thought of one day having a man—Will, hopefully—be so eager for her appearance that he had eyes for no one else. Once she'd taken her place on the small stage with Lily, the back doors opened again, and Lance and Cami appeared.

As the two slowly walked toward them, Amy looked at Josh and saw that the tense nervousness had left his face. His gaze was glued on his bride as she made her way to him, and Amy could see the love radiating between them. Oh, how anxious she was for the day she would be in Cami's position on her way to Will. Just before Cami reached the front, Amy looked out over the people gathered there, but still didn't find the face she sought. Though it was just family and close friends, they still managed to fill over half the pews. And more than one woman was dabbing at their eyes as they watched Josh take Cami's hand.

Resolutely putting aside her thoughts about Will for the moment, Amy turned to face the pastor when Josh and Cami did. She took Cami's bouquet and held it with her own as the ceremony got underway. Amy blinked back tears when Cami and Josh sang a song they'd written together just for their wedding and then listened as they pledged their love to each other before exchanging rings.

When the pastor pronounced them husband and wife, the people clapped and cheered. Amy couldn't help grinning when her brother wrapped his arms around Cami and gave her a long kiss. Her teenage heart soaked up the romance, and she sighed in delight.

As she followed the bridal couple up the aisle to the back doors of the chapel, Amy's gaze landed on Will and her heart skipped a beat. There he stood, looking tanned and a little more buff than she remembered. However, his dark brown was still cut short, and he had a familiar broad grin on his face as he clapped. He was looking at his sister and new brother-in-law, but it wasn't until she got closer to where he stood that Amy realized he wasn't alone.

Fighting a slow-spreading sick feeling, Amy forced her gaze away from Will and kept a smile pasted on her face as they left the sanctuary. She gave Josh and Cami a big hug, congratulating them. It wasn't long before the rest of the congregation spilled into the foyer as well. Amy stepped away from the crowd and pressed back against the wall so she wasn't in the way. She tried very hard to keep a smile on her face, but as she saw Will approach Cami and Josh, it was nearly impossible.

He hugged his sister, shook hands with Josh and then slipped his arm around the young woman standing next to him. Even from this distance, Amy could see the smile on Cami's face change as Will introduced the woman to them. Amy looked away, not wanting to meet her new sister-in-law's gaze. Thankfully, Cami's nieces, Rose and Addy approached her then, and Amy bent her head to talk to the young girls.

Back at the manor, the caterer had the food all set up for the reception. It reminded Amy of the Christmas they'd spent at Collingsworth when there had been a whole bunch of people gathered for the dinner.

"Are you okay?" Cami asked as she sat down. As the maid of honor, Amy was seated beside Cami, so there had been no way to avoid her.

"I'm fine." Amy hoped the smile she gave her would back up her words.

Cami took her hand and leaned close. "Listen, sweetie, I want you to hear this from me because I have a feeling he's going to announce it soon. The woman with Will, she's not his girlfriend."

Focusing on Cami's last comment, hope flickered to life. "She's not?" Amy met Cami's gaze and saw the sadness there. *No.*

"She's his wife."

Amy felt as if all the air had been squeezed from her lungs. His wife? How was that possible? She'd been so sure that God had wanted him to marry her. She stared down at her lap where Cami's hand still gripped hers.

God, I don't understand why You let this happen, but the least You can do is help me get through this. I don't want to ruin Cami and Josh's day.

She looked up at Cami and smiled. "I'll be fine."

"We'll talk about this later. Okay?"

At that moment, Amy was reminded again why she was so glad that Cami had married her brother. She'd never been super close to her own older sister, Bethany, and she had always suspected it had to do with more than just their age gap. In Cami, she'd found the relationship she'd always wanted to have with a sister. "Don't worry about me. Just enjoy your wedding. I'm so happy for you and Josh."

Cami pulled her close for a hug and then released her. "We *will* talk later."

The evening didn't follow the normal reception traditions. It resembled a big family dinner with a few of the guests dressed more formally than the rest. There had been no tossing of the bouquet or long speeches, and the evening hadn't dragged on as the wedding couple planned to head to a cabin about an hour away for their honeymoon.

Amy pulled her jacket close as she stood on the porch of the manor with the rest of the guests and waved goodbye when her brother and Cami pulled away in Josh's truck. As she watched the red taillights disappear, Amy suddenly felt very alone. No one knew how she was feeling except for Cami. Somehow she had to make it through the next few days before she and her family left for home. She didn't know when she'd next see her brother and sister-in-law, but she hoped it wouldn't be too long.

Once back in the manor, the family crowded around Will to offer their congratulations to him and his new wife. *Delia.* That was her name. Amy allowed herself to really look at the woman for the first time. She appeared to be Asian with long, jet-black hair and large brown eyes. As she stood next to Will, Amy could see that Delia was dainty, the top of her head not even reaching Will's shoulder. She had a beautiful smile and readily shared it with those around them.

The sick feeling wouldn't be suppressed any longer as she watched them. Pressing a hand to her stomach, she tried to look away, but she couldn't. On Will's face was the same love she'd seen on Josh's not that long ago. Only it wasn't directed at her like she'd dreamed. This dainty, exotic woman was the recipient of what she had thought would be hers. And if Delia was what Will wanted in a woman, Amy realized she would never have had a chance with Will anyway, because the woman he'd chosen to love was the opposite of her in pretty much every way.

Finally able to turn away from the sight of the happy couple, Amy climbed the stairs to her room. Just for tonight she would let herself weep for the heartache of a shattered dream. But tomorrow she would pull herself back together—she had to—and guard her heart much more carefully in the future.

❧ *Chapter One* ❧

E*IGHT Years Later*

"I can't thank you enough for being willing to come help us out," Lance said as he sank down onto one of the stools next to the counter.

Amy smiled. "I'm just glad the timing worked out for me to be here."

Lance nodded, exhaustion etched on his face. No doubt the man hadn't been sleeping well since they'd gotten the news that Jessa's pregnancy was in jeopardy, and she needed to go on bed -rest.

"I know it will take a huge weight off Jessa's mind knowing you're here. Rose has been a great help, but she has a job, and Addy is travelling with some friends down to Florida for a few weeks."

"Usually I have plans to travel once school is out too, but this year I just never managed to get anything together. I think God knew I would be needed here."

"Did Rose take Julia with her?" Lance asked, referring to his and Jessa's eight-year-old daughter. The only child they'd been able to have in the nine years they'd been married.

When Cami had called Amy to ask if she'd be willing to help Jessa and Lance out, she'd explained that since Julia's birth, Jessa had suffered four miscarriages. They'd occurred at varying times during each pregnancy but had been increasingly devastating for both Jessa and Lance.

"I hope you don't think Jessa is too demanding," Lance said, rubbing a hand across his forehead. "It's just that this is the furthest she's made it in a pregnancy since Jules was born. She—we—are desperate for this one to get as close to term as we can get it. We've agreed that she will do as little as possible, and when she's moving around, someone will be with her. I realize that might seem a little extreme—"

Amy held up her hand. "I understand completely and have no problem helping with anything she needs."

"Thank you. Again." Lance pressed his hands to the counter and stood. "I'm going to run into town and do a little work at the office. I shouldn't be gone too long, but I need to catch up on a few things that got pushed to the back burner when the bed rest command was given."

"I'll give you a call if anything comes up," Amy assured him. She picked up the small walkie-talkie from the counter. "And I'll keep this with me at all times in case Jessa needs something."

Lance nodded. "Just figured it might be easier if she needed you quickly than for her to try and type out a text message or something."

"It's perfect. Now off you go." Amy made shooing motions with her hands. "I've got this under control."

As her cousin left the kitchen, Amy moved around the counter to sit on the stool he'd vacated. She opened the notebook Jessa had given her earlier with information on what needed to be done. In addition to helping with Jessa, Amy had agreed to pick up what she could of the running of the bed and breakfast side of things now that the manor had been converted from just the family home to a B&B. She really hoped that she wasn't promising more than she could deliver. There was no doubt she wanted to help them out, but Amy didn't want to cause more work for anyone because of her inability to do something that was required.

The most daunting thing on the list was just over a week away. A wedding. A couple had booked the whole manor for the wedding party and family, and they were going to use the chapel for the ceremony. Jessa had made notes that Laurel and Violet would be helping out, too, so Amy wouldn't be completely on her own. The only reason the sisters hadn't been able to help out more with Jessa was because they each had families of their own and couldn't move into the manor.

Since she'd last seen them, Laurel and Matt had added two more children to their family. Another boy and a girl, which gave them two of each. Dean and Violet's brood had only grown by one in addition to Addy and Danielle, who had been born just a couple of weeks before Will and Cami's wedding. They'd gotten their boy so had apparently decided to stop at three. Cami and Josh had two—both girls—and from what her brother had said, they were quite happy with the size of their family. Given that their career required a lot of travel, it made sense they wouldn't try for a larger family.

In a few weeks, Cami and Josh would be arriving with the girls for their annual summer Collingsworth family get-together. Amy was excited to see them since it had been Christmas when they'd last been together.

In the meantime, the most pressing thing on her agenda was figuring out what she needed to get from the store for the breakfasts for the weekend. Laurel and Violet had already volunteered to help out with suppers for the family, but the breakfasts for the guests she'd have to handle on her own. Thankfully, her mom had made sure she knew everything about running a household—including cooking. It was just that she didn't have much opportunity to practice since she still lived at home where her mom did most the cooking.

Looking up from the notebook, Amy stared out the

window above the sink. It had been just over eight years since she'd last been to Collingsworth. Since Cami and Josh made their home in Nashville, there had been no reason for Amy to return after that heartbreaking visit for their wedding. Cami was still the only one who knew what had happened during that time. She'd apologized more than once for asking Amy to return to Collingsworth when she'd called last week, but Amy hadn't even had to think twice about it. Though it had taken some time, her teenage heart had healed. She still didn't completely understand the feeling she'd had that Will Collingsworth was the man God wanted her to marry, she had put it behind her.

Of course, Will was no longer a married man. She remembered the day she'd heard the news of Delia's death. There had been no joy for her because the circumstances had been just too awful. Pregnant with their first child, she'd had an aneurism and died just a year after their marriage. They had been able to save the baby—a girl—but there had been nothing they could do for Delia. Amy couldn't even fathom how someone dealt with something like that. She knew it had been difficult for Josh when his first wife had committed suicide, but it hadn't been a huge shock as she'd tried a couple of times already. What had happened with Delia—

Amy heard the front door open and turned on her stool. Had Lance had forgotten something. A man appeared in the doorway to the kitchen. Though she barely recognized him, her heart skipped a beat. He looked nothing like the man she'd loved with her teenage heart. Short, styled hair had grown out to a scruffier length, and it looked like he hadn't shaved in a couple of days. The hard, tenseness of his face gave him a somewhat gaunt look, and there was no twinkling in his eyes or smile on his face. Even though it had been almost six years since his wife's death, he looked as haunted by it now as he must have the day it happened.

"Hi," she said, standing up from the stool.

"Hello. I'm Will Collingsworth." He stared at her for a moment. "Are you a guest here?"

Telling herself there was no reason to be disappointed he didn't recognize her, Amy shook her head. "No. I'm here to help Jessa. My name is Amy."

"We've been away, so I just heard the news. I dropped by to see if there was anything I could do." He glanced toward the hallway. "Can you wait here, Isabella? I'll just be a couple of minutes."

Amy's gaze dropped from Will to the little girl who moved to stand next to him, and she understood with shocking clarity why he still wore the haunted look all these years later. The little girl was the spitting image of her mother. It was like she had all her mother's genes and none of her father's.

Isabella looked at Amy, her big brown eyes wide.

"Is it okay if she stays here with you?" Will asked.

"Sure. I could use some company." Amy smiled at the little girl. She was rewarded with a small smile in return.

"Be good, please."

"I will."

Will rested a hand on her shoulder for a moment before disappearing up the stairs.

Amy beckoned for Isabella to come to the counter. She noticed as the little girl approached that she was dressed in the most fashionable brand name children's clothes. As a teacher, she was aware of children's fashions, and Isabella would certainly outshine most in her first grade class.

"My name is Amy," she said as Isabella climbed onto one of the stools. "Do you want a cookie or something?"

"Yes. I'd like a cookie." Isabella glanced toward where her father had gone.

"Will you get in trouble if you have one?"

She immediately shook her head. "Daddy lets me have whatever I want."

Amy tilted her head. She supposed it would make sense that Will indulged his little girl. "Well, I don't want to spoil your appetite if you're going to eat lunch soon."

"It's okay. I'll just have one. I love Aunt Jessa's cookies."

"Me, too. I had a couple last night." Amy got up and circled the counter to grab the cookie jar. She picked out two and handed one to Isabella. "I'm going to join you. Any excuse for cookies is good."

Isabella smiled and once again Amy was tossed back in time. The memory of a similar smile had plagued her for months—years—after Cami and Josh's wedding.

"What's wrong with Aunt Jessa?" Isabella asked after she took a small nibble of the cookie. "Did something happen to the baby?"

"No. The doctor just wants her to get lots more rest so the baby can finish growing. While she's getting rest, I'm going to be helping out around here."

"Who are you?" Dark eyes gazed at her curiously.

"I'm Lance's cousin. I have the summer off since I'm a teacher, so I was able to come help them out."

"You're a teacher?"

"Yep. I teach first grade. What grade are you in?"

"I just finished kindergarten."

"Cool. You'll be in grade one when school starts."

Isabella nodded. "I did so well that when I asked Daddy for a tablet, he got me one." She gestured toward the floral bag sitting next to her on the counter. "My favorite color is purple."

"I know a lot of little girls who like purple."

"Is that your favorite color, too?"

"One of them," Amy admitted. "But I also like pink and blue and green. And sometimes red." She leaned close and with a grin whispered, "I try to be fair to all the colors, so they don't feel bad. Don't want anyone to feel left out."

Isabella giggled as she lifted her cookie to take another bite.

Someone cleared their throat, and Amy turned to see Will standing in the doorway once again. His hands were on his hips, and Amy wondered if perhaps Isabella had been wrong about her dad's reaction to a cookie this close to lunch.

"Ready to go, Isabella?" he asked.

"Amy gave me a cookie," she told him as she slid off the stool. Cookie in one hand, Isabella grasped the handle of her bag and pulled it from the counter.

Amy stood up. "I hope that was okay."

"That's fine," Will said distractedly. He reached into his pocket and pulled out his wallet. "Here. This is my business card. Please call if something happens with Jessa. And if you're unable to reach Lance, don't hesitate to contact me."

"Will do." Amy took the card, hating the fact that his nearness was leaving her breathless. She was supposed to have been over him.

Will looked at her more closely. "Do I know you? I mean, have we met before?"

For a moment, Amy wasn't sure how to respond. There was a tiny part of her heart that hurt when she realized he didn't remember her. Finally, she nodded. "Josh is my brother."

Will's brows drew together for a moment before comprehension dawned on his face. "You were here for Christmas when Jessa and Lance got married."

"Yes." Amy wasn't surprised that he didn't remember her from Josh and Cami's wedding. He'd been a little distracted at the time.

"You must have been here for Cami's wedding, too," he said.

"I was her maid of honor," she replied, hoping he

wouldn't delve too deeply into that day. She didn't think it was a place he'd want to revisit either, although for obviously different reasons.

"That was eight years ago. You've changed a bit," he commented. "I guess that's why I didn't recognize you right away."

"You've changed, too," Amy replied. She was well aware that she wasn't the thin teenager she'd once been. A love of good cooking and abhorrence of exercise had led to some weight gain over the years. Having gotten to the point where her curves were a few pounds away from pushing her into the "you need to lose weight" doctor lecture zone, she was trying to be more careful about what she ate.

Will nodded and turned to Isabella. "I guess we'd better go. Thank you for watching her."

"Anytime," Amy said with a smile. "I teach first grade, so I'm used to kids her age."

"I may take you up on that. See you around." Will laid a hand on Isabella's back, and they left the kitchen.

Amy waited for the door to close before sinking back onto her stool. Well, she'd known that the meeting would come sooner or later, so it was actually a relief to have it out of the way already. And it was also a relief to see that some of the things that she'd loved about him as a teenager were gone. There seemed to be very little left of the young man she'd set her heart on. Too bad there was still something about the man that caused her heart to react. It didn't bode well for the weeks ahead.

"She was nice."

Will glanced into the rearview mirror to see Isabella in her booster seat behind him. "Amy?"

"Yes. She was nice," Isabella repeated, her dark eyes serious.

"I'm sure that's true." He flicked on the blinker and leaned forward to check for traffic before pulling from the driveway onto the highway leading to Collingsworth. "She's Uncle Josh's sister, and you think he's nice, too, right?"

"Yes. I like him. And Aunt Cami. And Grace and Jojo."

"They should all be here in a few weeks, so you'll be able to play with your cousins again."

"She said she teaches kids like me," Isabella said, apparently not ready to let go of the subject of Amy Moyer just yet. "I think I'd like her to teach me."

"Unfortunately, I don't think she teaches school here."

"Where does she teach?"

Will tried to keep his impatience at bay. Isabella had been a curious one since she'd started talking and usually it wasn't a big deal, but when he didn't know the answers, it became a little irritating. "I really don't know. Maybe Texas. I think that's where Josh's family is from."

"Why is she here?"

"She said she's here to help Aunt Jessa until she has the baby." Will hit some controls on the dashboard. "Do you want to watch a DVD?"

Even as Isabella's favorite movie began to play, Will pushed down the guilt. He knew he shouldn't just shut her down, but he was hanging on by a thread. It was getting closer to Isabella's sixth birthday. The range of emotions associated with that day overwhelmed him. How did one celebrate a birth one day and grieve a death the next? Six years had passed, and he still hadn't figured it out. Every year he had to resist the urge to leave Isabella with one of his sisters and go to a remote cabin and just sleep the day away.

And this year was worse than ever. Having just finished kindergarten, Isabella had experienced friend birthday parties for the first time and was expecting nothing less than what her friends had for their special days. Much to his dismay, the days of low-key family only parties were gone.

Remembering what Isabella had said about Amy, Will wondered if he might be able to convince her to help him out. Being a teacher, she'd probably have some good ideas of what might work for a six-year-old's birthday party. As long as it didn't take away from what Amy needed to do for Jessa, she might be willing to help him out. He'd even be willing to pay her quite handsomely for her time and effort. Jessa might even let him host the party at the manor, since their apartment wasn't exactly conducive to entertaining a group of young girls.

Feeling a little better about the prospect of Isabella's party, Will headed to the restaurant he'd promised he'd take her to for lunch. He knew they ate out far too much, but he just didn't have the interest in cooking many meals. Laurel had invited Isabella to come over for the afternoon, so once lunch was over, he'd drop her off and then go to the office for a few hours. They'd just gotten back from visiting his family in California, so he needed to put some time into the work that had piled up in his absence.

୬ൟ

"Do you need anything, Jessa?" Amy said into the walkie-talkie. "I'm bringing you a sandwich. Do you want some fruit as well?"

"Strawberries? And maybe a glass of milk."

"Sure thing. Be right up." Amy placed the sandwich on a tray and then cut up some strawberries and poured a glass of milk. She grabbed a cold water bottle as well and headed up the stairs.

Jessa was propped up against pillows in a large bed. Her red curls were gathered on top of her head, and she wore no makeup which made her look a little more pale than Amy remembered.

"Thank you," Jessa said with a smile as Amy set the bed tray over her legs. "Did you eat already?"

"Not yet," Amy told her.

"Why don't you go get your lunch and come back and eat with me? No sense each eating by ourselves."

"Sure. I'll be right back."

When she returned a few minutes later, Amy discovered that Jessa had waited for her. "Guess it's kind of quiet up here." She set her plate and glass down on the nightstand and pulled a chair closer to the bed.

"Yeah. There's only so much TV I want to watch and so much surfing I can do. Guess I'm going to catch up on all the reading I haven't had time for over the past couple of years."

"I can give you some recommendations if you'd like. I love to read and have several favorite authors." Amy took a bite of her sandwich.

"I'd like that. I'm sure that my favorites don't have enough out there that I haven't read yet to last until the baby comes."

"How are you feeling today?"

"Less stressed now that you're here." Jessa smiled at her. "I really do appreciate you dropping everything to come. I couldn't believe it when Cami said you were willing to help us out."

"Not really much to drop," Amy assured her. "It's nice to be back in Collingsworth. I've always enjoyed my visits here."

"Did you talk to Will?" Jessa asked.

"Not too much. I had a longer conversation with his daughter." Amy knew that Jessa was unaware of her teenage feelings for Will. "She's a beautiful little girl."

"Yes, she is," Jessa said. "And the spitting image of her mother."

"It's been a while since I've seen Delia, but I noticed the resemblance right away. And it seems she's got a daddy who spoils her."

"She does have that," Jessa said, but her brow furrowed. "You were able to tell that from the short time she was with you?"

Amy laughed. "Not from her behavior. I asked if her daddy would let her have one of your cookies before lunch, and she informed me that he let her have anything she wanted."

Jessa sighed. "That's how Will loves her."

"That's not too surprising, is it?" Amy was a little confused by Jessa's reaction to how Will spoiled Isabella. "She seems like a nice little girl in spite of being spoiled."

"Oh, she is, but since the day she was born, Will has seemed to struggle with how he feels about her. Showering her with gifts and anything she asks for is his way of 'loving' her."

Amy swallowed the bite of sandwich she'd taken. "I'm sure it must be difficult to deal with the birth of a baby and the death of a spouse at the same time."

"Isabella was born a month premature. For the first two weeks after she was born, Laurel, Violet, Lily and I were the ones who stayed with her in the hospital. Once Delia's funeral was over, Will disappeared for a week."

❧ Chapter Two ❧

AMY hadn't heard much about what had happened during that time. She hadn't asked, and Cami hadn't volunteered any information. The less she'd heard about Will back then, the better.

"I would happily have taken Isabella home, but in the end, Will said she was his responsibility. He was the one who had wanted to have a baby. Delia hadn't."

"Really? Why was that?" Amy felt a bit like she was opening a can of worms. What she had assumed was grief on Will's part seemed a whole lot more complex now.

"She was adopted," Jessa said. She took a bite of her sandwich before continuing. "Apparently her biological mother died giving birth to her. The couple who adopted her were missionaries in the Philippines and found her in an orphanage over there."

Amy had just assumed that Delia had been someone Will had met on one of his mission trips. Which was what had happened, she just hadn't realized that Delia had been part of an American family. "So she was scared she'd die in childbirth, too?"

Jessa nodded. "Will tried to reassure her that it was different here than it had been in the Philippines with her mom. More medical advancements and such, but right from the start Delia struggled with the pregnancy. She was sick almost from day one, and it never stopped. By the time she was seven months she had a hard time moving around because she was so tiny, and her belly was so big. She was miserable. The day Will called to tell us that Delia..." She took a deep breath and blew it out. "She'd called to tell him that she was feeling really bad and was more sick than usual. He left work to go to her, but by the time he got to their apartment, she was unconscious. She never regained consciousness after that. They kept her on life support for a couple of weeks, but then had to deliver Isabella because Delia wasn't doing well."

"I'm sorry your family had to go through that," Amy said, her appetite long gone. "I didn't know the details of what happened. Isabella seems like a remarkably well-rounded girl, everything considered."

"We try our best to shower her with the love that Will can't seem to. Sometimes I want to just slap him in order to wake him up to what he's missing. But as Isabella's gotten older and turned into the spitting image of her mother, I wonder how he can get through each day. Delia's death changed him so much."

Amy nodded. "I could tell that right away. I'd only seen him a few times, but as soon as he walked in today I saw the changes in him."

"We keep hoping that maybe some woman will come along, and he'll find love again. For Isabella's sake, as well as his own."

Amy felt a twinge of something in her heart. "It would take a special kind of woman to be able to step into his life." And she knew that woman wasn't her. She didn't know what Delia had been like personality-wise, but in appearance they couldn't have been more different. If Delia was Will's type, Amy wouldn't be in the running, even if she wanted to be.

Which she didn't.

Jessa nodded. "It seems all of us Collingsworths are destined to go into relationships with baggage. We were so happy for Will when he married Delia. Out of all of us he seemed to have had the most normal upbringing and then such a sweet relationship with Delia. Well, until she got pregnant. Then it wasn't so sweet anymore." She plucked at the fabric of the bedspread. "I have to admit, I really don't understand God's thinking with regards to Delia. Her parents lost their only daughter. Will lost his wife. Isabella lost her mother. I just don't understand."

Amy had to admit she would have struggled to understand that as well. She glanced at Jessa and saw her face looking drawn. "Are you okay?"

"Yes, I'm fine," Jessa assured her. She laid a hand on her stomach. "Baby is doing great today. Lots of movement, but no contractions."

"That's good," Amy said, hoping to steer her thoughts from the sadness of Will's life. "Do you know if you're having a boy or girl?"

"I've had so many scans it would have been difficult to not find out," Jessa said with a grin. "We've been told several times that we've got a little guy on the way."

"Really? That's terrific!" Amy set the plate with her half-eaten sandwich on the night stand. She settled back in her chair. "Maybe Cami should try one more time. She might get her boy."

Jessa nodded. "I was shocked when they said it was a boy. Lance was thrilled. He loves Jules, but I knew he wanted a son. Now if we can just get this little one to term or at least close to it."

"Well, that's what I'm here for, so be prepared for a lecture if I think you're doing too much."

"No worries there. I'm not going to do anything I don't absolutely have to. Part of me feels this is my last chance. I'm almost forty, so I'm not getting any younger. Already they labelled me as advanced maternal age." Jessa tilted her head. "Do you have a boyfriend?"

Though the change of subject took her off-guard, Amy said, "Nope. I've dated a few, but I'm looking for something like Cami and Josh have. And you and Lance. When I see you guys together, I realize how important it is not to just settle. And my mom is always telling me it's better to be single than in a bad relationship."

"This is true," Jessa agreed. "You've still got lots of time. I was thirty when Lance and I finally found each other again. It is worth waiting for that person God has for you."

Amy winced inwardly at Jessa's words. She wasn't so sure she trusted herself to judge who God wanted her to be with. She'd been way off base the last time she'd tried to do that. "Hope God hits me over the head with a hammer to get my attention when the right guy is in the vicinity."

Jessa chuckled. "Some of us need that, no doubt. I certainly didn't think Lance was the one for me when I saw him again after all those years. Just keep an open mind...and heart. Love may surprise you."

They talked a little longer about the manor and the guests who would be arriving in the next few days. Then Jessa asked her to wait while she went to the bathroom. Amy knew that Lance hadn't wanted her to be alone when getting in and out of the bed and walking around, so she had no problem waiting until Jessa was settled back into the bed again.

"I think I'm going to try to sleep for a little bit. I haven't slept too well since the doctor put me on bed- rest. But now that you're here, I'm feeling much more at ease."

"I'm glad," Amy said as she gathered up their dishes. "Buzz me if you need anything."

Downstairs Amy spent more time reviewing what she needed to keep track of over the next few days. New guests would be arriving that afternoon for the weekend. Jessa had said two girls from town would be out around one o'clock to prep the two rooms that had been vacated shortly after breakfast. Once the young women showed up, Amy helped them with the rooms and by the time the first of the new guests arrived around three, everything was ready.

Laurel showed up with her family, Julia and Isabella just before five. Violet and Dean weren't far behind. And all came bearing food. Lance walked in the door as they were setting up the meal. After the sisters had made sure their kids and husbands had food, they disappeared upstairs to see Jessa.

Will walked in after everyone had started to eat. Amy noticed that Isabella didn't run to greet him as Julia had done when Lance had arrived. It also hadn't escaped her attention that Lance had gone to his niece and given her a hug and asked her how she was doing.

"How was Isabella?" Will asked Rose as he picked up a plate and began to dish up his dinner.

"She was fine, Uncle Will. She's always fine." Rose glanced over to where Isabella sat. "We had fun, didn't we?"

Isabella nodded. "Rose helped us make some cupcakes and let us put frosting and sprinkles on them. We brought them for dessert."

Will nodded, but no smile curved the corners of his mouth. "Sounds good. I'm glad you had fun."

Amy understood then why Jessa sometimes wanted to smack Will. Would he realize what he was missing out on before it was too late? As she watched each of the fathers there with their kids, she wondered how he could not see how different he was with Isabella.

At Amy's urging, once the meal was done, the dads took the kids outside to the play structure in the backyard.

"I'll help you clean up," Rose said as she stood and began to stack the plates.

"You go ahead and go with them, Rose," Will said. "I need to talk to Amy for a minute."

Rose looked from Will to Amy and then nodded. "If

you're sending me off though, you have to help with the dishes."

For the first time, Amy saw the hint of a smile on Will's face. "I think I can handle that."

Amy scraped plates into the garbage, figuring she wasn't going to make small talk with the guy. It was beyond her what he could possibly want.

He took the stack of scraped plates on the counter and began to load the large dishwasher. "Isabella tells me you're a teacher."

"Yes. I teach grade one at a Christian school in Dallas." Did he want her to tutor Isabella in something?

"I was wondering—since you have experience with kids Isabella's age—if you'd be willing to plan her birthday party."

Amy turned to stare at him. "Her birthday party?"

He nodded. "Usually we do a small family party, but this past year when she went to school, she learned all about friend parties and is insisting on one for her birthday."

"And you give her everything she wants," Amy said.

Will's brows drew together briefly. "I try to. I just don't know anything about planning that type of party. Laurel and Violet are busy with their own kids and Jessa... Well, I don't want to impose on her for obvious reasons."

"So you want me to plan her whole birthday?" Amy knew she'd have no problem doing that, but part of her mind was working to figure out how to draw him into this for his daughter's sake.

"Yes. You'd have an unlimited budget, and I'd pay you for your time."

Sometimes Amy forgot how wealthy the Collingsworths were. Josh and Cami were no exception, but, aside from the luxury bus they used for travelling, they didn't have many of the trappings of the rich.

She leaned back against the counter and crossed her

arms. "Okay. I'll do it, but under a couple of conditions."

Will gave her a wary look. "Conditions?"

"Yep. She's your daughter. I want you to help plan it."

"And?"

"And I won't take any pay for doing this. Consider it a labor of love."

"A labor of love? You don't even know her," Will pointed out.

"She's a child. What's not to love?" Amy said with a smile. "Do we have a deal?"

"What kind of help are you talking about?" Will was obviously not going to agree to anything without a few more details.

"Nothing too elaborate. Just some help with decisions. And maybe a piñata or two."

"A piñata? Why would you need help with that? Wouldn't you just buy it?"

Amy grinned. "Never! I have the perfect recipe to make one. And you're going to help."

He regarded her for what seemed like forever before nodding. "Okay. Deal."

"Perfect. When is her birthday?" Even as she asked the question, Amy was mindful of the other memory the day held.

"Two weeks from today."

"So it's on a Friday? Would you be willing to maybe have it on the day after? Sometimes that's easier if parents work during the week. Maybe have it Saturday afternoon?"

His face clouded for a moment, but he still said, "That would be fine. I'll just explain to her that because she wants a friend -party she'll have to wait an extra day. Somehow I think she'll be okay with that."

"Great! Maybe you could drop her off here a couple of times so we can spend some time together. That way I can get a feel for what kind of party she'd like. We'll need to get invitations out pretty quickly. Do you know her friends' addresses?"

Will shook his head. "But I think Laurel or Violet can help with that. They volunteer at the school so they might know how I can get the information."

Amy began to gather up the remaining dishes. "I'll give you my email address so you can send them to me once you have them."

"Thank you. I appreciate your willingness to help me out."

"You're welcome. I love kids, so this will be fun."

He stared at her for a long moment. "I guess if you're a teacher you need to love kids, eh?"

"It certainly helps," Amy said. "But I've always loved children of all ages."

"I'm sure your students must love you. Isabella was talking about how nice you were, and she was only with you for a short time."

"Ah. How sweet." Amy put the detergent in the dishwasher and turned it on. "She's a lovely little girl."

Will shifted from one foot to the other. "Well, I'm going to go see Jessa and ask her if we can borrow her backyard for the party."

"That would be perfect," Amy said. "It would be easier for me to be able to do the preparations since I need to be here for Jessa."

Will nodded then left the kitchen. Amy stared after him for a moment before turning her attention back to the remaining things that needed to be put away. She was putting plastic wrap back on the food Laurel and Violet had brought when they both came into the kitchen.

"Hey, hun, let's just transfer the leftovers into Jessa's

containers. I don't want to take anything home," Violet said. She opened a drawer and began to pull out some containers and lids.

"Me either," Laurel agreed. "I made extra so there would be some leftovers." She glanced at the bowls on the counter. "But it looks like we had some hungry people here tonight."

"I heard Will ask Jessa about having Isabella's party here," Violet said. "And he told her you had agreed to help plan it."

Amy nodded. "He found out I was a teacher, so I guess he figured I might have an idea of how to plan a friend party for her. I agreed...with a couple of conditions."

"Conditions?" Laurel asked looking very much like Will when he'd said the same thing.

"One had to do with him offering to compensate me financially for my help. I told him I wouldn't take pay. The other was that he be involved."

Violet's eyes widened. "And he agreed?"

"Yep. Even with the threat of having to make a piñata."

"Wow." Laurel glanced at Violet then back to Amy. "I'm impressed. Normally he's quick to pass off stuff like that when we try to get him involved."

"I guess time will tell if he'll actually make himself available," Amy said.

"True." Violet settled on a chair at the table and plucked a cookie from the plate Amy had set out. "I just hope that he doesn't realize there are people who would have happily taken his money and done all the work without his help."

Amy pressed a finger to her lips. "Shhh. Too late for him now."

The three of them laughed conspiratorially.

"Of course, we'll help you, too," Laurel assured her. "But I am super curious to see how much you manage to get him to do."

Conversation on the subject stalled when Will walked back into the kitchen.

"Did she agree?" Amy asked.

Will nodded. "So we just need to decide on the time for the invitations." He turned to his sisters. "I'm going to need help getting the addresses to send them to. You know a lot of the moms at the school, right?"

Laurel nodded. "We can get that for you."

"Thanks." He pulled out his phone and glanced at Amy. "You were going to give me your email address."

"Right," Amy said and rattled it off for him, repeating it once to make sure he'd input it into his phone correctly.

"I'll email you once I have the information from Laurel and Violet." He slid the phone back into his pocket. "I think Isabella's grandparents might fly in for her birthday. My folks won't likely come since we were just there, but we'll see."

Amy finished wiping down the counters while Violet and Laurel talked with Will about Delia's parents. She wondered if they found comfort in how much Isabella looked like their daughter. And if they knew how much Delia had struggled with her pregnancy. Amy shared almost everything with her mom, but she knew that wasn't always the case for all mothers and daughters. She was curious to meet the grandparents and see how they interacted with Isabella and Will.

Soon Will excused himself and went to the backyard. Within a couple of minutes, all the dads were traipsing back into the house with the kids, most none too happy at having been dragged away from their play time.

Will and Isabella were the first to leave, but the other two families followed shortly afterward. Lance and Julia disappeared upstairs to spend some time with Jessa before it was bedtime for the little girl.

Amy finished cleaning up and chatted with a couple of the

guests who had returned after spending the day at a nearby beach. When Lance came down after putting Julia to bed, they went over what they anticipated the next day would hold. She was glad her cousin was detail oriented, too. It helped to know what they expected of her and what she needed to do. It made things much easier for her.

Before falling asleep, she emailed Cami with details of the last couple of days and then phoned her mom to touch base. Then in the darkness of her room, Amy prayed for God's wisdom and understanding as she dealt with Will and Isabella. She felt drawn to the little girl who had no mother to love her and a father who apparently couldn't love her. Given that Isabella's age was the same as the kids she usually worked with, Amy felt that maybe God had another purpose for her time in Collingsworth in addition to helping Lance and Jessa.

❧ Chapter Three ❧

WILL put his hands on his hips as he stared down at Isabella. Stubbornness was stamped all over the little girl's face. It had been one battle after another since she'd gotten up. He'd suggested the wrong thing for her to wear. He'd done her hair wrong. He hadn't offered her the right things for breakfast. And the latest was his denial of her request to go to the manor and see Amy.

"We're not going to the manor," Will repeated, more firmly than the first two times he'd said it.

Isabella crossed her arms. "Why?"

"I have some work I need to get done. You can read or draw or watch television."

"You're mean." She poked out her lower lip.

There had been more of these episodes lately, and Laurel and Violet had both suggested that his indulgence of her in everything was most likely the reason. They had advised him to not give in to her every demand, but he had a feeling that was a bit like closing the barn door once the cows had already escaped. It was a losing battle, and he was just about ready to phone Lance up to see if he could drop Isabella off to spend some time with Amy. That would be the easy way, but even Delia's parents had told him the last time they'd visited that he needed to take a firmer hand with her. Their advice had surprised him since he figured they, of anyone, would understand why he found it difficult to say no to Isabella.

"I'm sorry if you think I'm mean, but the answer is no." This sticking to his guns thing was not easy or fun. "You can bring your things into my office if you want to work in there with me, but we're not going to the manor."

With a final glare at him, Isabella spun on her heel and marched down the hallway to her room. Will winced when her door slammed shut then let out a long sigh. He really was the worst father on the planet. Nothing he felt or did for Isabella was right. He knew it was his guilt over how he just couldn't seem to love her the way that Lance, Matt and Dean loved their children. Every single time he looked at her, all he felt was guilt.

Maybe if Delia had wanted the baby as much as he had, he wouldn't carry this burden of guilt. But she had been distraught throughout the pregnancy. There had been barely a day when she hadn't said how much she wished she wasn't pregnant. It was his insistence that they have a family that had taken Delia's life. He could blame no one but himself, and Isabella was a constant reminder of his failure. He knew it wasn't her fault, but he just couldn't get past the guilt and the feeling of responsibility for her mother's death.

He ran a hand over his face and, with one last look at the closed door of Isabella's room, Will walked into the study off the living room where he had a home office. Sitting behind the desk, his gaze went to the picture he kept there of Delia and himself on their wedding day. They'd married late in the afternoon on a beach in the Philippines. The sun had just started to set as they'd been pronounced husband and wife.

It had been a whirlwind courtship starting on the first day of his short term mission trip to the Philippines. There had been a huge potluck supper to welcome them the night his team had arrived. Delia had attended it with her parents, who were also part of the mission. He'd been immediately drawn to her beautiful smile and big brown eyes. At first he'd thought she was too young for him, but after a few subtle questions, he'd discovered that she was, in fact, twenty-one.

They'd gotten to know each other really well, and when he'd had to leave at the end of the summer, it had been horrible. They agreed to try the long distance thing for a bit since she was still going to be in the Philippines for several more months helping out with her parents' clinic. In the end, neither of them wanted to continue that for too long. Without telling his parents or the rest of the family, he'd flown back to the Philippines after Christmas that year to surprise her. He'd asked her father for her hand in marriage and once they had her parents' somewhat reluctant blessing, they had decided to get married right away.

In some ways, he regretted not telling his family. He could have flown them all there to be part of the wedding, but it had been a complication he really hadn't wanted at that point. Though his mother had never voiced how disappointed she was, he'd known she had been.

Will picked up the picture and stared down at it. He thought he'd had everything at that point. A wonderful wife. A career he loved. Enough money to make life easier. And he'd felt confident he and Delia would continue to serve the Lord whenever the opportunity arose. The only thing he had wanted to complete their life together had been a child. Only the very thing that should have completed their family had torn it apart.

Hating himself for the thought, Will put the picture down and flipped open the file he'd put on his desk earlier with the expenses for their latest project. No doubt Isabella would be back for round ten soon. He needed to get work done while he could.

Amy sank down onto a chair at the table and let out a long sigh. Her first breakfast for the guests had been an unqualified success. Though she knew how to cook and bake all kinds of things, she couldn't remember the last time she'd actually cooked a meal for strangers. They had been generous with their praise, and she felt more confident about being able to handle the weeks ahead.

"Jessa said it was delicious," Lance announced as he walked into the kitchen. "And I agree!"

"Thank you." Amy stood up to take the tray from him. She set it on the counter and began to take the dishes off of it. "I have to say I'm glad it's just the one meal a day I have to make for the guests. I about had a panic attack over this one."

"I figured your mom would have made sure you were well equipped in the kitchen." Lance filled a cup from the coffee pot. "As I recall, she was a great cook. My mom always used to tell us that we had Aunt Michelle to thank for anything good she made."

Amy stuck the plates in the dishwasher. "Yeah. I remember Mom talking about how she taught your mom to cook when she and your dad got married."

"That's why I didn't hesitate to give Cami the go ahead to ask you to come help out. I figured if anyone could handle what we have here, it would be you."

"I hope your confidence in me isn't misplaced. This is only day two," she reminded him.

"Well, just to put your mind at ease a little., Jessa and I decided this morning to honor all current bookings at the manor, but to not take any further reservations until after the baby is here, and they've both had a chance to adjust."

"So you won't need me the whole summer?" Amy asked, strangely disappointed by the thought.

"Well, we have reservations scattered throughout the summer, so I'd like you to stay on as originally planned. Plus,

I can always use some help with Julia, and I think Jessa enjoys the company when I'm not here."

Lance's phone rang, and as he answered it, he walked from the kitchen. Amy finished cleaning up the remainder of the dishes then went upstairs to check on Jessa. She found Julia curled up on the bed with her reading books. Deciding not to interrupt, she went on to her room and settled down with her laptop. She kept the walkie-talkie close as she wrote emails and chatted online with a couple of her friends. It was definitely a slower pace in Collingsworth than what she was used to in Dallas, but she figured she could handle it for a couple of months.

The next morning, Amy went to church with Lance and Julia. Jessa had insisted they all go after promising to not try to get out of bed at all while they were gone. Still, Lance made sure they sat at the back of the sanctuary, and she noticed he kept his phone in his hand. She enjoyed the service which was much like the ones at her church in Dallas, a nice blend of contemporary and traditional. Once it was over, Lance left to get Julia while Amy waited by the front door for him.

She spotted Laurel and Rose headed in her direction and waved.

"We're just swinging by the house to pick up a few things before we come to the manor," Laurel said once they were close. "Vi and Dean ended up going into the city to see his folks, so they won't be joining us."

Amy had just opened her mouth to reply which she was tackled around the hips in a tight hug. Having experience with those types of hugs, she quickly regained her balance and looked down. She smiled at the beautiful little face staring up at her. Running a hand over the girl's glossy hair, she said, "Well, if it isn't Miss Isabella. How are you today, sweetie?"

"I'm good!"

The girl seemed reluctant to release her, so Amy wrapped an arm around her shoulders. "Were you in junior church?"

"Yep. We learned about David and Goliath. Except I already knew that story."

"Well, there are some stories you just can't hear too often," Amy assured her with a smile.

"Isabella."

Amy looked up to see Will approaching them. The man looked worn out and stressed. Dark circles lay beneath his eyes, and he appeared even more tense than he had two days earlier. "Hey, Will. Did you lose something?"

His gaze met hers briefly before dropping to the girl still attached to her hip. "I think you can let go of Amy now, Isabella. We're going to the manor for lunch, so you're going to see her again in a little while."

"We are?" Isabella loosened her grip and turned to look at him. "You didn't tell me that. You should've told me."

Amy could hear the reproof in the little girl's voice and nearly smiled. But didn't.

Will put his hands on his hips, and almost instantly Isabella assumed the same position. Though Isabella faced away from her, Amy could imagine the look on the little girl's face. She glanced at Laurel who just shrugged.

"Frankly, after the hassles you gave me this morning and yesterday, I wasn't sure you deserved to go." Will let out a sigh. "And if you don't check that attitude, we're going home."

Immediately Isabella dropped her hands from her hips but her head and shoulders remained lifted. "Sorry, Daddy."

Amy knew manipulation when she saw it. She had no doubt the little girl's apology lacked sincerity, but Isabella was smart enough to know she wasn't going to get her way without it. Amy felt sorry for Will, but, unfortunately, he'd kind of created this situation.

As she expected, Will gave a nod and said, "Okay, but no more attitude today, please."

Though Amy knew she had no right, she really wished she could give Will some advice. She wasn't a mother, but she did have experience with the age, and none of the children that came through her classes were perfect angels. She had run into a few children like Isabella, and though they had been a challenge for her, she'd loved them and found that by the end of the year, with some gentle guidance, their interactions with her had improved.

"Ready to go, Amy?"

She turned to see Lance approach with Julia in tow.

"Yep." She gave Isabella a smile. "See you guys shortly."

Once back at the manor, she helped Lance get things together for the barbeque. Jessa was planning to come down and join them for a bit. Lance and Jessa had decided that as long as she didn't do anything else while she was downstairs, it would be okay. Amy agreed, figuring that being out in the fresh air with her family would do Jessa a world of good.

Lance got the barbeque fired up and was just putting the meat on when the others arrived. All the younger children ran off to the large play structure. Jessa had come down and was settled on a lounge chair that allowed her to keep her feet up.

"It's so good to be outside again." Jessa lifted the glass of ice cold water Amy had brought her and took a sip. "I miss my gardens and the sunshine."

"It will all be worth it," Lance said as he bent to press a kiss to the top of her head. "Wish we could share the bed rest."

"I don't know about Jessa," Laurel said, "but I'd rather have shared the labor."

The women laughed when the men looked pained. Amy wondered how Will felt hearing these jokes about pregnancy and delivery when his own experience had been anything but funny.

"By the way," Lance began as he returned to the barbeque to flip the steaks and hamburgers. "I invited Maura to join us."

"Really?" Jessa exclaimed. "I didn't know she was back."

"Just got back yesterday, apparently." Lance laid down the spatula that he'd been using to turn the meat. "Gareth wasn't with her in church, so I'm not sure if he's back or not. And it sounded like they were going to be leaving again in a week or so."

Amy saw Jessa frown at her husband's words. "I hate that they keep having problems."

"I think they bring those problems on themselves," Laurel commented. "I mean, they seem to thrive on their disagreements."

Jessa sighed. "Yes, I know what you mean, but man, when they're on the outs it's miserable for all of their friends."

Before anyone could say anything more, Maura appeared around the side of the manor, with a tall lanky man right behind her. Though Amy remembered Maura from previous visits, she didn't recall having met her husband.

"Gareth, glad you could make it," Lance said as he walked to greet them.

Maura moved quickly to where Jessa sat. "I couldn't believe it this morning when Lance told me what had happened. Just let me know if you need anything." She gave her friend a hug and then looked around to greet the others. When her gaze landed on Amy, there was a spark of curiosity. Maura glanced at Will then said, "So Will, you've finally got yourself a girlfriend?"

It took everything within Amy not to glance at Will. She smiled at Maura and shook her head. "I'm here to help Jessa for the summer."

"That's Amy. Josh's sister," Lance said. "She is generously giving up her summer to help us out around here."

"Ah, sorry about that," Maura said with a sheepish grin. She went to Will and gave him a hug and a pat on the cheek. "One of these days you'll take my advice."

"I guess stranger things have happened," Will said with a slight lift of the corner of his mouth. It didn't seem to be the first time they'd had a discussion over his relationship status.

Still, when Maura turned back to Amy, her gaze held a glint of curiosity. "I remember you now. You were one of Cami's bridesmaids, right? Her maid of honor?"

Amy nodded. "Good memory."

"It was the hair. You have the most beautiful multi-color curls. Is it for real?" Maura reached out and touched a strand where it lay on Amy's shoulder.

"Yep. All my own."

"Lucky duck. Just wait until you get to our age." She motioned to Jessa. "Then we end up with multi-color hair we wish we didn't have."

Amy laughed, remembering now the quick wit of Jessa's best friend. So far her husband sat in silence on a chair beside Matt. There didn't seem to be tension between them, but Amy wasn't familiar enough with them to know for sure. Since no little ones had shown up, she assumed they didn't have any children.

When Lance asked for a platter for the meat, Amy turned to grab it from the table. As she looked up, she found Will's gaze on her. She froze for a second but then glanced away as she handed the plate to Lance. She hadn't been able to read anything in his expression and wasn't sure what to make of it. She hoped he didn't think that Maura's comment had put any type of thoughts into her head where he was concerned. Been there. Done that. She wasn't going back for round two when she'd be competing against a memory. God was going to have to put that one in neon lights—flashing ones—if He wanted her to consider Will as anything other than a friend.

As it turned out, the reason for Gareth's absence from

church didn't appear to have been because of a conflict with Maura. They sat together throughout the meal, and when Gareth slid his arm around her waist at one point, she didn't pull away. At least it would be one less thing for Jessa to be concerned about, because Amy was sure that she did worry about her best friend. Amy knew that she would have.

"Ready to go back upstairs?" Lance asked, once the meal was done, and they'd had some time to visit. Maura and Gareth had left already, and Laurel and Matt were rounding up their kids to leave as well.

"Not really, but I know I need to," Jessa said with a sigh. "This was lovely."

As Lance helped Jessa back into the manor, Amy began to gather up the few remaining things on the table.

"Here, let me help with that," Will said when she turned to carry the tray into the house.

She hesitated then relinquished it to him. "Uh, thanks."

He's just being nice. Do not read anything into it.

She repeated the warning a few times as she followed him into the house with the empty juice pitcher and a bottle of ketchup. Will set the tray on the counter and moved aside as she began to empty it. She didn't look at him as she worked, not sure she wanted to see the expression on his face. Whatever it was, good or bad, she didn't want to see it.

"I should be getting the list from Laurel and Vi this week for the invitations."

"The sooner, the better," Amy said, opening the fridge to put the condiments away. "Some might not be available since it's summer and people go on vacation."

"True. I didn't really think about that. I hope Isabella's not disappointed if they can't all come."

"The not-so-fun part of having a summer birthday," Amy commented.

"You have experience with it?" Will asked.

"Yep. But I've also experienced it with my classes. I try to plan a party near the end of school to celebrate all the kids' birthdays who didn't have them during the school year. That way no one feels left out." Amy dampened a dishrag and wiped down the tray before putting it away.

"My birthday was always during the school year, so I never really thought much about it. And my siblings were all during that time, too, come to think of it."

Amy smiled at him. "You were among the lucky students then. Most everyone would have been available for your birthday parties."

Will leaned a hip against the counter and crossed his arms. "Was it that bad? Just wondering what I'm in for with Isabella. This is just the first of many summer birthdays."

"Nah. It worked out fine. As she gets older, she'll have a group of friends she'll want to invite. She'll be more flexible with when she has the party in order to make sure they can come. I'm sure you'll do whatever you can to make her parties memorable."

"I suppose you think I overindulge her like my sisters do," Will said, his expression once again unreadable.

Amy shrugged. "That's not my place to say. I'm sure you're doing what you think is best for her."

"Maybe." He straightened from the counter. "Or maybe just what's easiest for me."

Before Amy could say anything, Lance walked into the kitchen. He looked from Amy to Will and back again. "Am I interrupting something?"

∿ Chapter Four ∾

NOPE," Amy said as she wiped down the counters. Surprisingly, a part of her wished he had, but alas, that was not the case. "We were just talking about Isabella's birthday party."

"Oh, right. Jessa said you wanted to have it here. Sounds like fun." Lance pulled a couple of water bottles from the fridge. "Do you mind keeping an eye on Julia for a bit, Amy? I want to spend some time with Jessa."

"Sure. I'm sure Jessa would enjoy the company."

"I would, too," Lance said. "I've missed having her around down here."

Amy smiled, happy her cousin and his wife still had such a close relationship after almost ten years. She was fortunate to have been surrounded by several examples of strong, healthy relationships. Her mom and dad had been married for almost forty years and still did almost everything together. Beth and Josh both had good marriages. Amy could see the importance of waiting for the person God wanted her to be with.

"Well, don't rush back down. Julia and I will find plenty to do."

"Are you hanging around a bit?" Lance asked as he turned to Will.

"Probably. I don't think Isabella will be all that anxious to get back to the apartment."

"You need to get yourself a place with a little outdoor space one of these days," Lance said with a smile.

"One of these days," Will agreed.

"See you in a bit," Lance said as he headed out of the kitchen.

"Mind keeping an eye on Julia for a couple of minutes?" Amy asked. "I'd like to get out of these church clothes."

Will nodded. "I'll head back out there now."

Not sure how she felt about spending part of her afternoon with Will, Amy climbed the stairs to her room.

Will opened the can of pop he'd gotten from the fridge as he settled down into one of the lawn chairs. The girls were still happily playing on the huge wooden structure Matt and Lance had built for the kids. It had a playhouse in addition to the sandbox, slide and swings. Isabella loved it, and Will knew he needed to take Lance's advice and get a place with some yard. The problem was he already had a place. It just wasn't livable yet, and he wasn't sure when he'd ever be able to bring himself to completing the project. Plus, it really was too big for just him and Isabella. He couldn't sell it in the condition it was in, so it would continue to sit empty for the time being.

"I can't believe how beautiful it is up here even on a summer day. Down in Texas I'd be sweltering on a day like this."

Will looked over to see Amy settling into the lawn chair next to his. She drew her legs up to sit cross-legged as she set a glass on the table beside her chair. The church clothes had been exchanged for a pair of white shorts that accented the tan of her long legs. She wore a white tank top underneath a large bright pink t-shirt that slid off one shoulder. Her hair was now gathered back in a ponytail which left the soft curve of her jawline visible.

Pulling his gaze from her, Will tried to remember what she'd said. "Uh. Yeah. The nice summers make up for the lousy winters."

"I still remember the winter we were up here for Lance's wedding. That was super cold. Cami and Josh's wedding was marginally better."

"There are days I wonder why I moved here from California," Will admitted.

"Why did you?" Amy asked.

Will thought back to the day he'd made the decision. "Lance offered me a job with his company. It seemed like the perfect way to be able to spend time with the family I was finally getting to know. Then it was just easier to stay here after everything happened. And now Isabella loves being around her cousins. I don't really have a good reason to take her away from them."

"It's nice she has that kind of relationship. I don't really have any cousins my age. Most are around Josh and Beth's age. But they spent most their early years in Kenya so they didn't have much contact with our cousins either. Josh is fortunate that Lance reached out to him when he did. I think Josh would say Lance is his best friend now. Well, aside from Cami."

"Guess they'll be heading this way in a few weeks," Will said.

"Yep. I can't wait to see them."

"Are you planning to stay for the whole summer?"

"Yes, because even if the baby comes early, Jessa will likely need help around here while she recovers. And it will give me a chance to see Josh and Cami."

They sat in silence for a few minutes before Will said, "Listen, I'm sorry about what happened earlier with Maura."

Amy glanced his way. The corner of her mouth lifted in a half-smile, and she shrugged. "No big deal. It was an understandable conclusion since she didn't realize who I was."

"She's been trying very hard for the past year or so to get me back into the dating world."

"It does seem that people in relationships like to encourage others to follow their example." Amy laughed. "I'm not sure if it's because they want everyone to be as happy as they are or if misery loves company."

"Do you have a boyfriend?" Will asked before he could stop himself.

Amy shook her head. "Not at the moment."

"Do you have people trying to set you up?"

"Nah. I still live with my folks, and I think my mom would be just as happy if I stayed with them forever." Amy picked up her glass and took a sip. "A couple of my friends are in serious relationships and every once in a while will try to talk me into a blind date. Haven't given in yet."

"You're still young," Will said.

"Not as young as I used to be, but I'm not rushing into anything. I kind of like being single. Gives me flexibility to do things like come here to Collingsworth for the summer. Besides," Amy glanced at him, a contemplative expression on her face. "I dealt with a broken heart as a teenager and haven't been too keen to repeat the experience."

"Really? Teenage boys can be mean, that's for sure." Will wasn't sure why he'd allowed the conversation to wander into this territory. Between Isabella's reaction to Amy, and Maura's comments, he found himself looking at Amy in a new way. A way that appealed to him more than it should have.

Amy didn't address his observation. "My mom always tells me it's gonna take a real special guy to catch my attention. And my dad says I can be a real handful sometimes. I, personally, have no idea what they're talking about." When she glanced his way again, Will saw a glint of humor in her eyes.

"I'm sure you're nothing compared to the handful Isabella's going to be." Will watched as his daughter pumped her legs on the swing to send it soaring.

"You may be right there," Amy agreed. "But there's still time for you to help her learn a different way of dealing with you and others around her."

"It's gotten worse in the past year since she went to school. Suddenly she wanted everything her friends had and, frankly, it was just easier to give in than try to argue with her."

"I'm not a parent, but I do have a little experience with this through my teaching." Amy uncrossed her legs and stretched them out in front of her, wriggling her pink polished toes. "But it really shouldn't be an argument. You are the parent and have the final say."

"That's easier said than done," Will remarked. "But I have a feeling my sisters, who *are* parents, would agree with you."

"I'm sure it must be difficult being a single parent," Amy said, her voice soft. "Especially in your circumstances."

"It certainly wasn't what I had planned for my life." He watched as Isabella slid off her swing and set off running, Julia hot on her heels, both girls shrieking.

"And I haven't done a very good job accepting that." Will surprised himself with that revelation. He hadn't shared that with anyone before.

"I know what it's like to plan one thing and have it turn out way different than you thought it would. Although obviously not to the scale you have."

When Will looked her way, he found that she was now

watching the girls, a distant expression on her face. He found it interesting how easy it was to talk with her. He hadn't let his guard down much around the single women of Collingsworth. And he would never have spent a Sunday afternoon chatting with one of them after a family dinner. He supposed it had to do with her not even being remotely interested in trying to snag him.

While Will did understand why women might view him as a catch—his sisters said he wasn't bad looking and he did have some of the Collingsworth millions—he just hadn't been interested in any of the women who had crossed his path so far. Ever since Isabella had gone to kindergarten she'd periodically brought up the fact that other kids in her class had a mother and a father. He'd finally told her about Delia, but that hadn't stopped her from wanting a mommy of her own. However, it wouldn't be fair to a woman to marry her just because Isabella wanted—and maybe needed—a mother.

He hoped that her fascination with Amy wouldn't put any ideas in her head. While Maura's little slip-up had been awkward, it would be nothing compared to Isabella setting her sights on Amy for the role of mother. His little girl was used to getting what she wanted, but Amy would be the one thing he wouldn't be able to give her. For now, Will was trying to keep Isabella focused on how Amy was a teacher and how she loved little kids like Isabella because of that. If he could keep her thinking *teacher* when she interacted with Amy, they might be able to avoid any awkwardness during the next couple of months.

"I've been meaning to ask," Amy began, "where's Lily?"

"Who knows." Will watched as she took another sip of her water. "Last I heard she was hanging out in Paris."

"Really? What happened to the guy she was with? Nick?"

"Nate. He's still here. Apparently she wanted to travel and tried to convince him to go with her, but he had responsibilities here. None of us have seen her in a couple of years. Kinda reminiscent of Cami, from what I've heard."

"Maybe she'll come around like Cami did."

"We hope that will happen. I know Jessa worries a lot about her. She basically raised Lily, so I think she feels more responsible for her."

"Did she go to college?"

"Not here. I know she wanted to study art or fashion or something." Will sighed. "I'm sorry. I sound like a horrible brother. I was kind of in my own little world during the time she up and left. I just know what I hear periodically from the girls."

"It's okay to not be as close to one sibling as you are to others," Amy said. "That's kind of how it is with me and my older sister, Beth."

"You don't spend much time together?"

"Not really. She was around thirteen when I was born, and I've always gotten the feeling she resented the fact that I was a girl. Once I arrived on the scene, she wasn't the only little princess anymore. That's why I absolutely love Cami. She's been so great to me, and I feel she's more like a sister to me than Beth is."

"Family relationships can be a real challenge," Will said. "Thankfully, my parents worked hard to make sure we all got along. And then to find out I had a whole other family was an interesting discovery."

"I think your family is terrific. I'm so glad that both Josh and Lance married into it. Makes me almost family, too."

Will smiled, surprising himself. "I'm sure they'd happily claim you as sister."

"I'm sure you're not looking for another sister. They've already got you outnumbered five to one."

Will realized he wasn't, in fact, interested in having her as a sister. Nothing he'd thought about her since that first morning in the kitchen had included viewing her as a sibling. "Yes, I do have plenty of sisters, but I'm up for a friend."

"A person can never have too many friends," Amy said as she flashed him a smile.

"Daddy!"

Isabella's yell drew Will's attention back to the girls. He watched as she skipped in his direction, a determined look on her face. Bracing himself for what was to come, Will straightened in his seat.

"What's up?" he said as she approached, Julia not far behind her.

"It's hot. We want ice cream."

"Ice cream?" Will looked from Isabella to Julia, who nodded her agreement. "I'm sure there's some in the freezer."

"Yep, I'm pretty sure I saw some in there," Amy agreed.

Isabella's hands went to her hips. "Daddy. That's not the kind of ice cream we want. We want Dairy Queen. Right, Julia?" She glanced at her cousin who once again nodded.

Will turned to Amy and found her watching him, humor glinting in her eyes. Something told him she was trying very hard not to laugh at his predicament.

"Ice cream does sound good," she said with a grin.

Given that he couldn't say no to one little girl, there was no way he was going to be able to say no to three of them. "Okay. Fine."

The girls cheered as he stood from his lawn chair. When Amy didn't get up, he pinned her with a look. "No way am I taking these two on my own. You sided with them, so you get to enjoy the pleasure of their company, too."

"If you insist," Amy said, her soft green eyes twinkling.

"Oh, I do," Will replied and held out a hand to pull her up from the chair.

Following a hesitation so brief that he wondered if he'd actually imagined it, Amy gripped his hand and came to her feet. After releasing her hand, he turned to the girls. "Go get your shoes on."

"I should probably let Lance and Jessa know where we're going," Amy said as she reached for her phone. "And I need shoes, too."

"I'll text them. No need to disturb them if they're napping," Will said as he followed her onto the porch and then into the kitchen.

Amy nodded as she headed up the stairs.

Once they had their shoes on, Isabella and Julia waited on the front porch, fairly dancing with excitement. Will pulled his keys out and led the way to his SUV. He helped the girls get into the back and then started it to cool the interior down. He leaned against the side of the vehicle and sent a quick text to Lance while he waited for Amy to reappear.

When she did, he noticed she'd changed from her shorts into a pair of white capris. Her hair was down again, and she wore a pair of large sunglasses.

He straightened and opened the passenger side door for her. After she was settled, he closed it and went around to slide behind the wheel.

"Wow," Amy said. "Is this a car or a spaceship?"

Will picked up his sunglasses from where he'd left them earlier on the dash and slid them on. He put the SUV in gear and headed out toward the highway. "Unfortunately, the Escalade spaceship model was all sold out. They only made a handful, and I wasn't quick enough, so I had to settle for the car model."

When there was no response from Amy, he glanced over at her. She sat staring at him. Her glasses hid her eyes, but the corners of her lips turned up. "Did you just crack a joke?"

❧ *Chapter Five* ❧

GUESS so," Will said, his gaze back on the road. He was a bit surprised himself. Though he appreciated humor as much as the next person, he hadn't really initiated it much over the past few years. "I have a weakness for nice cars."

"You have more than one of these?" Amy asked, her tone incredulous.

"No, but I do have a truck that I use for visiting job sites or moving stuff."

"So this is your Sunday go to meetin' ride?"

This time Will chuckled. "Among other things."

Amy ran her hand over the dashboard. "I don't think I've ever ridden in something so luxurious. This is crazy cool."

Will knew that of all his siblings, he'd been the one to indulge himself with the inheritance money, although they all had larger homes than he did—not counting the one that sat empty not far from the manor. He was generous with his money, and even though he didn't go on the missions trips like he had before, he tried to support missions as best he could.

"What do you drive?" Will asked.

"A bike," Amy replied.

"Like a motorcycle? You don't strike me as the biker chick sort."

"Nope. A bicycle. You know. Two wheels. Pedals. Handlebars."

"Seriously?" Will glanced over to see her nod. "Why wouldn't you have a car?"

"Haven't really needed one. The school where I teach isn't far, so I can ride my bike to work. If it's raining or I need to go somewhere that the bike won't get me, I can borrow my mom's car. It's just an unnecessary expense for me. Trying to watch my pennies where I can."

Will felt a little embarrassed by the obviously unnecessary opulence of his vehicle. It had been years since he'd been concerned about money and had kind of forgotten how that was. "I hope you spent some money for a good helmet at least."

"Well, sure," Amy said. "I don't skimp on the important things."

"That's good to hear. Isn't it a little chilly in the winter though?"

"On the really cold mornings or if it snows, my mom will insist I take her car. I usually don't argue too much. But honestly, there's nothing like a little brisk ride to wake a person up."

"Here you get that brisk shot of cold just walking from where you park your car to where you're going."

"Hard to imagine it can be that cold when it's so nice out," Amy commented.

"That's true," Will agreed as he turned off the highway onto Main Street. "I think the nice summers lull us into sticking around. Then winter arrives, and we're wondering why we're still here."

He found a parking spot not far from the Dairy Queen and pulled in. He helped Isabella and Julia out and then found Amy waiting on the sidewalk for them. His mom had always taught him to open doors for ladies, but it was hard when he had a child to take care of, too.

"You guys know what you want?" Will asked as he guided them toward the restaurant.

Amy stood beside Will as they waited in a short line to place their order. The girls were busy discussing what they planned to order and were trying to finagle their way into getting the biggest size possible. It had been a little while since she'd been to Dairy Queen, but Amy knew what she was going to indulge in. Ice cream was a weakness of hers. She ate it when she was happy. She ate it when she was sad. There was never a reason to not eat ice cream. Except that if she ate as much as she wanted, she'd no doubt have to buy a whole new wardrobe.

"Do you know what you want?"

She glanced over to see Will leaning toward her. His sunglasses, like hers, were now on the top of his head, so she could see his blue eyes. Having them focused on her like that did funny things to her stomach. "Yep. I do."

As the people in front of them finished their orders, Will put a hand on each of the girl's shoulders to keep them from darting forward.

"Hi, Marissa!" Julia and Isabella said in unison as they approached at a more sedate pace.

The girl behind the counter smiled at them. "Well, hello you two. I bet you're here for some hotdogs, right?"

Both girls shook their heads so vigorously their hair swirled around their shoulders. "We want ice cream," Isabella informed her.

The young woman looked up and smiled at Will and then her gaze slid to Amy. Curiosity was clear on her face. "So, what kind of ice cream can I get you?"

The girls placed their orders first then Will turned to Amy. "What do you want?"

Though she had debated on a small Blizzard, Amy threw caution to the wind and ordered a medium. Will asked for a chocolate shake as he pulled out his wallet. After he'd paid, they stepped to the side to wait for their order.

"Marissa babysits for Isabella and Julia sometimes. Her family goes to our church, too."

"She's lots of fun," Julia said. "She'll let us fix her hair and sometimes brings us makeup to put on her."

It definitely sounded like a fun time for six- and eight-year-old girls. "She seems very nice."

"Well, Jessa found her, and you know Jessa wouldn't let just anyone watch her little princess," Will said. "And I figured if she was good enough for Jessa, she was good enough for me."

"Here you go," Marissa said as she returned. She handed them each the item they'd ordered. "Thanks for coming, guys."

Amy could still see the curiosity on the young lady's face, but she was obviously too polite to ask.

"Do you want to eat here or go back to the manor?" Will asked.

Before Amy could say anything, the girls put in their votes for staying in the restaurant. When Will looked at her, she nodded. "I don't think you want some of us in that spaceship of yours with ice cream anyway."

"True," Will said as the girls took off in search of an empty place to sit.

They ended up at a table in front of the large glass window. Each girl went in one side of the booth, so they sat across from each other. Amy slid in next Julia while Will sat down beside Isabella, his legs bumping hers.

Thankfully, the girls kept up a running conversation as they ate, so Amy didn't have to try and think of what to say. It was all she could do to keep from closing her eyes and savoring those first few bites of her Blizzard. It had been a while since she'd last had one, and it tasted so good.

"You like ice cream?" Will asked.

Evidently some of the pleasure she was deriving from her treat must have shown on her face. "No. I don't like ice cream, I absolutely love it. I'd eat it every day if I could get away with it."

Will lifted a brow. "So you're one of those girls who sit and eat a pint when they're upset?"

"Yes, I can be. I can also eat a pint when I'm happy, which is why I rarely have ice cream in the house."

"You must burn off some calories riding your bike," Will observed. "I would think that would balance out an indulgence in something you enjoy."

"I don't ride that much. The school is only about six blocks away. Trust me, what I'd have to do to burn off the ice cream I'd like to eat each day would never happen. As much as I love ice cream, I detest exercise. So I just try to eat healthy most the time and stay active."

"Seems to be working for you," Will commented.

Amy dipped her head to take another bite of ice cream as she felt the heat rise in her cheeks. She knew he didn't mean anything by the comment, but just the fact that he'd looked at her figure to determine that did funny things to her stomach.

"Hello, Will!"

A woman's voice interrupted her moment of mortification. Amy looked up to see a woman standing at the table with a tray of ice cream containers in her hands. She had a smooth bob of black hair and striking blue eyes. She looked to be in her thirties and, like Marissa, her expression was curious.

"Hello, Trish," Will said as he stood from the booth. "How are you doing?"

"Can't complain," she said with a wide smile. "Definitely enjoying the summer off. We're heading to Hawaii for a week next month."

"That's great. We went to California to see my folks, but that's about it for us for traveling this summer."

The woman looked at Amy. "And who is this lovely lady?"

Amy shook hands with the woman and said, "I'm Amy Moyer."

"She's here helping Jessa with Julia and the manor now that she's on bed rest," Will said.

"Moyer?" the woman asked.

Amy nodded. "Josh is my brother, and Lance is my cousin."

"Ah, so you're just like family," the woman said. "I'm Trish Salverson."

"Nice to meet you," Amy replied, not sure what to make of the *just like family* comment. The woman wore a wedding ring on her left hand, so clearly she wasn't after Will.

"How long are you here for?"

"Probably until the middle of August. I have to get back to Dallas before school starts since I have a job there."

"You're a teacher? So am I."

"Yes, I teach first grade," Amy said.

"Ah, you teach the young ones. I teach middle school math."

"I really enjoy the kids around Julia and Isabella's age, so teaching first grade is a dream for me."

After a couple beats of awkward silence, Will said, "Well, be sure and say hi to Emmitt. Hope you have a good vacation."

"We will, I'm sure. Tabitha isn't going though, so maybe you could keep an eye on her."

Will shrugged. "I'm sure she doesn't need that. But if she does need something, I'm certain your parents or brother would be able to help her out."

Amy ducked her head to hide a smile. She took another small bite of her Blizzard. It wasn't too surprising to find that Will was a hot commodity among the single women in Collingsworth. It seemed this wasn't the first time he'd brushed aside attempts at matchmaking.

"So I'm guessing Tabitha's single?" Amy said once Trish had left their table, and Will had sat back down.

"Oh yes. For the moment. The woman has been through three husbands and way too many boyfriends to count. I have no desire to become part of the *I've dated Tabitha* club. She's nice enough, just can't seem to settle on one guy."

"Maybe the right one hasn't come along yet," Amy suggested.

"That's possible, but maybe she should just focus on other areas of her life while she waits instead of dating every single guy that comes along."

Amy's phone chirped an alert. She pulled it from her purse and read the message.

Plz bring me ice cream. Pretty please! Xoxox

She smiled at Jessa's text. "Jessa wants some ice cream. Good thing we hung around here."

After getting a text with what Jessa and Lance wanted, Will went back up to the counter while Amy finished up her ice cream with the girls.

"Thank you," Amy said as they walked to his SUV a short time later. "That was lovely."

"You're welcome." Will opened the back door for the girls and then the front one for her. Once she was settled, he handed her the tray holding the ice cream for Jessa and

Lance.

"Hope it's not soup by the time we get there," Amy said as they headed out of town.

"No worries," Will assured her. "This thing can spit ice cubes if I crank the A/C."

Sure enough, by the time they got back to the manor, Amy had goose bumps. She waited for Will to come around and open her door after he'd let the girls out. He took the tray and stepped back so she could slide off the seat. Once out, he returned the tray to her.

"I'll let you deliver that to Jessa. I'm going to go see what the girls are up to." They'd darted off around the side of the house as soon as they'd been freed from the vehicle.

Amy walked beside him and waited as he opened the front door of the manor for her. "Thanks again for the ice cream."

The corner of his mouth lifted. "Anytime."

She laughed. "You might regret that."

"I doubt it," Will said as she began to climb the stairs to the second floor.

Amy resisted the urge to respond. *He's being nice because he's a nice guy.* That was what she had to keep reminding herself. She was not about to revisit past heartache, and she had no doubt that allowing herself to feel anything for Will would only lead right back there. There was no way she wanted to be this man's second choice. She couldn't imagine being involved with a guy who still mourned his wife.

She rapped lightly on the door to Jessa and Lance's suite of rooms. It opened right away to reveal Lance. He smiled as his gaze fell on the tray she held.

"C'mon in." Lance stepped back. He'd changed into a white t-shirt and a pair of shorts, and his hair stood up on end in spots like he'd been sleeping.

Jessa was curled on her side but pushed to a reclining

position on her pillows when she spotted Amy. "Oh, you are my favorite person."

"Don't thank me. Isabella and Julia came up with the idea to go, and Will paid for it. I'm just the delivery girl."

Lance took the containers off the tray and handed one to Jessa. He sank down on the bed next to her and stretched his legs out. "Thanks for watching Julia."

"You know she's no problem. She and Isabella get along very well."

"Is Will with them?" Jessa asked.

"Yep. I think they are in the backyard. He said he'd keep an eye on them while I brought you the ice cream."

"You and Will getting along okay?" Lance asked.

"Sure. He's not the chattiest man I've ever been around, but he kind of reminds me of how Josh was before Cami. He did crack a joke, so I assume he can be interactive when he wants to be."

"He cracked a joke?" Jessa asked.

"Yeah. We were talking about his car."

"A joke about his car?" This time it was Lance. "I'm impressed."

Amy looked back and forth between them. "Why? He doesn't usually joke?" She'd thought him rather serious compared to how he'd used to be, but had thought it was maybe just with her since he didn't know her.

"Not that I've heard. He'll sometimes laugh at other people's jokes, but never cracks any himself."

"Guess we'd better mark this one on the calendar," Amy said with a smile.

Jessa glanced at Lance as she said, "Yeah, we'd better."

"I'm gonna head down. Did you need anything else?"

"Nope. We're good," Lance said. "I'll be down in a bit."

Amy detoured to her room to change into her shorts and then gathered her hair back up in a ponytail. Her mother had always frowned on her going out in public in shorts, and she'd never gotten out of the habit of changing before leaving the house. Shorts were, however, definitely more comfortable on a day like this.

She stopped by the kitchen, and made a pitcher of juice and put it on a tray with some glasses. Will was in the same seat he'd had before they'd left. He was looking at something on his phone but glanced up as she approached. He slid the phone into his pocket as he stood and reached for the tray. He set it on the glass-topped table in front of the chairs and poured some juice into the glasses.

When he handed one to Amy, she took it and said, "Thanks." She settled back into the lawn chair and took a sip. "Jessa and Lance were certainly enjoying the ice cream when I left. Must be one of her pregnancy cravings."

"Yes, I seem to remember Lance mentioning something about that."

"Come push me, Amy," Isabella yelled from the swing set.

"She knows how to swing," Will commented.

Amy smiled as she put her glass down and stood. "I don't mind giving her a few pushes."

"Are you going to push me?" Isabella asked as she got herself up on the swing.

"Are you going to ask nicely?" Amy replied.

Isabella sat for a moment then said, "Would you please push me?"

"Certainly," Amy said and smiled. She walked behind the girl, relishing the feel of the fresh grass beneath her bare feet. "Hang on."

୫ఞ

Will watched Amy push Isabella on the swing. He hadn't missed her request for Isabella to ask nicely. As he observed

Amy's interactions with his daughter, he could see that he had failed in more places than he'd realized. Even asking politely was something he hadn't forced her to do. It was just easier to give in. He didn't know how it was when his sisters watched Isabella, but they seemed to be wary of insisting she toe the line when he was around. Amy, on the other hand, had just put it out there that if Isabella wanted something, she was going to have to ask nicely.

He knew he wasn't doing his daughter any favors by allowing her behavior to continue. Maybe he needed to talk to his sisters about helping him out in working with Isabella. Watching Amy with his daughter brought an ache to his gut. Delia should be the one spending time with the little girl. When his eyes stung, he lowered his sunglasses to cover them. Sometimes he wondered what he'd do differently if he'd had the chance to go back. Would he listen to Delia and not push for children? That would mean he'd have Delia but no Isabella. He didn't know what he'd choose. He wanted a family. He still didn't understand why God couldn't have let him have both.

As he sat there though, Will realized that he may have wanted both, but he wasn't doing very well with what God *had* given him. It was becoming more and more apparent to him that he needed to change his outlook where Isabella was concerned. He did love her, but had such a difficult time showing it. In a way it had felt a bit like he was betraying Delia by loving the child she hadn't wanted. However, he *had* wanted that child and yet here he was, acting like he hadn't.

"Hey, bro." Lance sat down in a chair on the other side of Will. "How's it going?"

"It's going. How 'bout with you?"

"I feel bad Jessa is cooped up in that room. She would love to be outside."

"Couldn't she just sit out here?"

"I think we're both too scared of what might happen. Sitting out here for the little bit that she did earlier was good for her, but she wouldn't come out again now. I know we may seem extreme in our approach, but I honestly don't know what another loss would do to her. To us."

Will understood the pain in Lance's voice. He knew that with each passing day their hopes rose for a successful delivery. He didn't blame them at all for doing what they could to achieve that objective. There would be many Sunday afternoons that Jessa could enjoy outside with her family once the baby was born.

He saw Isabella slow her swing and slide off. As she joined Julia in the playhouse, Amy made her way back to where he sat with Lance. It was hard to not notice her long tanned legs and the curves of her figure as she moved gracefully toward them.

"Hey, Lance," Amy said as she joined them, but she didn't sit back down. "You out here for a bit?"

"Yep. Unless Jessa needs me."

"If it's okay I think I'm going to go in for a while." She picked up her phone and her glass of juice. "Just text me if you need something."

"Don't worry about anything. We'll be fine."

"Thanks again for the ice cream, Will," Amy said with a smile.

Though he wanted to watch her walk into the house, Will turned his gaze back to where the girls were playing. The last thing he needed was to do anything that might give Lance— or anyone else—the wrong idea where he and Amy were concerned. Of course, he needed to keep that in mind for himself as well. She clearly saw him as a friend—maybe even a brother—and nothing more, which was probably a good thing. He found her interesting and appreciated that she seemed at ease with him. But that was no reason to start looking at her as anything more than the friend of the family that she was.

❧ *Chapter Six* ❧

AMY climbed the stairs to her room, her phone clutched in her hand. She hoped her departure hadn't appeared to Will and Lance to be the frantic escape it had really been. She'd seen Will watching them while she'd pushed Isabella on the swing. A part of her had reacted to his attention even though she knew it was most likely centered on his daughter, not her. That long-buried fifteen-year-old part of her had sprung to life, yearning for the attention of the man she'd thought was lost to her. It had taken her by surprise, and Amy knew she couldn't allow those thoughts and feelings to take hold.

"This isn't funny, God," she muttered under her breath as she sank down on her bed, grateful to be in the sanctuary of her room.

Eight years ago, Will's attention was all she'd craved. That was definitely not what she wanted now. There were just too many screwed up dynamics in the situation. Not the least of which was that he was no more interested in her now than he'd been eight years earlier. Besides, Amy enjoyed how things were in her life now. She was content to wait for a nice, uncomplicated man to love her.

Or so she kept telling herself.

She stared at the screen of her phone before touching it to place a call to her best friend. Sammi hadn't known her when she was a teenager, and Amy had never told her about what had happened back then. She was prepared to tell her now and to ask for advice and for her to pray.

As she waited for Sammi to answer, she walked to the window seat and sank down on its cushioned surface. She had a room along the front, so her view was of the tree-lined driveway. Which was just as well. She didn't want to be looking down on the back yard where Will was with Isabella.

"Hello, Miss Amelia," Sammi answered with a laugh.

"Hey, Samsam. You busy?"

"Nope. Just sitting in front of the A/C trying to keep cool. What's up?"

Amy let out a long sigh and spilled the whole story. "Maybe I was naïve or just plain stupid, but I didn't expect to feel this way about him again."

"So you're telling me that back when you were just fifteen, you felt God wanted you to marry Will?" Sammi asked.

"Yes. I can't explain it. I know it sounds dumb and very teenage drama-ish, but it was such a strong feeling back then. So when he came back married, I was beyond crushed. For the next couple of years, I walked around feeling like I had an open wound on my heart. Again, I know, dramatic, but even now, if I let myself, I can still feel the pain, and it takes my breath away."

"Then why in the world would you agree to go there to help out knowing you'd see him again?"

Amy twisted a strand of hair around her finger. "I don't know. They needed help. Cami had told me he'd changed. And honestly? I thought I didn't feel anything for him anymore."

"And now? What's happened?"

"He's not the same person I felt so strongly about as a teenager. And it was fine—at first. We'd spent some time together with the family, and there was really nothing there. Then today, he's here with his daughter, and I was pushing her on the swing. I happened to look up and saw him watching us—for all I know he was just watching her—but suddenly everything came rushing back."

"Teenage Amy was back?"

"Yep. Just like that all the emotions and feelings were there. And suddenly I'm thinking things like *I wonder if he likes this color I'm wearing. Or, maybe I should've left my hair down.*" Amy pressed her fingers against her forehead. "Where did it come from? I can't be thinking like that anymore."

"Why not?" Sammi asked. "He's available. You're available."

"But that's the thing," Amy said, "I don't think he's really available. Yes, in the physical sense, he is. I noticed he's not wearing a ring. But emotionally, I don't think he's there yet."

"You think he's still caught up with his wife?"

"Yes, I do. His daughter is the spitting image of Delia. How could he not be reminded of the woman every single day? I only saw Delia a few times when we were here for Cami and Josh's wedding, but as soon as I saw her daughter, it was like I was right back there." Amy sighed. "I wouldn't want to be the one he settles for because he can't have the wife he lost so suddenly."

"Do you think he feels anything toward you?"

"I doubt it. If Delia was his type, I'm the exact opposite of her. This has nothing to do with there being a possibility of a relationship between us—there isn't. This is me trying to keep myself from being hurt all over again. I need to figure out how to get teenage Amy to go back to wherever she came from and stay there."

Sammi chuckled. "You know it doesn't work that way.

Emotions are not something so easily ignored."

Amy swallowed hard, her throat tight. She knew she sounded crazy. It was why she'd never told anyone aside from Cami about what had happened back then. And even with Cami she'd never told her how much hurt she'd felt when she'd realized Will was married. So much of her hurt had not come from Will's actions, but from the feeling that God had betrayed her. She'd been so sure Will was to have been hers.

"Listen, Aims, you don't know that maybe what you felt back then was right," Sammi said, her voice more serious.

"What? No." Even though Sammi couldn't see her, Amy shook her head vigorously. "No."

"Maybe God did mean for you and him to be together. Just not then. You would have had to wait anyway, because I'm pretty sure there's no way your mom and dad would have of approved a relationship between the two of you when you were fifteen or even sixteen. It could be that now is the fruition of what God impressed upon your heart all those years ago."

"Don't say that, Sammi. Please don't say that," Amy pleaded. "Don't I deserve to have someone's whole heart? I don't want to share his heart with a woman who was taken from him so horribly. I think it would have been easier if he and Delia had divorced because then at least he would have chosen to separate himself from her. She was taken from him, and he's still mourning her loss six years later. I can't deal with that."

"You don't know that he won't love you with his whole heart. God can ease that grief in his heart and fill it completely with love for you."

"Sammi, he can't even love his daughter the way he should," Amy said. "He gives that little girl everything she could ever want or ask for...except for his love."

"Why? Who can't love a child?"

"A man who feels that that child is the reason his wife is no longer alive."

"Surely he doesn't blame her," Sammi insisted. "It's hardly *her* fault."

"Actually, I don't think he blames her. I'm pretty sure he shoulders that blame all himself, but every time he looks at her he is reminded of why she is here and why Delia isn't. If he can't love his daughter, how could he even begin to love someone like me?"

There was silence for a few seconds then Sammi said, "I'm sorry, Aims. I'll be praying for you. Trust God that He might still have something wonderful planned for the two of you. Don't shut the door out of fear."

"But I don't want to feel this again. I don't want to start counting the minutes until I see him. I don't want to think of him when I'm trying to consider what to wear. I just really don't want those emotions to have so much power again."

"Sometimes you have to take the risk of hurt in order to reap the joy. Don't let the fear bind you from at least being open to what God might have in store for you."

Amy knew that her friend was right. It was something she would have said to a friend herself, but taking that advice now was not something she wanted to do. "I'll pray about it."

"I will too," Sammi assured her.

Watching out the window, Amy sucked in a breath as she saw Isabella appear on the porch. She skipped over to the SUV as Will followed more slowly. He opened the door for her but before she climbed in, the little girl happened to glance up and spot Amy in the window. Isabella waved enthusiastically at her.

Will turned, and Amy felt her breath catch as he waved a hand in her direction. She returned the wave and then watched as he helped Isabella into the back seat of his vehicle. He rounded the hood to the other side and opened the door. Amy thought he'd get right into the car, but he paused and looked up at her again. He wore sunglasses, so it wasn't like their gazes met, but he was clearly looking in her direction.

Frozen, she waited. He didn't wave again but gave a slight nod of his head before disappearing into his SUV. As she watched them drive away, his fancy car glinting in the afternoon sun, she remembered the question they used to be asked in elementary school. What super power would you like to have and why? Back in grade school she'd never had a ready answer, but right then Amy wished she had the ability to read minds. She'd give just about anything to know what was going on in his head.

"Amy? You still there?" Sammi's voice broke into her thoughts.

"Yeah. Sorry." Amy slid off the window seat and went to curl up on her bed. "Will and Isabella just left."

"Where are you calling me from?"

"My bedroom. I could see them from my window."

"Listen, just remember why you're there. You agreed to help your cousin and his family. Focus on that."

"I'll try. It would have been easier if I hadn't agreed to work with Will on Isabella's birthday party. And her birthday is, of course, also the date of Delia's death."

"You can do it. Just be your normal perky self," Sammi advised. "When are Cami and Josh arriving?"

"Probably right around the time of the birthday party, I think. I don't have a definite date."

"Well, focus on the fun you'll have when they arrive. I know you're excited to see them again."

"Yes, I definitely am," Amy agreed. "That was one of the reasons I agreed to come help out."

"Hang in there. And if you need some back-up, let me know. I'd happily trade this heat for a more moderate temperature."

"I may take you up on that offer. But in the meantime, thanks for the listening ear. I really appreciate it."

"I just wish you'd told me about this before. Any other secrets I should know?"

"Nope. That was the biggie. I didn't tell you before because I knew how dumb it sounded, and I really thought it was in the past and wasn't going to be an issue again. Anyway, tell me what you've been up to."

After chatting for another twenty minutes, Amy ended the call with Sammi and sprawled back on the bed, staring up at the ceiling. While it felt good to have shared her turmoil with someone, she still didn't have any answers. And aside from flat out avoiding Will, she didn't know how she was going to keep those teen emotions from flaring every time he came around. She kind of wished she hadn't agreed to help with the party, but for Isabella's sake, she wouldn't back out.

Somehow she'd figure out how to get through this without getting hurt again. Even if Sammi thought she should be open to how things might unfold, Amy really didn't relish getting burned once more when the pain had never completely faded from her memory. It would be like when she'd burned herself twice in the same place while making cookies one time. Burn upon burn. Pain upon pain. She had been able to go a long time without feeling it, but now she felt every single stab of agony she'd experienced back then.

"Nope. Not going to let that happen again," Amy murmured to herself. If God truly wanted this to work out with Will, He was going to have to make it very clear. So clear that everyone else, including Will, could see that it was what God wanted. Otherwise...no go.

৬৽৵ৎ

Uncertain what to make of what had transpired Sunday afternoon, Will had purposefully steered clear of spending any time at the manor. Though he'd had to go by there each day to drop Isabella off, he hadn't gone in with her. She spent mornings with either Laurel's or Violet's kids and afternoons at the manor with Julia. So even though he hadn't seen Amy since Sunday, he'd heard plenty about what she'd done with the girls. Isabella was completely smitten with her and that worried Will. He knew her time at the manor was temporary, and he hated the idea of Isabella being upset when she left.

He had emailed back and forth with Amy a couple of times since he'd gotten the list from Violet for the people to invite to Isabella's party. She hadn't mentioned anything about him helping again, and he wasn't sure if she'd changed her mind, forgotten or if it was still pending. Will hadn't decided yet if he would remind her or not.

Laurel had called him earlier to say they were going out there for supper and invited him to join them. Never one to turn down a meal he didn't have to cook, Will agreed. That day Julia and Isabella had actually spent the afternoon with their cousins since Laurel and Violet had taken them all to a waterpark. The girls would be arriving with them.

The manor was quiet when he got there Thursday afternoon. Lance had left the office early because the bride and groom who had booked the chapel for their wedding were arriving to prepare for the weekend. He assumed that Lance and Amy had both gone to show them where their ceremony was taking place.

He settled on a stool at the counter and pulled out his phone. He was waiting for a couple of emails in response to some he'd sent earlier in the day. One had been to his parents to see if they'd made a decision yet on coming for Isabella's birthday. He was pretty sure they were going to say no since they'd just been there to visit them, but he wished they would just make their decision already.

As he sat there reading other things on his social media, he heard the chirp of a text alert. He glanced over and saw a phone sitting on the counter at his elbow. The display was lit up, and before he realized what he was doing, he'd read the short message.

Hey sweetie! Just wondering how you're doing. <3

It was from someone named SamSam. The phone chirped again, and another message appeared.

Been worried since our convo on Sunday. Hope you're doing okay. Been praying for you!

Trust God to guide both you and him. Don't dismiss this without making sure it really isn't His will.

Will tore his gaze from the phone before another message appeared. It sounded like even though Amy had said she didn't have a boyfriend, there was someone on the horizon. And why would she have told him that when they'd talked about dating earlier? She didn't know him from Adam. If she'd found someone to love, more power to her. She seemed like a sweet girl, and he hoped she could find happiness with some guy who treated her like a queen.

It helped him understand Sunday afternoon a bit better. He'd thought maybe being with him—especially after Maura's comments—had made her a bit uncomfortable, even though she'd been too polite to say anything. Apparently she'd had another guy on her mind the whole time. That made him feel a little better. Or did it? Suddenly he wasn't sure. At the very least it would be easier to spend time with her knowing she didn't care at all about the insinuations of Maura's comments.

He returned his attention to his phone and even though the phone chirped two more times, he didn't look. When the back door opened a short time later, Will glanced up to see a young couple enter the kitchen followed by Amy and Lance. As he watched the couple, he thought how in love they looked. So much like he and Delia had been. They looked young...and happy. He hoped that they enjoyed their happiness for many years.

As Amy approached the counter, he noticed she also looked young. The light green sleeveless shirt she wore had several buttons open to reveal a white tank top underneath which was tucked into jean capris. Her blonde curls were up in a high ponytail. He didn't know how old she actually was, but right then she looked about eighteen.

"Hey, Amy," he said.

"Hi," she replied with a smile as she reached out and picked up her phone.

Out of the corner of his eye Will saw her touch the screen. He was only half-listening to Lance as he talked to the couple. At one point Amy's head jerked up, and he felt her looking at him. Will kept his gaze on Lance, not wanting her to suspect that he'd read her messages. He felt horrible about having done it, but there was no way he could confess without making it awkward all around.

Amy ducked her head again, and he could hear her quickly tapping out a message. Once done, she crossed her arms, tucking the phone against her side.

"So the rest of your party is arriving tomorrow?" Lance asked.

"Yes," the bride replied. "Our parents are staying here with me and my sisters, but everyone else has rooms at the hotel with Jim."

"Rehearsal will be at four as you requested, and reservations have been made at the restaurant you wanted for six. Hopefully, that will give you enough time."

"Sounds perfect," the groom said. "We tried to keep it small and simple, but it's still gotten a bit bigger than we anticipated."

"Yeah, I remember that from my wedding. All that planning and then having things tend to take on a life of their own," Lance said with a laugh.

After the couple had thanked them, Lance walked them to the front door.

"Are you involved in planning for this wedding?" Will asked.

Amy glanced up from her phone. "Uh. No, not the planning. I will be helping Violet and Laurel with decorating tonight. I guess Jessa likes to have the decorations up before the rehearsal so the bride can approve it. She brought everything with her and gave some instructions on what she wanted."

"Sounds like...fun," Will said. That was one area he'd left to Delia and her mom, and they'd outdone themselves. At least it had seemed that way from his male perspective.

Amy smiled, her eyes lighting up. "Weddings are always fun. Usually I just attend them, so it will be fun to help prepare for this one. I remember helping Cami decorate here for her wedding, too."

"The chapel has been put to good use since then."

"I'm not surprised. I hope whoever I marry doesn't mind a destination wedding, because I'd love to get married in the chapel here."

Will wondered if the guy she had her sights on would agree to that. "The combination of the manor being a bed & breakfast and having the chapel was a great idea. It's just too bad that Jessa is down for the count at the moment. I know she enjoys this part, too."

Her phone chirped again, and she looked down at it. Her brow furrowed, and she gave a slight shake of her head as she typed out a response.

"Trouble?" Will asked when she tucked the phone back under her arm.

Amy shook her head. "Just my best friend giving me some advice. I love Sammi to death, but when she gets her teeth into something she's a bit relentless."

"Friends are usually that way," Will commented, realizing as she said the name that SamSam from the text message was a girl. "Out of the best of intentions most the time."

"Oh yes, I know she means well. She just doesn't see things quite the same way I do."

"Hope it doesn't cause problems for you two."

"Not a chance." Amy grinned. "Neither of us can get rid of the other that easily."

A racket from the front of the house drew Will's attention. He turned on his stool to see his nieces and nephews spill into the kitchen from the hallway. Their cheeks were rosy from their afternoon at the pool. He spotted Isabella and watched as her gaze searched for—and found—Amy.

"You should've come," Isabella told her after giving her a hug. "We had so much fun."

"I'm sure you did." Amy ran a hand over the little girl's hair. "Hey, look who's here."

Isabella glanced in the direction Amy gestured. "Hi, Daddy."

Before he could return the greeting, she turned back to Amy, her expression open and full of excitement. "I went down the slide a thousand times."

"A thousand times? That's pretty impressive," Amy said as she glanced his way.

Isabella's dismissal of him stung, but he knew he had no one to blame but himself. He couldn't deny that she was never as animated or excited to share things with him as she was with Amy right then. And Amy appeared to soak it all up like she'd never heard anything so exciting in her whole life. How could this woman who had known his daughter for just a week love her like that? And strangely enough, he didn't doubt she really did love Isabella. He didn't think Amy could fake the affection she showed to Isabella. And what was it she'd said the first day they'd met? *She's a child. What's not to love?*

Matt, along with Laurel and Violet, had joined them in the kitchen.

"Dean not coming?" Will asked.

Violet plopped down in a chair at the table. "He'll be here in a little bit. He's stopping to pick up pizza."

"Pizza!" all the kids said in unison and cheered.

"I'm going to go see Jessa for a couple of minutes," he said as he stood up. "Or did you need me to do anything?"

"Nope. Go keep her company," Laurel said.

Upstairs, Will walked through the open door of the suite and then knocked lightly on the bedroom door.

"Come in."

Will pushed open the door and stepped into the bedroom. The curtains were all wide open and lots of light spilled into the room.

"Hey, sis. How're you doing?" Will asked as he sank down on a chair near the bed.

Jessa set down the book in her hands and turned over on her side, so they faced each other. "For someone who can't get out of bed, I'm doing pretty well. How about you?"

"I'm doing good." Will stretched out his legs and laced his fingers over his stomach. "Being replaced in my daughter's life, but otherwise, doing good."

Jessa's eyebrows rose. "Amy?"

"Yep. They just got back from swimming, and Isabella couldn't have cared less that I was here. All she wanted to do was tell Amy every detail about their time swimming."

"I love you dearly, Will, but honestly, you have no one to blame but yourself. She's hungry for someone to be with her the way Amy is. Someone who makes her feel special and that what she has to share is important. Don't you remember wanting that as a kid? How you felt when your mom or dad didn't have time for you for some reason? I'm guessing Isabella feels that way more often than not."

❧ Chapter Seven ❧

WILL'S breath caught in his lungs at the harsh words spoken in Jessa's gentle voice. He did remember how it felt to not be able to share something super important with his mom or dad because something—or someone—had demanded their attention first. Despite what Jessa said, he *did* listen to Isabella, just not with the enthusiasm and excitement Amy had shown her. And apparently to a six-year-old, that made all the difference in the world.

Before he could say anything in his defense, Jessa continued, "She knows that Laurel has her own kids and so does Violet, but Isabella discovered that Amy doesn't, and she's claimed her. That should have been you, but while you may have given her everything in the world, what she really wants is someone to give her their undivided attention." Jessa paused as if waiting for him to argue with her. He didn't because he knew that everything she said was true. "I've seen them together a bit, but Lance has seen it more. He's mentioned how Amy treats Isabella like she's the most special little girl in the world. And you should see how Amy gets her to behave. It's like she'd do anything to make Amy happy. She loves her. Of course, Amy is very lovable. She's been a real answer to prayer for me."

"And what happens to Isabella when Amy leaves?" Will asked. "It's going to break her heart."

"Yes, I know." Jessa stared at him for a moment. "At the risk of upsetting you, Will, I'm going to put it right out there. You need to man up."

"Man up?"

"Have you heard the saying that anyone can be a father, but that it takes a real man to be a daddy?"

Will shifted in his seat, his gaze sliding from Jessa's for a moment.

"You need to man up and become the daddy Isabella needs. You need to put aside whatever grief, guilt and anger you're feeling about everything involving Delia. I know it's not easy when Isabella looks so much like her, but you need to start seeing her for who she is. She's not responsible for the circumstances of her birth. She can't help how she looks. She's a little girl who needs a daddy, especially because she doesn't have a mommy. Especially because the woman she loves will be leaving her in the months ahead."

Swallowing hard, Will pressed his chin to his chest and stared at his hands. "Why are you saying this to me now? I'm sure you've been thinking about it before."

"Yes. I have, and I've tried to subtly bring it to your attention, but either you didn't pick up on it or you just didn't want to listen."

Will knew it was probably the latter. "And now?"

"And now I'm a mother doing what she can to save her baby. I don't think I can handle another loss. I need you to see Isabella for the gift she is and be thankful for her." Jessa pressed a hand to her stomach. "Don't take her for granted. It can all change in the blink of an eye. You should know that more than anyone. You have something that people the world over are struggling to have. She deserves to be loved and cherished just because she is. Follow Amy's lead. I'll bet you'll see changes in Isabella you never imagined, and maybe even in yourself. It's time to move forward, Will."

Everything Jessa said was like a stab in the heart. He knew she was right, and though he wasn't sure how to change things, he knew that he needed to. A child was what he'd wanted and now that he had one, he wasn't taking care of her the way he should. "Thank you."

"Come here," Jessa said with a wave of her hand.

Will slid from the chair to his knees next to the bed. Jessa wrapped an arm around his neck. "I love you. I wasn't sure I would when we first met. I resented that you'd been blessed with a great family while us girls had to struggle with Gran, but in the end I couldn't help but love you. And now I hurt for you. I want to see you happy, and I think the first step to that happiness is with Isabella."

"You're right. And I love you, too." He sat back a bit when she loosened her arm and grinned at her. "You were the prickliest of the bunch, but I knew I would win you over sooner or later."

There was a light rap on the door, and Will looked over to see Lance standing in the doorway.

"Everything okay?" he asked as he walked toward the bed.

"Everything's fine, babe," Jessa assured him. "Are you going to let me go downstairs for a little while?"

"Only if you promise to sit on the lounge chair and not move," Lance replied.

Will pressed his hands against the bed as he got to his feet. "I have a feeling she'd agree to just about anything to get downstairs."

"I'd carry her if I weren't so worried about dropping her," Lance said as he held out his hand to help Jessa into a sitting position. "Need to use the bathroom before we go?"

Slowly sliding off the bed, Jessa said, "Yes, please."

"On that note, I'm going to join the others. See you in a

few." As he left Jessa and Lance, Will felt a pang of loss. Not so much grief for Delia, but just a kind of longing for the closeness of a relationship like his sister and brother-in-law shared. He and Delia hadn't quite reached that point before her death. They'd still been getting used to being married when she'd gotten pregnant, and the months following that had been terribly difficult for them both. Delia's resentment had grown as had his frustration and guilt. It had not been an environment conducive to nurturing closeness.

The kitchen was empty when he got downstairs, so he went out to the back porch and found the family gathered there.

"Lance and Jessa will be right down," Will said when Laurel saw him.

Once they'd arrived, and Jessa was settled in her chair, Lance said a prayer for their meal, and they dug in.

Isabella stuck to Amy like glue through dinner. Anyone watching Will might have assumed he was watching Amy even though he was actually looking at Isabella. It was just that where one was, so was the other. Afterwards, she finally broke away to go play with her cousins. Keeping an eye on her as she brushed aside her cousin's offer of help on the swings, Will realized that her personality had made it easy for him to distance himself. From very young, she'd been an independent little girl. He'd lost count of how many times a day he'd hear *I do it*. And in later years that morphed into *I can do it*, or *I don't need help*. In talking with his mom and with Delia's, it was clear that she had been destined to be a stubborn little thing. Apparently both he and Delia had manifest similar traits as children.

His gaze went to Amy where she sat chatting with Violet, her blonde curls falling across her shoulders. It was because of her presence that he had truly seen his failings as a father, and even though it had been a painful realization, he was grateful for it. He closed his eyes and leaned his head against the back of the chair. Jessa's words echoed in his mind. *She's not responsible for the circumstances of her birth.* No, if anyone was, it was him. Will knew he needed to make changes, particularly now because heartache was coming for his little girl. When the summer ended, so would Amy's time in Collingsworth. Isabella was not going to want her to leave.

Someone kicked his foot. "You asleep?"

Opening his eyes, he saw Laurel sitting on the chair next to his. "Nope." He straightened in his seat. "Not yet anyway."

"Isabella should sleep well tonight. She had a ton of fun at the waterpark."

"Thanks so much for taking her." Will once again sought her out and saw the little girl climbing the stairs to the playhouse. "She actually seems to always sleep really well. I think it's because she doesn't stop much during the day. I'd love some of her energy."

Laurel laughed. "I think we'd all like a little of our kids' energy. I'm convinced that they are actually energy thieves. If they touch me, they take some of my energy and add it to their already boundless supply."

"I honestly don't know how you keep up with all of them. I can barely keep up with one."

"She's sure taken with Amy," Laurel commented, her voice low. "During our time at the waterpark I heard an awful lot about her."

"Yes, she has decided that the sun rises and sets on Amy."

"Are you worried about that?"

"Not in the short term. I'm glad she's enjoying spending time with Amy. In the long term, however..." Will shrugged. "I'm not looking forward to when Amy leaves. I know it's going to devastate Isabella." He looked at Laurel. "Do you think I should keep her from spending too much time with Amy in order to prevent that outcome?"

Laurel frowned. "I think that might make things worse. At the very least, she'll make your life miserable."

"One way or the other, I'll be dealing with one very

unhappy little girl." Will sighed. "Short of convincing Amy to move here, it's the end result."

Laurel smiled. "You could always try."

"Not sure she wants to live here. It sounds like she's quite happy with her life in Texas."

"Given enough incentive, she might be willing to consider it," Laurel commented.

"Money? Somehow she doesn't strike me as someone who makes decisions based on money."

"Money. Or love."

Will arched a brow at Laurel, glad that they were sitting a distance from Amy, who was still engrossed in her conversation with Violet. "Love?"

"Yeah. Perhaps I should try introducing her to some of the nice men at church. Maybe if she fell in love with someone she'd consider moving to Collingsworth."

Will frowned at her suggestion, trying to figure out why he really didn't like it. "But then she'd probably spend most her time with the guy, and Isabella would be left out in the cold. I really don't think her moving here is the best idea. I guess Isabella is just going to learn at a young age that even when you love someone desperately they can be taken from you."

"Ugh, Will." Laurel scowled and smacked his arm. "Don't put it that way. Fine, I'll skip the matchmaking. Sometimes you can be so dense."

Before Will could respond, Laurel stood up and left him staring after her, not sure what had just happened. She made her way over to where Amy and Violet were sitting and joined them. Will looked from Laurel to Amy, wondering if there might indeed be a way to keep her in Collingsworth. He could afford to hire her in some capacity, but as what? Plus, she did have a job waiting for her in Texas. There was no doubt that no matter what he did to change things between him and Isabella over the next few weeks, she was still going to be devastated at Amy's departure.

჻

"So, Amy, would you ever consider moving here to Collingsworth?"

Laurel's question took her off-guard. "Um. I haven't really thought too much about it, to be honest."

"But you *have* thought about it?"

"The summer is definitely more tolerable than Dallas, but I'm not sure it would make up for the cold winters you guys have up here. And I doubt teaching jobs are any easier to come by in Collingsworth than they are in Dallas."

Laurel settled back in her chair. "What if you fell in love with someone here?"

It took all her might to not look in Will's direction. Was that what she and Will had been talking about? "I guess it would depend on if the guy were really tied here or if he'd consider moving to Dallas. My family is there, after all."

Laurel nodded. "But sometimes love will make you consider crazy things."

"Tell me about it," Amy muttered. "I don't really foresee that being an issue though."

"You don't think we have any guys worth considering here?" Violet asked, getting in on the discussion.

"Well, no, it's not that," Amy said, a little confused by the direction of the conversation. "It's just complicated."

Laurel's eyes widened. "Are you already involved with someone? I thought Cami said you weren't dating anyone."

They'd been discussing her love life with Cami? "I'm not. Like I said, it's complicated."

"Ah...that's never fun," Violet said.

Amy gave her a weak smile. "The heart works in mysterious ways. For now, I'm just praying about the situation."

If these two women hadn't been Will's sisters, she might have been willing to divulge more, but she had no idea what they would think of the situation. She had trusted Cami not to say anything in the past, but still hadn't told her about the latest turn of events. For now, Sammi was the only one she would confide in.

"If you need us to put in a good word with someone, just let us know," Violet said with a grin. "We'd be happy to talk you up."

"Thanks, but I don't think that will be necessary," Amy assured her. "I'm just in a holding pattern right now and that's fine. I'm in no rush since I'm not really sure how I feel."

Laurel stared at her. "You seem rather pragmatic about it. This is love we're talking about, you know."

Amy sighed. "Well, I've just been down this road before. Last time I ended up with a badly broken heart. I'm not hoping for anything really. And there are lots of other issues to be considered as well. So for now...just praying about it."

"I guess that is the best thing to do," Violet agreed. "Even though I'd really like to meet this guy and help you out."

"Yeah, me, too," Laurel said.

Ah, if they only knew. She smiled but didn't say anything more. As it was, she'd probably said too much.

Amy wrapped the last of the leftover pizza in plastic wrap then opened the door of the fridge to find a spot for it.

"So when are we doing this piñata thing?"

She shoved the pizza onto a shelf and closed the fridge to find Will standing there, hands on his hips.

"Piñata?" Amy wasn't sure why she'd asked him that since she knew what he was referring to. "Oh. Well, I guess whenever is convenient for you. I just have to get a few supplies. Do you get a newspaper?"

Will tilted his head. "A newspaper?"

"Yeah, we need newspaper to make the piñata. So if you have any, don't throw them away."

He looked a little skeptical but nodded. "How does Saturday afternoon sound?"

"Maybe Sunday would be better. I think we should do it here so we can do it outside. However, the wedding is here on Saturday so we probably shouldn't be out in the yard getting all yucky when guests are wandering around."

"That's true," Will agreed. "Sunday it is. So between now and then I will save up any papers I can get my hands on."

"And you might want to bring a change of clothes if you're coming over here right after church," Amy said. "For you and Isabella."

"Sounds like it's going to be quite an adventure."

"Oh, it will be. One you'll likely never forget." Amy grinned. "Or want to repeat."

She tried to ignore the flutter of excitement in her stomach at the prospect of spending time with him. Still uncertain about how to handle it, Amy had tried to pray about things. But even then, she wasn't sure what to pray for. In the end what had worked best had been *Whatever Your will is, God*, but there was a large part of her that didn't want His will to be her loving Will. Maybe it was selfish, maybe it was naïve, but like she'd told Sammi, she wanted to be loved with someone's whole heart. She didn't want to have to share. Delia would always be Will's first love, and Amy wasn't sure she could ever accept that he could love her as much.

"Well, I'd better get to the chapel to help with the decorating," Amy said, trying, as she did each day, to act normally around Will.

"I'll come with you," Will said as he followed her from the kitchen out the door to the back porch. "You never know when you might need a guy to climb a ladder."

"I have a feeling that's where you'll find your daughter anyway," Amy told him. "I think she and Julia went with Laurel and Violet when the guys left with the rest of the kids."

She noticed that Will shortened his strides a bit for her as they crossed the yard to the chapel. He was a few inches taller than her five foot seven height. She guessed he was right at six feet and given his long stride, his extra inches were all leg. Up until she'd turned eighteen, she'd favored her dad's build as well as height. She was taller than both her mother and Bethany, but somehow along the time with becoming an adult, her more angular body had begun to soften into curves she hadn't anticipated.

Will opened the door of the chapel once they reached the wide porch. He held it for her as she stepped into the foyer area. The lights were all on, and voices drifted from the sanctuary.

"How exactly did she want these set up?" Violet asked as Amy walked into the area where they were working. She glanced over and smiled. "Hey, you two. Welcome to confusion central."

"What are you wondering about, Violet?" Amy asked, looking at the greenery she held.

"How did she want this and those candles set up?"

Amy moved to look into the boxes sitting on the front pews. "The bride put a photo album in here that had pictures of how everything was to be arranged. She showed it to me this afternoon."

Violet set down the greenery and began to look in the boxes as well. "Aha! Here we go."

Things progressed much more smoothly once they had the pictures to work from. The little girls were put to work placing candles into glass jars which Amy then put on the wide window sills along with some greenery. Violet had Will up on a ladder replacing a few of the white lights that had burnt out.

Amy neared where Will was working just as he climbed off the ladder.

"So Amy, do you sing?" he asked.

"Well sure. Don't you?" She smiled at him before turning to put the next display together.

"Funny. Not exactly what I meant. I just wondered if you have a talent for singing like your brother."

"Certainly not to his level, but yes, I do sing. I'm on the worship team at church and also sing special numbers when asked."

"You never wanted to do it professionally?"

Amy shook her head. "Nope. I enjoy music very much, but have never wanted to do it the way Josh and Cami do. I had other ideas for my future."

"So you've always wanted to be a teacher?" Will moved the ladder to the next section of lights, but didn't climb it right away.

"No, actually, for about a year when I was fifteen I wanted to be the Doctor's next companion."

She glanced at him to see his reaction. Will lifted an eyebrow. "You're a Doctor Who fan?"

Amy grinned, pleased that he'd understood her reference. "I was a bit more fanatical when I was younger. I figured that with my name, I was a shoo-in, but then realized there would only ever be one Amy for the Doctor, and it wasn't me."

"Amelia Pond," Will said with a nod. "But you'd need a Rory."

"Oh, I had my Rory all planned out. Unfortunately, it wasn't meant to be." Amy put the last display in place then turned to watch Will climb the ladder. "Are you a Doctor Who fan, too?"

Will reached to grab a strand of lights. "Like you, I was a bigger fan when I was younger, but I still like to catch the odd show on television."

"A couple of years ago I saved up money like mad in order to make a trip to London. My best friend came with me, and we had a blast doing a tour of places that were of significance to Doctor Who. She's not quite the fan I am, but she was a good sport."

"Sounds like fun. I never thought about going on a tour like that. Most my traveling had to do with missions work. I haven't travelled just for sightseeing purposes in a long time."

"I usually try to save up enough money through the school year to do some travelling during the summer. This year, for some reason, I never managed to get my plans together, and it turned out that was a good thing. I was at loose ends when Cami called to ask if I'd come up here."

"Funny how things work out like that sometimes," Will said as he stepped off the ladder and closed it.

"What's next?" Amy asked Violet, who was working with Laurel on a display for the unity candle.

"Those bows need to be attached to the end of each pew, and it looks like she wants to have that rope strung between each row along the aisle."

"Good idea," Amy said with a nod. "Best way to keep people from spilling into the aisle to take pictures and blocking the view of the professional photographer."

Violet nodded. "We actually recommend it to people, although at some weddings it seems to be less of an issue than others. The younger the guests are, the more likely it is to run into this with everyone wanting to snap shots on their phones."

"I'll definitely be doing that at my wedding," Amy said as she picked up the rope.

"Planning already?" Laurel asked with an arched brow.

"Doesn't every girl?" Amy replied. "Well, I know Cami said she didn't, but I've been planning mine since I was a little girl. Every wedding I attend gives me more ideas."

"I was like that," Laurel admitted. "But in the end, Matt and I had a very simple wedding with just a handful of people. And you know what? It was perfect, and I wouldn't change a thing."

"I figure I'd better have my ducks in a row because if Mister Perfect shows up and asks me to marry him, I'm not gonna give him time to reconsider."

Violet snickered. "Good plan."

"I'm already an old maid by my family's standards. My mom married my dad when she was nineteen, and Beth and Steve married when she was twenty."

"You can't be that old," Laurel remarked. "Certainly not near spinster status just yet."

"I'll be twenty-five on my next birthday," Amy said. "But honestly, I think my mom would be happy if I never married and just lived with them forever. I was her surprise baby, and she's been reluctant to let me try out my wings too much."

"Is she worried about you being here?" Violet asked.

"Not for safety reasons of course, but I think she's praying I don't meet a guy here and decide to stay." Though Will wasn't contributing to the conversation, Amy got the feeling he was listening. She told herself it was just natural since there was no other conversation going on...but she couldn't help but wonder what was going through his head once again.

"Those apron strings are hard to cut," Laurel said as she laid out the last of the ribbon on the candle table. "Rose is getting close. I hope she sticks around for a while though."

"Where is she tonight?" Violet asked.

Amy moved to the first pew and began to thread the rope through the hooks on the ends.

"She's out on a date," Laurel said and then sighed. "She's growing up too fast."

Wow, even an eighteen- year- old had a busier social life than she did, Amy mused. As she reached the last pew, she turned to see how evenly the loops were spaced and bumped into Will.

❦ Chapter Eight ❧

OOPS. Sorry about that." Amy tried not to pay attention to the whiff of his cologne she got. Or how her heart skipped a beat at his nearness. "Trying to see if the loops look the same."

Will stared at her for a moment then said, "Yeah. Your side looks better than mine."

Amy glanced at the other side of the aisle and tried not to smile. "There is a bit of unevenness."

Will scoffed. "A bit? I'm not cut out for this wedding decoration stuff."

"Here, let me see if I can line them up with the other side." Amy bent to slide the rope a bit at each hook.

Once they were looped to Laurel's satisfaction, Amy and Will began the task of hanging bows on each hook with the help of Julia and Isabella.

"This looks so wonderful," Amy said once they were done. "I remember how beautiful it looked for Cami and Josh's wedding, too."

"That was a really beautiful wedding," Laurel agreed. "I think partly because it was such a long time coming. I was starting to wonder if your brother was ever going to pop the question."

"All of us were," Amy said. "But I think he just wanted to make sure it was the right decision. After having such a rough time with his first marriage, he didn't want to rush into anything."

"I'm glad it worked out so well for them," Violet said as she began to close up the boxes. "And I think they are just perfect for each other."

"I know," Amy said wistfully. "Watching them together has reinforced for me the importance of waiting for the right person and not just settling. I know I talk about wanting to get married, but honestly, I'm in no rush. I'm trying to just trust God to do His work in that area of my life."

Amy hoped she sounded more convincing than she felt. It was easier said than done to let God do His work in that part of her life when she still felt the sting of pain from the last time she'd trusted Him with it.

"And that's how it should be," Laurel said.

"Will, can you help us take these boxes to the storage room?" Violet asked. "We'll leave them there to box everything back up after the wedding."

Since the boxes were light, it didn't take long to get them put away. They stood at the rear of the sanctuary for one last look, and Violet declared it perfect.

As they walked back to the manor, Amy felt a little hand slide into hers and looked down to see Isabella skipping beside her. In the dusk of the evening, she smiled at her. She had begun to formulate her plans for the birthday party and really hoped that Isabella would love it. At some point in the next few days, she needed to get together with Will to run a few things by him...and ask for the use of his credit card or some cash.

Back at the manor, Violet and Laurel went upstairs to update Jessa on the wedding plans. Amy headed for the kitchen with Isabella and Will.

Mindful of Isabella, Amy looked at Will and said, "Can you give me a call in the next day or two? I have a couple of questions."

Will nodded. "Yes, I was thinking we needed to touch base about that."

"I'd also like it if maybe you could stop by on your own one time," Amy suggested, hating that it sounded so clandestine but hoping that Isabella wouldn't pick up on what she was saying.

"Will do." Will turned to look at Isabella. "Think it's time we headed for home."

Isabella protested but finally, after saying an extended goodbye to Amy, followed her father out to the car. Amy let out a long breath as she sank down on a stool at the counter. It was hard to push aside the emotions that being around Will had brought to the surface again. But she was determined to not let anyone suspect anything, in hopes that one day the feelings would go away, and no one there would be any the wiser. She had to find that happy balance between not spending too much time with him and yet not avoiding him.

తSo

Will opened the door for Isabella to climb out of the SUV. "Did you have fun today?"

Isabella glanced up at him, her brow furrowed. "Yes. Auntie Violet said I swim like a fish."

"I'm sure that's true. You always did love your swimming lessons."

"I wish we had a pool," Isabella said wistfully as they rode the elevator to their fifth floor apartment. "Then I could go swimming all the time."

"We'd have to move if we wanted a pool," Will told her.

"I'd like to move. I want to live in a house like Julia. She can go outside and play whenever she wants. And Uncle Lance built her that super cool playhouse. I want that."

Will knew that it was a bit ridiculous to continue to live in an apartment with a child when he could afford a home that would give her the things she wanted. He just needed to make up his mind about the beginnings of the house he already had. He'd put the building on a temporary hold once they'd decided to move from Collingsworth, but Delia's passing had made it permanent. So while the outside of the building was basically complete, the inside was empty. No walls. No furnishings. Nothing.

"We'll see about moving," Will said, hoping he wouldn't regret telling her that. "But it won't happen right away, so you need to be patient."

"Really?" Isabella fairly danced around him as he unlocked the door to the apartment. "I promise not to bug."

Mindful of Jessa's words about being a daddy, not just a father, Will tried to help Isabella with her bedtime routine. Her independent streak was wide and well established, however, and she just kept saying she could do it herself.

Finally, after she'd turned out her light and crawled under the covers, Will knelt beside her bed. "Listen, Bella." The ease with which the nickname rolled off his tongue took him by surprise. Yet in that moment, she truly was his Bella. Swallowing hard, he said, "I want to talk to you for a minute. Okay?"

There was a beat of silence. "Am I in trouble?"

"Oh, no. Nothing like that," Will assured her. "I realized today that I haven't been a very good daddy for you. It was very hard for me when your mommy died."

"'Cause I made her die?" Isabella asked.

Will felt the breath squeeze from his lungs. "Why do you say that?"

"I heard some of the mommies talking at Megan's birthday party. They said it was so sad that my mommy had died so I could be born."

"That's not true," Will said, trying to keep the anger he felt toward those women from his tone. "Your mommy had something wrong in her brain that we didn't know about. Yes, she was pregnant with you when it got really bad, but it wasn't your fault. You were born early because of what happened to your mommy, but you didn't make her die."

"Really? I thought maybe you didn't love me because of that."

Will's eyes closed briefly, and he prayed that God would give him the words to say. "I'm sorry, sweetie. I hurt really badly when Mommy died. I loved her very, very much. After she died, I was scared to love you that much in case something happened to you too. I didn't want to hurt like that again."

"So you do love me?" Isabella asked.

"Oh yes, I do," Will said as he placed a hand on her silky soft hair. "I'm sorry I haven't done a good job showing you, but I'm going to try to do better."

"Are you going to be like Uncle Lance is with Julia? Or Uncle Matt and Uncle Dean with their kids?"

"Is that what you'd like?"

"Yes. I've wanted a daddy like them."

Will let out a long sigh. "I'm going to try my best. Be patient with me, okay?"

"Okay."

"Goodnight, sweetie." Will leaned forward and pressed a kiss to her forehead. "See you in the morning."

As he left the room, Will hoped that he would be able to fulfill his promise to her. For the first time since her birth, he really wanted to. And when he'd said he loved her, he knew the words came straight from his heart. He just wished it hadn't taken him so long to come to his senses. He was a fool. A stupid, selfish fool. But he was going to try to make it up to her as best he could.

He went to the kitchen and made himself a cup of coffee before heading for his study. After setting the mug on the desk, Will removed his phone from the holder on his belt and settled into his chair. As he turned on his computer monitor, he found his thoughts going to Amy. He needed to give her a call. He glanced at the time in the corner of his monitor. It was still early enough that he could probably call her.

He picked up his phone and scrolled through his contacts to find where he'd entered her information earlier.

When she answered, he said, "Hey. It's Will."

"Hi. Hang on a second."

He heard her rustling around and wondered if he'd gotten her out of bed.

"Okay. Sorry about that," Amy said. "Just wanted to grab my notebook where I'd made some notes."

"Notes?"

"Yes. For the party. You don't throw a party like this without some organization," Amy informed him.

"I'll have to defer to you on that, having never thrown a party like this before."

"Just be glad it's not her wedding. I'd be sending you spreadsheets and documents in addition to asking for your credit card."

"Well, in that case, I'm glad we're starting off small."

"I hope you don't regret asking me to do this," Amy said. "Because this is going to be a party to remember."

"So I take it you have some ideas?"

"Oh, you bet. Based on my conversations with Isabella over the past few days, I've determined that we're going to do a forest fairy party."

"I get the fairy part. She's nuts about fairies, but the forest?"

"Yes. That's why I want you to come by when you can. I want to show you a spot I found in the woods where I think we can have the party."

"You want to have the party in the woods?"

He heard Amy sigh before she said, "Don't you have any imagination at all?"

"Not when it comes to fairy parties, apparently," Will said, trying not to laugh at the exasperation he heard in her voice. "You're going to have to paint me a picture."

"It will be easier to do that when you can see what I'm talking about. I'll show you in more detail when you stop by. But in addition to that, I want a face painter. Do you know of one?"

Will hated to disappoint her again with his lack of information, so he offered up the first thought that popped into his mind. "You might ask Rose. She used to color all the time and, I believe, has moved into painting. She might be able to help you out."

"Oh, that's perfect. She'd make a beautiful fairy, too. Good idea," Amy said. "Let me write that down. She's supposed to be here tomorrow, so I'll ask her."

Hoping he'd come up a few notches in Amy's opinion of his abilities, Will was still a little uncertain how this was all going to come together. "Um, there are no such things as male fairies, right?"

"Well, of course there are," Amy said. "I figure I'll get you an outfit like Peter Pan's except with wings."

The mouthful of coffee Will had just taken spewed all over his monitor and desk. "Say what?"

"You need to be in character if you're going to be at this party," Amy told him. "You should probably be able to wear a pair of women's tights. Finding green ones might be a bit of a challenge though."

"Green tights?" Will could barely get the words out. He was trying to be a better daddy, but he was going to have to draw the line at green tights. He really didn't think being a better daddy required him to chuck his manhood card out the window.

"Yep. You've got some long legs though. Probably will need the long and leggy ones. Any chance you'd shave your legs? I know from experience that wearing tights with hairy legs can be a bit bothersome."

"No. Absolutely...no. Just no. No." Will managed to get the words out. He waited to hear her disappointed response, but the only thing coming from her end of the phone was gasping breaths, and he realized she was laughing at him. "Very funny."

She erupted into full-fledged laughter then. Finally, she composed herself enough to say, "You should have heard the horrification in your voice. I only wish I could have seen your face."

"Horrification? Is that even a word?"

"Of course it is. My word. It's a cross between horrified and mortification."

As she dissolved into another fit of giggles, Will found himself smiling and then laughing with her. Partly because he was relieved, but mainly because her laughter was so infectious. It had been too long since he'd laughed like that. It was like something slowly loosened within him. The tendrils of negative emotions from the past six years slowly began to unwind themselves from around his heart, and, for the first time in far too long, he felt happiness.

"Okay. Point for you," Will said when their laughter finally died down. "You really had me going there. You've got a mean streak in you."

"Ah, admit it. You thought it was funny, too," Amy said.

"Well, yes, once I realized I really wasn't going to have to wear green tights. I would never have lived that down."

"On the plus side though, you probably wouldn't have had too many women chasing after you."

"True, but I think the women are the lesser of two evils in this particular situation." Will leaned forward to snag a tissue from the box on his desk and began to wipe up the coffee he'd sprayed everywhere. "Are you planning to dress as a fairy?"

"Definitely. I'm already planning my and Isabella's costumes. Which brings me to my next point."

"You have points?"

"Yes, I'm an organized person who enjoys making lists. Focus."

"I can respect that," Will told her. "I, myself, prefer things to be well organized."

"Well, this will be as organized as a party with twelve six-year-olds can be."

"Twelve? How many did we invite in total?"

"Fifteen. Twelve have responded already. The others still have some time to reply, so we might end up with all of them. Plus her cousins."

"That seems like a rather big party, isn't it?"

"Yes, maybe a little, but we couldn't just not invite some of the girls from her class last year. At this age, it's kind of an all or nothing situation. But we didn't invite any boys."

"Well, that's a relief. I'd hate to see how you'd want to dress them up."

"Haha. I'm not in the habit of emasculating young boys."

"Just thirty-something men?"

"Yep. Now, back to my next point," Amy said. "I need your credit card."

"Okay. I'll give it to you tomorrow when I come by to see the spot you found."

"I really wish you'd give me a budget for this party. I don't want you to get your credit card statement and fall over from shock."

"Exactly how much do you think it might run?" Will wasn't at all worried about being shocked at the cost of the party. He'd already decided he'd pay whatever it took to give Isabella the party of her dreams. He knew he was supposed to be cutting back on indulging her, but it seemed important to still give her this.

"I don't know for sure, but definitely not over a thousand. Maybe not even five hundred."

"That's fine. Just buy whatever you need to make this party memorable for her. Don't cut corners. If you want something, buy it. Don't worry about the cost. Believe me, unless you're buying her a brand new car, my credit card can handle the cost."

"I won't disappoint you. I think you'll see that you got your money's worth."

"Seriously, Amy, I'm not worried about that. Just have fun and buy what you need."

"Sorry, I'm just not used to operating without a budget or keeping an eye on the bottom line."

"Well, enjoy yourself," Will told her. He leaned back in his chair, stretching his legs out. "And I don't want to hear anything more about money."

Amy sighed. "Okay."

"Do you have any more points we need to discuss?"

"No, I think that was it." Amy paused then said, "Do you find Isabella's birthday difficult because her mom died the same day?"

Will was a bit surprised by Amy's question, and it took him a few seconds to come up with a response. "Actually, Delia didn't die on Isabella's birthday. After she collapsed, they put her on life support. She was on that for two weeks, in hopes of giving the baby more time. Unfortunately, her blood pressure began to climb, and soon it wasn't safe for Isabella to be inside. They ended up delivering her just before midnight. We discussed it and made the decision to wait until the next day to take Delia off the life support. Everyone agreed that it would be better for Isabella to not have her birthday be the same day as her mom's death."

"I didn't realize that. I'm sorry, by the way, for your loss. I'm not sure I ever told you that."

"Thank you. It's been a long road, but I think things are changing. And it's partly due to you."

There was a beat of silence before Amy asked, "Me?"

"Yes. I've seen how Isabella is with you and realized that I haven't been the parent I should have been with her. I've had my reasons—none of which are really valid—but I'm working to change that now. She's just soaked up the love you shower on her. She's not even your child, and you love her. I knew I needed to do better. She deserves that."

"Oh, I'm so glad to hear that. Yes, she does deserve that, but so do you. There can be a really special bond between a daddy and his little girl. I hope the two of you find that now."

"I hope we do, too." Will wanted to say more, but wasn't sure exactly how to put it into words. But then the moment passed.

"Well, I need to go. I told my mom I'd call her tonight," Amy said. "So you'll come by tomorrow, you think?"

"Yes. I'll drop Isabella off at Laurel's and then come over before I go into the office. Will that be okay?"

"Hopefully we'll be done with breakfast by then."

"Oh, I forgot about that. How about I come out around ten instead?"

"That would work much better. And don't forget your credit card."

Will laughed. "Spoken like a true woman. I won't forget."

As he hung up the phone, Will tried to analyze what he

was feeling. The lighthearted conversation with Amy had been just what he'd needed. But he didn't know if the other feelings swirling around in his heart had to do with what had transpired with Isabella or something more.

❧ Chapter Nine ❧

THE next morning Amy was up early to make breakfast for the wedding party members and family who had already arrived. Thankfully Lance was there to help. He was amazingly adept in the kitchen, which Amy enjoyed teasing him about.

"I figured learning to cook would look good on my husband resume," he said with a grin as he flipped the French toast. "Of course, in the end it didn't matter. Jessa didn't know I could cook until after I proposed. Lucky me. She was willing to take me on whether I could cook or not."

"Well, I'll be sure and ask any guy I'm considering marrying if he can cook. I think it's a definite asset."

As the guests began to show up, Amy and Lance worked to get the rest of the food onto the table. It was a full house, and though Amy hadn't minded the cooking, the clean-up wasn't going to be fun. But Lance stayed until the meal was done and helped with the clean-up as well. Sometimes Amy wondered why they needed her, though she wasn't complaining. It just seemed that Lance really had it all in hand, and Julia was a big help as well.

Shortly before ten, Amy went to her room to freshen up. As she stood in front of the mirror, she took a couple of deep breaths. Though she kept telling herself to just put aside what she was feeling until God made it really clear that this was what He wanted for her, Amy found herself attracted to this Will in ways she hadn't been to the Will of eight years ago. That was making it much harder to ignore her feelings.

When she went back downstairs, Will had arrived and was talking to Lance in the kitchen. It sounded like it was business related stuff. She set her notepad and pen on the table and retrieved her phone from where she'd left it earlier.

"Ready to go?" Will asked when he saw her.

"Yep."

Lance glanced back and forth between them. "Where are you off to?"

"I'm taking Will to a spot I found that I think would be perfect for Isabella's forest fairy party."

"Forest fairy party?" Lance looked at Will.

Will held his hands up. "Don't look at me. It's all your cousin's idea. I'm just along for the ride. And the use of my credit card."

"Brave man," Lance murmured as he moved toward the fridge. "I'm just going to take some juice up to Jessa before I head to the office. I'll have Julia stay with her until you get back."

"We won't be too long," Amy said. "It's not far."

As Lance headed for the stairs, Amy went out the back with Will following.

"How did you find this spot?" Will asked as they followed a narrow path into the woods.

Keeping an eye on the path, so she didn't trip, Amy said, "I took the girls exploring a couple of days ago, and we happened to stumble across it. It was actually Julia and Isabella who gave me the idea. They started pretending to be fairies."

"That sounds familiar," Will said. "Isabella has been in love with fairies ever since she saw some Tinkerbelle movie."

"I hope she'll like what we do for the party." Amy lifted her hand to hold back some branches.

"This isn't going to be the easiest place to bring in a lot of stuff," Will commented. "I'm assuming you're going to want tables and chairs along with the decorations."

"Yes. That's the only drawback, but I figured we have enough strong men in this family to help cart stuff out here."

As they arrived at the clearing, Amy moved to the side so he could stand next to her. She hoped he would have some patience while she explained what she wanted to do. "I want to get some tulle and ribbons to hang from the branches of the trees. I figure it would be great if we could get low tables and chairs that are more the size of the girls."

"Not sure where we'd get those. I know they must be available somewhere because schools have them. I found that out the hard way when I went to one of Isabella's parent-teacher meetings and had to sit on one of those miniature chairs at a dinky table."

Amy clapped her hands together. "Yes. That is exactly what I want. And then I want to have a place where they can decorate their wings."

"Decorate their wings?"

"Yes. I'm going to have wings for each of the girls along with some tutus. After all, what's a fairy without wings? And each girl will get a flower crown when they arrive. Rose will also do their face paint as they arrive." Will hadn't objected just yet, but Amy could see that he didn't quite get her vision. "Then I'll need some tables set up with the food and drinks and the cake. I'd also like to hire a photographer to take pictures."

"You might check with my sisters about a photographer. If I recall correctly they've had someone take family pictures in the past."

Amy nodded as she scribbled a note in her book. "That's good. I'd rather use someone they've had experience with." She looked up to find Will watching her, his blue gaze intent.

"You're taking this very seriously. Thank you."

"Party planning is a serious endeavor. Especially for a little girl's first big friend-party. And I love Isabella."

"And for that, I thank you too. She's needed someone like you to come along." Will paused. "Not just her but me too."

Amy's breath caught in her lungs. He'd made similar, although more vague, comments before. What was he saying? She'd tried to push her feelings about him aside so that she could deal normally with him, but all it took was the slightest hint that he might feel something for her to bring it all to the forefront once again. "You?"

Will shoved his hands into his pockets and nodded. His head dipped. "Like I said last night, I've really been struggling since Isabella was born. I know it wasn't her fault that Delia died. The doctor said that in all likelihood, the aneurysm would have killed her sooner rather than later even if she hadn't been pregnant." He sighed. "I was so wrapped up in my grief it was like there wasn't room in my heart for love. And then it was just easier to not let myself feel anything. After all, what if something happened to Isabella, too? I didn't think I could handle yet another loss."

"She looks a lot like Delia," Amy commented.

Will looked up and met her gaze. "Yes, she does. That has been difficult, too, but having you come into our lives has made me look at her in a new light. She is her own little person even if she looks a lot like her mother. And I watched as you, who had no blood connection, just opened your heart to her. It was like a slap in the face. A real wake up call. Jessa also took me to task for how I'm raising her. Giving her everything but my heart."

Amy smiled, even though disappointment had replaced

that initial spark of hope. If only she would learn to not let things he did affect her. "I'm so glad for you and for Isabella, too."

"I still can't believe it took Josh's little sister to help me see the light. I'm happier than ever that he married Cami." Then, glancing around the clearing, Will said, "Was there more you needed to show me here?"

Josh's little sister. She should have known better than to read things into what he'd said over the past couple of days. All the things he credited to her having to do with him were in relation to Isabella. There was no *you make me want to love again.* Or *you've opened my heart to love again.* "No. I think that just about covers it. Just need your credit card."

Will grinned as he reached into his back pocket. "Now you sound like a wife."

Amy felt her cheeks flush even though his words about her being Josh's little sister still rang in her ears. "Well, one would think your wife would have her own credit card."

He chuckled as he opened his wallet and slid a card out. "That's true."

"You can trust me with it," Amy said when she took it from him. "I promise not to spend too much."

"I'm not worried. Like I said last night, don't skimp. Get what you need to make this the party you have envisioned."

Amy tapped the card on her notebook before sliding it into her pocket. "I guess we're done here." She turned and led the way back along the path to the house. "Are you bringing Isabella here after lunch?"

"Yep. She would be most distressed if she weren't allowed to come spend some time with you."

As they walked out of the woods onto the lawn, Will said, "I'm going to head into town. See you later."

Amy watched his long strides eat up the yard as he walked to where his car sat. Her resolution to not allow her feelings for him to deepen was being tested. She had thought she could be around him and still manage to keep what she felt under control, but her reactions to him earlier were proof that wasn't working. Maybe it was time to put a little distance between them, especially since he'd made it clear not that long ago that he saw her as only Josh's little sister. If she could do it subtly without raising any red-flags, maybe she could rein things in.

As his SUV headed down the driveway, Amy turned and went to the back door and let herself into the kitchen. He would be back shortly with Isabella, but hopefully he'd just drop her off and return to work. And maybe it was time to ask Lance for a little time off. Rose had offered to come hang with the girls in the afternoon if Amy ever needed a break.

Back in the house, Amy climbed the stairs to where Julia was spending time with Jessa. She knocked on the door and, after hearing Jessa's response, stepped into the room.

Jessa lay back against a stack of pillows while Julia sat cross-legged on Lance's side of the bed. A bed tray sat between them with a card game on it. "How was the tour of the site?"

"It was good. And I got Will's credit card, so I'm ready to do some shopping."

Jessa grinned. "I wish I could go with you. I'd love to put a dent in his credit limit."

"I promised him he could trust me with it and that I wouldn't go hog wild." Amy sank down on the end of the bed, careful to not upset the cards on the tray. "But I'm wondering if you'd be okay with me asking Rose to come out here this afternoon. I'd like to do a little shopping."

"That would be fine. I don't want you to feel you have to be here every minute of the day," Jessa said. "And like I told you, you're welcome to use my car any time you need it."

"Thanks. I'll probably be gone over supper, but I'll make sure everything for dinner is ready before I go."

Jessa tilted her head. "Is everything okay?"

"Yes. Why?"

"You seem a little distracted."

Amy smiled. "My mind's going in a million directions with ideas for this party. I just need to start getting things so I can cross stuff off my list."

"I think it's so sweet you're doing this for Isabella." Jessa glanced at Julia. "Even if it's going to mean the other little girls in the family are going to want super great parties like this one from now on."

"Well, let's just see if I can pull it off before anyone gets too jealous." Amy stood up. "I'll let you guys finish your game. Let me know if there's anything you need. I'll just be downstairs. I think Will is going to be dropping Isabella off shortly."

Back in the kitchen, Amy settled down at the table with her notebook and laptop. She made a list of places to go to that she'd seen in town and what she needed to look for at each place. It was likely that she would have to order some things online, so she would need to ask Will about using his credit card for places like that. Before she could reconsider, Amy picked up her cell and placed the call to Will.

"Hey, it's Amy," she said when he answered.

"Miss me already?"

Her heart clenched at his teasing. Though her throat was tight, she tried to keep her tone light when she responded. "Something like that." *He only sees you as Josh's little sister.* "Just wondered how to deal with ordering a few things online. I don't know how you feel about me using your card that way."

"Are they reputable sites?" Will asked.

"They should be, but I'd actually feel better if I just use my card and then you can reimburse me. If my card gets hacked, there's not too much damage they can do."

"If you're sure you have the room. Just give me the receipts as soon as you get them, and I can get you the money."

"Okay. I'll feel better doing it that way." Amy ended the call and got up to get something to drink. She sat back down at the table and stared out the window over the sink. *Please, God, don't let him break my heart twice. Why are You letting me feel this all over again? Wasn't one heartbreak enough?*

She'd been horribly naïve to think she could come here and be around Will again without having any of her old feelings for him surface. And even worse than the old feelings were the new ones that had been showing up as well. Resting an elbow on the table, Amy pressed her forehead against her fist. This time around, however, she wasn't a fifteen-year-old girl with raging teenage hormones. She should be able to deal with this and not let it overwhelm her like it had before.

Determined to get herself some space, Amy phoned Rose and confirmed that she would be able to come out to the manor a little later that afternoon. Will and Isabella often ended up staying for supper, so Amy planned to be gone for that as well.

Thankfully, Will just dropped Isabella off and headed back to town. Amy took her laptop out to the picnic table and looked through some websites while Isabella and Julia played together. Once Rose arrived, Amy showed her what was planned for supper. Laurel and Violet were both going to be arriving at the manor soon for the wedding rehearsal in case anything was needed. Amy was glad that Rose had agreed to come early to help her out. Once the wedding party left for the rehearsal dinner, the family would have their own dinner at the manor.

"Thanks for coming early, Rose," Amy said as she took Jessa's keys from the hook by the door.

Rose smiled. "I'm glad to be able to help. And I'm excited about helping with the face painting."

"I found a couple of sites with costumes for us that aren't

totally inappropriate for a children's party. I'll forward them to you so you can choose which one you want."

The young woman rubbed her hands together. "I can hardly wait. This is so much fun."

"Well, I'm going to head off and see what I can find in Collingsworth before resorting to buying online. I have my cell if anything should come up." Amy slipped the strap of her purse over her shoulder. "Thanks again for coming to watch the girls."

"You go and have fun shopping. Everything is going to be fine here."

Once in Jessa's car on the way into town, Amy took a deep breath and let it out. She hadn't realized how much she had needed a break until right then. And maybe if it hadn't been for the complication of the situation with Will, she wouldn't have needed one at all. But shopping was as good an excuse as any for putting a little distance between her and the man who was slowly bringing all her feelings for him to the surface once again.

⚫⚫⚫

Pulling to a stop in front of the manor, Will noticed dark clouds gathering and casting a gloomy pall over the late afternoon sky. It looked like a storm was brewing to the west, and while he liked storms, he hoped this one didn't bring destruction in its wake. The first drops of rain hit him as he took the front steps two at a time and let himself into the manor. Immediately, he was met with the scent of dinner, and his stomach growled.

In the kitchen, he found the family gathered around the table and the counter. With the impending storm, there would be no eating outside that night.

"Hi Daddy," Isabella said as she skipped toward him.

Will bent to hug her. "How was your day?"

"Good." But then her brow furrowed. "But Amy left."

He was surprised at the jolt of alarm he felt at her statement. Will glanced up and caught Laurel's gaze. "Amy left?"

"Not permanently. She just went into town to do some shopping for the party."

"And she's not back yet?" Will asked.

"She said she was just going to grab something to eat while she shopped."

Perplexed by the near- panic he'd felt at Isabella's words and the relief he'd felt when Laurel had clarified, Will took the plate Violet handed him. Neither reaction made a lot of sense, but he told himself it was just because he didn't want to have to handle Isabella's party all by himself. Yeah, that had to be it.

A loud clap of thunder caused Lance to pause in his prayer for the food. When he continued, he prayed for safety for Amy and that no one would be injured during the course of the storm.

After the prayer was done, Violet turned to Dean and said, "Babe, should I call Amy and have her wait out the storm at the station? She might not be used to driving in this kind of weather."

Will thought of Amy at the station with Dean's deputies and found it didn't sit too well with him. He knew most of them, and while they were nice enough, the single ones could really lay on the charm. The thought of them turning their attentions to Amy twisted his gut. What was wrong with him? He guessed he felt some sort of responsibility for her. Josh wasn't there to watch over her so he'd taken up the task. Even as he thought it, Will knew that wasn't entirely true either.

"If you think she'll need a place to wait," Dean said. "But she might be more comfortable at McDonalds or the diner."

Will hoped Violet would take Dean's suggestion and tell Amy to go somewhere else. Any place but the station. If only he'd known she planned to go shopping in town, he could have picked her up and gone with her. Then, at least, he could have waited out the storm with her.

Not wanting to dwell on what he was feeling, Will dished up his plate and, after realizing the women were going upstairs to Jessa, joined the other men in the dining room. Conversation inevitably turned to work since three of the four of them worked for Lance's company. Dean, while not part of the company, was well informed about it and joined in the shop talk as well.

Will shifted his chair so that he could watch the lightning through the dining room windows. Mother Nature was putting on quite the show. Rain streaked madly down the glass as the storm continued. None of the kids were scared of storms so even when the thunder boomed, no one got upset. He just hoped Amy stayed put until the rain let up a little. Rain could create a whiteout situation similar to snow, and the twists and turns on the road from Collingsworth to the manor could be dangerous in these wet conditions.

Thankfully, the storm gave him a reason to hang around the manor. Will already knew he wouldn't be leaving until Amy was home safe and sound. He just didn't want it to be obvious to the others there.

❧❧

Amy sat in a booth next to the window of the McDonalds. The rain sluicing down the glass blurred the lights of the cars on the street, and every few minutes there was a flash of lightning and a boom of thunder. She slowly ate the meal she'd bought knowing that it was best she stay in town until things died down a bit. Violet had called to suggest the same thing, but she'd already made up her mind. The storm had brought on an early twilight, and since Amy hadn't driven the road at all before today, she wasn't going to risk it in both darkness and rain.

Her phone rang, and she saw from the display it was her mom. Happy to have someone to talk to while she waited,

Amy answered it.

"Hey, Mom," Amy picked up a fry and dipped it into the ketchup.

"Hi, sweetie. How are you doing?"

"Fine. Just waiting out a storm in town."

"A real gully washer?"

"Yep. And a nice light show, too." Amy took another bite of French fry. "How are you and Dad?"

"We're doing pretty good. It's been hot here. We could use some of the rain you guys have."

Amy frowned. Her mom's voice sounded tense. "Is something wrong, Mom?"

❦ Chapter Ten ❧

THERE was a pause and then her mom sighed. "Yes, sweetie. I'm sorry."

Amy's stomach knotted. "What's happened? Are you and Dad okay?"

"Everyone is fine, sweetheart. It's just...there's been a fire."

"A fire? Did something happen to the house?"

"Not the house. The church." Her mom paused. "And the school."

"The school?" Amy felt dread pooling in her stomach. "What happened? Were they able to save it?"

"No. They had been working in the school, painting, varnishing and stuff. They think an electrical short caused the fire and with so much flammable stuff in the building, it went up in flames quickly. Because it was late at night, no one realized what was happening right away. The sprinklers and alarm system seemed to have been shut off or malfunctioned because they didn't kick on. The church was burn a bit, but the school was completely gutted."

"Was anyone hurt?" The thought of the damage done to the buildings was bad enough, but if someone had been hurt as well, that would be terrible.

"Because it happened so early in the morning, no one was in either of the buildings."

"What are they going to do? About the school?"

"Your dad met with the board this afternoon because they realized parents needed to be able to make alternate plans for the school year."

"Alternate plans? So they're not going to try to relocate the school?"

"They spent time putting out feelers to parents while they also looked for possible alternatives. A lot of parents weren't willing to have their kids go to a school across the city since it would mean long bus rides, especially for the younger ones. The church is too damaged to be able to use it for classes. They are recommending that parents look into other Christian schools in the area or consider the public schools."

Amy stared out the blurred window. "What about us teachers?"

Her mom sighed. "They aren't able to offer any of you anything at this point. Your dad said they were hoping that they will be able to rebuild by next school year, but right now they just don't have many options with the school year so close. All the equipment, the books and everything would have to be replaced. It just isn't possible to get everything into place before school is scheduled to start."

"So I have no job," Amy stated without emotion. What was she supposed to do now?

"I'm sorry, sweetie. Your dad and I just feel horrible. Of course, you always have a place with us, so don't worry about that. And I'm sure you'll be able to find something."

"Schools already have their teachers in place for the new year. No one is hiring now. I could maybe get a job subbing." Amy slumped in her seat. All she'd ever wanted to do was teach, and she had been well on her way in that career. Until this news. She'd planned to teach at this school for several more years, but now she was out of a job with no prospect of another.

"I know it's upsetting, but it could have been so much worse. At least you have us to help you out."

Amy knew that what her mom said was true, but part of her wondered how much worse. Right now she felt like her life had been devastated. After her broken heart at sixteen, Amy had carefully plotted out her life in hopes of avoiding anything quite so painful again. She'd planned to teach for a few years, get married and then have a couple of kids. It hadn't been a complicated plan. In fact, she'd tried to keep it simple. But here she was...her life suddenly spinning out of her control and off the track of her careful planning.

First the whole thing with Will. She'd seen another heartache coming from that direction. Had already begun to brace for it. But this latest twist with her career had blindsided her. Of all the things she'd expected to go wrong in her life, that hadn't been one of them.

"Are you going to be okay, sweetie?" her mom asked. "I wanted to be the one to tell you once we had an idea of what the church planned to do about the school."

"I'll be fine. God must have a plan in all this, right?"

"That's right. Trust God even when things don't look rosy." Then her mom sighed. "Though I will admit to questioning God a bit about this on your behalf. But at least you don't have to worry about paying rent to a landlord or having a car payment. I know you've been careful with your money."

"I've certainly tried, but that was in order to travel some, not pay my bills while I was unemployed."

"Sometimes what we plan is different from what God wants for us. Trust Him that all this will work out for good."

"Thanks, Mom." Amy knew she couldn't let her mom

know how upset she really was about everything. Right then she just wanted to end the call and get home to her room at the manor. She glanced at the window and saw that the rain continued to streak down the glass, and lightning flashed. It appeared she wouldn't be going anywhere for a little while.

As her mom went on to discuss other things, Amy tried to focus on what she was saying, but it was a challenge. Her mind was wildly racing trying to figure out solutions to the problems that had cropped up. It was a relief when her mom finally ended the call. Usually Amy loved talking with her, but right then she needed to be alone with her thoughts to process everything.

Amy dumped the remnants of her meal in the garbage and dashed through the rain to Jessa's car. She knew she couldn't drive out to the manor yet, but needed the privacy the car would give her. Once inside, she grabbed a tissue and wiped the rain from her face.

Rain streaked the windshield like it had the windows of the restaurant, but soon Amy realized the blurring of her vision was less from the rain and more from the tears that had sprung into her eyes. She blinked and felt hot moisture slide down her cheeks. Though she wasn't normally given to tears, Amy let these come. She felt so alone. Yes, she had her parents, and they would help her, but she felt keenly the responsibility for her own life and the decisions that lay ahead. There was no one there to share the burden with her. No husband. Not even a boyfriend. Just her.

Sitting with head bent, hands clasped in her lap, Amy sank into a miry pit of tears, self-pity and helplessness.

༄ஓ⟳

Will helped clear up the dishes and then played a few games with the kids while waiting for the storm to die down. And for Amy to return.

"I think we're going to venture out," Dean said a short time later. "It looks like it's letting up."

Will leaned against the counter to look out the window over the sink. "Any reports of damage from your guys?"

"Not yet. It seems the rain was the worst of it. We always have more issues when the wind is high."

"Hopefully everything dries up tomorrow before the wedding. I know they want to do pictures on the lawn afterwards," Laurel said. "I'm grateful we didn't lose any trees this time around."

Will watched as Dean and Violet gathered up their family and left. He hoped that meant that Amy would soon be on her way home. He really didn't want to leave until he was sure she was safe. No one else seemed too concerned about her though. Not long after Dean and Violet had left, Matt and Laurel loaded up and headed out as well.

"Mind if we hang around for a bit?" Will asked Lance. "I'd like to see how things went for Amy. She was shopping for the you-know-what."

Lance nodded. "That's fine. I'm going to go see how Jessa is doing."

"Can Isabella come to my room and play until you leave?" Julia asked.

"Yep. That would be fine," Will told his niece.

After the two girls had followed Lance up the stairs, Will settled in a chair at the table where he had a good view of the driveway. He spent some time on his phone checking email and other messages while he waited. It was almost twenty minutes later that he saw the sweep of headlights. He stood up and returned his phone to the holder on his belt as he walked to the front door.

He opened it in time to see Amy dash toward the manor, her head bent. There was still a light drizzle which no doubt accounted for the speed with which she crossed the distance between the car and the steps. As she got to the top step, she lifted her head. Will saw surprise cross her face before she dipped her head down again.

She stepped past him into the foyer. "Thanks."

"No bags? I figured you'd come home laden with stuff," Will said as he took in her damp blonde curls and wet clothes.

"They're all still in the car. I figured I'd wait to unload them until after the rain stopped. Some of that stuff won't do well if it gets wet." She ran a hand over her hair then plucked at the front of her wet shirt, still not looking at him. "I'd better go get dried off."

Will placed his hands on his hips as he watched her walk toward the stairs. Something was off. Wrong. Her usual bubbly, light step seemed weighted down as she climbed to the second floor of the manor. Had the shopping been that bad? In the brief glimpse he'd had of her face, he'd seen something else there besides surprise. Unfortunately, he couldn't quite pinpoint it, but the thought crossed his mind that it looked like she'd been crying. Not that it was easy to tell given that her face was already wet from the rain.

He wondered if she'd come back down. Part of him wanted to wait around to find out, but he told himself that his plan had been to make sure she made it home safe and sound. She was back at the manor now, so there was no need for him to stick around. If she didn't want to talk tonight, they could discuss how the shopping trip went another time.

Will climbed the stairs and knocked on Julia's bedroom door. "Isabella? We need to go, sweetie."

The door opened right away. Isabella stood there with a frown on her face. "I don't want to leave yet. I want to say goodnight to Amy."

"You can talk to her tomorrow. She got wet from the storm, so she's getting changed. We need to go home."

Isabella's chin lifted, and her hands went to her hips. As she stood there, Will realized that while she may have gotten her looks from Delia, she got a lot of her mannerisms and temperament from him. He also stood there with his hands on his hips.

He sighed. "You got a chance to see her today. You can wait until tomorrow to talk to her."

"I want to say goodnight to her. You said I could."

"I know, but she was wet when she came in and needed to change. She's probably ready for bed now. It's late."

"It's okay."

Will spun to see Amy standing in the hallway behind him. She wore black leggings and a large black sweatshirt with the words "Don't mess with Texas" in bright pink on the front of it. Her hair hung in ringlets over her shoulders, and her face was bare of makeup. She looked much younger than her age of twenty-four. Though she smiled briefly at Isabella, it faded quickly and left her looking...sad.

As he watched her hug Isabella, he had a flashback. Though he'd known they'd met before, Will had no real clear recollection of any interaction with her until that moment. He realized that it was the expression on her face that had jarred the memory. He now remembered seeing her on the staircase of the manor after Josh and Cami's wedding. His gaze had met hers briefly, and there had been sadness on her face that day, too, which had seemed out of place at a wedding. He hadn't spared it but a passing thought that day, but it lingered now as he watched her drop to her heels to talk to Isabella face to face.

He wanted to ask her what was wrong. But more than that, he wanted to make it better.

"Everything okay?"

Will looked up to see that Lance had joined them in the hall, a concerned expression on his face as he looked from Will to Amy.

Amy straightened and gave him a smile. "Yep. Just saying goodnight to Isabella."

"She was refusing to leave without seeing Amy," Will said then looked down at his daughter. "You ready to go now?"

This time she nodded and, after giving Amy one last hug,

walked to his side and took his hand. She looked up at him. "Will we be back tomorrow?"

"We'll see how the day goes. There's a wedding here, so maybe we should just stay out of the way." He was glad she didn't press the issue right then. He looked up and smiled at Amy. "I'd like to hear how the shopping went today. Hope you were able to find what you needed."

She returned his smile, but it didn't reach her eyes. "It went well. I'll still have to get a few things online though."

They said their goodnights and headed downstairs and out into the damp night. Isabella kept up a running conversation for the duration of the trip home, but it didn't require any response on his part, for which he was grateful. Amy still preoccupied his thoughts, and he wasn't entirely sure how he felt about that.

᷍᷍᷍

By Sunday morning, Amy felt marginally better. The wedding had gone off without a hitch. Everything had dried up enough for the wedding party to get the outdoor pictures the bride wanted. And thankfully, Will hadn't showed up at all. Seeing him there Friday night when she'd gotten home had been a surprise. She'd been so distracted by everything, she hadn't even noticed that it was his truck sitting in the driveway. In the dark, it had looked like Lance's.

With the distraction of the wedding, she'd been able to push aside her problems. Though it had been poignant to watch the young couple marry, while her own future was in such disarray. Now as she sat in church listening to the prelude playing, Amy still tried to keep her dour thoughts at bay. There was really nothing she could do about it right then. She planned to call Sammi later that day to see if she had any ideas for possible jobs.

"Amy!"

At the sound of Isabella's voice, Amy looked toward the end of the pew. The little girl stood there with Will right behind her. "Can I sit with you?"

"If it's okay with your dad." She moved down on the pew to make room for Isabella and then moved a bit further when she realized Will intended to sit down as well.

Amy had planned to stay home with Jessa that morning, but Lance had insisted she come. He said that he'd stay with Jessa, and they'd watch the service online together. Julia had come with her but had darted off with her cousins when Laurel had shown up with her brood in tow. Normally Amy would have joined them at the front of the church, but today she had found the first empty pew and sank down into it.

"Good morning," Will said as he settled down next to Isabella. He wore a light green shirt tucked into a pair of black slacks. The smile he gave her set her heart pounding.

In return, Amy smiled what she hoped was a normal smile but it was tiring to keep up the pretense that everything was okay. Thankfully the worship team began to sing, and her attention could safely leave Will and Isabella without appearing rude. The little girl was very well-behaved, singing along with the rest of the congregation. When they'd stood to sing, Isabella had slid her hand into Amy's and every once in a while, she'd squeeze it. When Amy had glanced at Isabella, she'd seen the little girl smiling up at her.

Each time Amy looked at Isabella, she felt a little hitch in her heart. She was supposed to have had a class full of little faces just like hers, and now she didn't. As they sat down after the singing was done, Will stretched his arm out on the pew behind Isabella. His hand bumped her shoulder, and for a moment she wanted to scoot closer to the little girl. To be included in the embrace he gave his daughter. But that wasn't her place. Never would be.

Sadness crept further into her heart. She wasn't one to wallow in self-pity, but right then it felt like the most natural and appealing place to be. What more could possibly go wrong?

Suddenly Isabella stood, and Amy realized the children had been dismissed for their own worship time. Will shifted sideways to let Isabella past him into the aisle to join the other children making their way to the front of the church. When he straightened again, he ended up a little closer to her. Amy glanced at him, and their gazes met for a moment. She couldn't read his expression, but she got the feeling he was trying to see deep into her soul. Maybe he sensed something wasn't right with her. That thought alarmed her a little, and she turned her gaze to the man standing behind the pulpit at the front of the church.

After the pastor had finished saying a prayer over the children who had gathered, they began to file out of the sanctuary. Isabella waved at them as she walked back by where they were sitting.

Amy braced herself for the sermon that was to come. It seemed every time she was struggling with something, the pastor would speak directly to whatever it was. She figured this time would be no different. Clasping her hands in her lap, she listened as he read a passage of Scripture and then bowed her head while he prayed. So far, so good. Surprisingly enough, while the sermon on Christian living was a good one, it didn't speak specifically to what she was dealing with. In some ways, she was relieved. She really didn't want a lecture on how she wasn't handling the latest bumps in her life the way she should.

Trust God.

So easy to do when things were going smoothly. Unfortunately, all of this had dredged up feelings she thought were long dead in relation to her spiritual life as well. After finding out Will had married Delia, she'd struggled to not be mad at God for leading her on. For letting her believe so strongly in something that wasn't to be. And now that she was having to watch her life fall apart around her once more, Amy couldn't help but feel like she'd been let down again. What was it about her that God couldn't just let her live her life? She didn't think she'd asked for much. A career she enjoyed. A good man to love and spend her life with. And maybe two or three children down the road. She wasn't longing for fame or fortune, but it seemed even her simple dreams were not to be easily attained.

Though the sermon hadn't been a particularly convicting one, Amy was glad when the service ended. Will stood and stepped into the aisle to allow Amy to exit the row. She moved toward the doors at the back of the sanctuary, conscious of Will following her. Once inthe foyer, she looked around for Laurel. Before Will could say anything, Amy headed in her direction.

"Hey, Laurel."

"Hi, Amy. How're you doing?" Laurel asked with a smile.

"I'm fine. Just wondering if you'd be able to take Julia back to the manor with you. I need to take care of a few things this afternoon."

Laurel's brow furrowed momentarily but then she nodded. "One of us will have room for her." She paused, laying a hand on her arm. "Are you sure you're okay?"

Amy felt an urge to spill everything, but held it in and nodded. "Besides, it will give you guys time with just your family. You've been so good about including me, but I think you could use some family time."

"You know we don't feel that way about you," Laurel said. "You're just like family to us."

Not exactly what Amy wanted to hear, but she smiled and nodded. "I appreciate that."

"That said, I can understand that you might need a break from us, too," Laurel laughed.

"No. It's not like that. Just need to do a couple of things. I'll be back a little later. Don't wait lunch for me."

Laurel nodded. "See you later."

Glancing around, Amy saw that Will was talking with a couple of people, and Isabella hadn't shown up yet. She figured it was best she slip away before the little girl saw her, or she'd have a harder time leaving.

❧ Chapter Eleven ❧

OUTSIDE the church, the day was warm and sunny. Perfect for what she needed. After a stop at a gas station to get directions to a nearby lake that had a park surrounding it, Amy ran into Walmart and picked up a few things for lunch. Normally she would have just gone through the drive-thru somewhere, but fast food places didn't have her favorite cookies and right now she wanted a bag of them.

It didn't take long to find the park the attendant had given her directions to. She parked Jessa's car and gathered up her purse and the food she'd bought. There were others there, but after walking for a bit she managed to find an empty picnic table under a big tree near the water. She settled onto the seat facing the lake and let out a long breath. For a while, she just sat there absorbing the sights and sounds of nature.

Summer in Minnesota was lovely, but right then she was really missing her folks and her life in Dallas. She wanted to hunker down for a long chat with Sammi. She wanted to go for a walk with her mom. She wanted to help her dad in the garden. The Collingsworths had all been so welcoming to her, but the people she connected with more deeply were all so very far away. And the one person she wanted to connect with saw her as nothing more than another sister to add to the five he already had.

Amy reached into her purse and found her notebook and pen. She set them on the picnic table and then pulled out some of the food she'd bought, along with a bottle of water. After a brief hesitation, she turned off her phone. She didn't expect anyone to try to get hold of her, but the longer she sat there, the more Amy knew she just needed some time to think through everything without distractions.

She found a blank page in her notebook and picked up her pen. Before she began to write, she bowed her head and asked God for peace and wisdom as she tried to figure out what to do. Though she still wasn't happy with what God had allowed to happen, Amy knew that she did need to trust Him. She said the words in hopes that her heart would truly fall in line with that desire.

Back in high school, the Bible class teacher at her Christian school had challenged them to memorize verses. As part of an extra credit project, they were to pick a word from a list the teach had and then memorize as many verses at they could with that word in it. Since she was in the midst of her "trusting God about Will" phase, she'd chosen the word trust.

As she sat there, she reached back into her memory to find those verses. They had given her hope back then, but that had been before everything had gone wrong. Now she needed the reminder to continue to trust God when things weren't going as she had planned. As a teenager, she'd been confused about how to continue to trust God when it seemed like what He'd let her feel had been wrong. She had a bit more maturity now though, but still she struggled with trusting Him.

She let out a long breath and picked up her pen. Slowly she began to write on the lined paper.

Commit your way to the Lord, trust also in Him, and He shall bring it to pass. Psalm 27:5

Whenever I am afraid, I will trust in You. Psalm 56:3

In God I have put my trust; I will not be afraid. What can man do to me? Psalm 56:11

Trust in Him at all times, you people; Pour out your heart before Him; God is a refuse for us. Psalm 62:8.

It is better to trust in the Lord than to put confidence in man. Psalm 118:8

Amy paused, surprised that she had remembered that many. Even with their references. She stared out at the water, watching as birds swooped down and then soared again. There was still one more verse in her mind. One that she knew should be the verse she clung to, but it was hard.

Bending over her notebook again, she wrote *Trust in the Lord with all your heart, and lean not on your own understanding; In all your ways acknowledge Him, and He shall direct your paths. Proverbs 3:5-6.*

That had been a verse she'd been required to memorize several times throughout her years in Christian school and Sunday school at church. So recalling it came easily, but putting it into practice was much more difficult.

She rested her hands on her notebook, running her fingers up and down the smoothness of her pen. Trust God. It was something she'd heard her whole life. It was so easy to say. Clearly she was guilty of spouting the words without putting it into practice. And now she was faced with the reality of having to do it, even though it was a struggle. How could she trust God when she still felt that sting of hurt from all those years ago?

Bottom line was she was scared. Scared of what her future held now that she didn't have a clear view of what lay ahead. Scared of the feelings in her heart. Scared to trust God to lead her down the path He wanted her to go. She was scared of the heartache that might lay that way once again.

Amy swallowed hard, wishing it was just as easy as saying the words. And she realized how easy it was to say she trusted God when things were going well. Now faced with stuff falling apart or happening beyond her control, that trust was hard to come by.

But she knew that even though she should be trusting God, she still needed to do her part. It wasn't likely He was going to just drop another job into her lap. Amy had to do her part.

She flipped a page in her notebook and began to write a new list.

1. Search for other schools in Dallas

2. Call and ask if they have openings for teachers or subs

As she continued to write, for the first time since hearing the news of the fire, Amy felt a sense of control returning. And a teeny, tiny bit of peace. Not a lot, but enough to give her a bit of hope and a sense of direction.

❦

"Why are we going home, Daddy?" Isabella asked as they headed back to the apartment after church. "I wanted to go to Julia's."

Will sighed. "We're going. We just need to swing by the apartment to change and pick up a few things."

Amy hadn't called or texted to tell him the plans for the afternoon had been cancelled, so Will was going to assume they were still on. Once at the apartment, Isabella changed quickly and urged him to get a move on.

"C'mon, Daddy. They're going to eat without us," Isabella said as she danced from one foot to the other.

He finished stuffing the requested newspapers into a bag and grabbed his keys from the counter. They were taking the truck this time because if he was going to get messy, he wasn't going to drive the SUV in that condition. He had brought another clean t-shirt just in case it was worse than he was anticipating.

"Okay, let's go."

Isabella skipped to the elevator and then out to the truck once they left the building. He loaded up the playlist he had of Isabella's favorite songs in hopes that she'd sing on the way out to the manor instead of asking him a bunch of questions.

They only had time for three songs before they arrived. He helped Isabella out and then reached in for the bag of newspapers. He turned in time to see Isabella open the front door of the manor and dart inside. Following more slowly, he stepped into the foyer and closed it behind him.

"Hey, Will," Violet said when he walked into the kitchen. "Can you bring that?"

Will picked up the bowl of potato salad she'd motioned to and headed out the back door. A breeze greeted him as he stepped onto the porch. It was rare for them to eat indoors during the summer. The kids loved to play, and Will always enjoyed the lazy Sunday afternoons spent with the family. Being raised in California had meant an adjustment to the northern winters, and there were some days he tolerated it better than others, but right then, he was glad to call Collingsworth home.

Seven years ago, however, he had come to accept that Collingsworth was not to be his home. The winter before Isabella was born had been brutal, and Delia had been beyond despondent. Finally, a month before Delia's death they had made the decision to move. Will knew that as long as they lived in Collingsworth, Delia would not be happy. So he had agreed to move once the baby was born. And in the midst of one of her more miserable bouts with morning sickness, Will had agreed to Delia's request that they have no more children.

It had been particularly difficult for Will to accept both decisions. He'd put roots down in Collingsworth with his birth family, but he knew his adopted family would be happy to have them come live in California. Since her parents were still overseas, it made sense to settle close to his family.

With those two concessions in place, Delia had been

happier than she'd been in a very long time. Realization had dawned on Will that it hadn't just been the difficult pregnancy that had depressed her. He was glad now that the final month they had together had more happy moments than sad ones. They'd spent time preparing for their move along with the birth of the baby. He had agreed without argument to Delia's choice for a name for their baby girl. After all, she'd suffered the most during the pregnancy. It seemed only right that she should get to pick the name.

"Earth to Will."

Will glanced over to see Violet standing next to him. "Hey. Here's the potato salad."

"You were deep in thought," Violet said as she took the bowl. "Something going on?"

If only she knew. "Just thinking how nice the summers are, and how much I enjoy hanging out here."

"You need to get a place of your own, so you can enjoy the outdoors more than just Sunday afternoons," Violet told him. "Isabella needs space, too."

Will looked over the where Isabella was playing with her cousins. "I've been thinking about moving."

"Why don't you finish up your house? I was all set to be super jealous of you once it was done."

He shrugged. "I'm not sure about doing that."

"Because it was supposed to be your house with Delia?"

"It wasn't ever going to be that." Will shifted from one foot to the other. "We were going to be moving."

Violet turned from where she'd been rearranging the dishes on the table. "Moving? To where?"

"California."

She straightened, her brows drawn together. "You were going to leave Collingsworth?"

"Yes." Unsure why he was revealing this now, Will shoved

his hands into the pockets of his jeans. "She was very unhappy."

"So you were willing to uproot your life here because of that?"

Will sighed. "I loved her."

"William Collingsworth, what have you done?"

Will swung around at the sound of Laurel's voice. She stood a few feet away from him, hands on her hips.

"What do you mean, what have I done?" Will crossed his arms and scowled at Laurel.

"Well, both times Amy has made herself scarce recently it has been when you're here. Friday night and then again this afternoon. It's like she's avoiding you."

Amy wasn't there? Again? Was Laurel right? After all, they had plans to work on the piñata that afternoon. It didn't seem like her to have forgotten their plans. "I haven't done anything. She was fine when we went to look at the location for the party on Friday. I've treated her no differently than I do you guys."

Laurel and Violet exchanged glances, and Laurel said, "She says nothing's wrong, but I don't quite believe that."

Will hadn't believed it the other night, and he didn't believe it now. From her pale, drawn appearance of Friday night to her quick escape after church that day, he wasn't convinced everything was okay. But he certainly didn't see how it could involve him, despite what Laurel may think.

"Maybe she likes you, Uncle Will," Rose suggested. "And if you are treating her like a sister, she might not want to be around you."

Shocked, Will stared at his niece. "That's highly unlikely. She hasn't given any indication of anything like that."

Violet laughed. "And how would you know? You've basically tuned out women for the past few years. The only ones you know are interested in you are the ones that make it blatantly obvious."

"Still." Will shrugged. "I doubt that's the reason she hasn't been around lately."

"You better not be messing with her feelings," Lance warned. "I love you, Will, but she's my little cousin, and I don't want her hurt."

Will held up his hands. "Seriously! I have no idea what's going on with her."

Laurel's phone rang, and she picked it up to look at the display. "It's Cami."

She tapped the screen to connect the call. "Hey, little sis. How's it going?"

Since she'd placed the phone in the middle of the table on speakerphone, everyone could hear Cami's reply. "I'm fine, but I'm a little worried about Amy."

Will saw Laurel and Violet exchange glances once again.

"Why?" Laurel asked, leaning toward the phone.

"I've been trying to get hold of her for the past hour, and it just goes right to her voice mail."

"She told me at church that she needed to do a few things. Is there something more that's concerning you?"

There was a pause and then Cami said, "She didn't tell you?"

Will felt his stomach tighten. Something *was* wrong.

"Tell us what? She said she was okay when I asked her if everything was all right."

"Everything isn't all right," Cami stated. "Mom said she called her Friday night to let her know that the school where she teaches was burned down."

"Like completely gone?"

"Yes, the school was gutted which means she has no job in the fall. I wanted to make sure she was doing okay with the news."

"She didn't say a word," Laurel said, a frown on her face. "Why wouldn't she tell us?"

"She wouldn't have wanted to burden you with the news. I think she probably figured it wasn't your problem and didn't want to worry you."

Will let the news sink in. It certainly did explain her disposition Friday night, but he felt a pit in his stomach at the thought of her dealing with it all on her own.

"Well, I guess we owe Will an apology," Violet said.

"What do you mean?" Cami asked.

"They accused me of upsetting her somehow," Will said loudly in the direction of the phone.

There was silence on the other end of the phone for several seconds. "Was she upset before she got the news about the fire?"

Will leaned his hands on the table and stared at the phone. "Are you also suggesting that I upset her in some way?"

"No. Not at all," Cami said far too quickly. "Anyway, could someone have her call me when she gets home? I just need to make sure she's okay."

"When are you guys coming?" Violet asked.

"We plan to be there at the end of the week."

Will partially tuned out the sound of his sisters' chatter as he pondered what Rose had suggested as well as Cami's reaction to what he'd said. Was there something he was missing when it came to Amy? For a minute, he let himself seriously consider that Amy had feelings for him. And then he thought about how he felt about that. The flutter of butterflies in his gut took him off-guard.

He hadn't felt anything like it in the years since Delia had died. But what if they were all wrong, and she really didn't have those types of feelings for him? If he approached her and she wasn't interested, it would make things awkward between them. He was very rusty at the subtleties of wading into a potential new relationship. And he hadn't given it much serious thought until that moment.

As he sat there, Will realized that if he'd been open to the idea of a relationship, he might have figured out sooner that, in fact, he didn't think of Amy as a sister. The concern he'd felt for her on Friday night should have been a big clue. Or the way he found himself loosening up around her. And laughing with her. She'd brought light and laughter into Isabella's life, but she'd also brought those same things into his. And though she'd been responsible for some of the changes in his relationship with Isabella, she had also been responsible for some of the changes in him.

What was he supposed to do now? Before the news of the school had come, she'd been planning to leave at the end of the summer. That wouldn't have given him enough time to figure things out. Maybe he could start by suggesting she hang around Collingsworth. He could hire her as a nanny for Isabella—not that he really needed one—but he was willing to consider anything to keep her there long enough to find out if what he felt was really genuine, and if she felt anything for him in return.

But then Will had to give his head a shake. What would a twenty-something beautiful young woman want with a man like him? There were probably any number of guys who would happily be in a relationship with her, and none of them likely came with the baggage he did.

"Earth to Will!" Violet snapped her fingers in front of his face.

Will turned to scowl at her. "What?"

Violet lifted a brow at his response. "Just wondering what you thought about the news about Amy's school."

"It's horrible." Will asked. "I feel bad for her."

Laurel nodded. "Me too. It's hard to believe something like that could happen."

"What do you think she's going to do for a job?" Violet asked. "I'm sure it must be upsetting for her."

"Her parents will make sure she's taken care of," Lance said. "But knowing Amy, I'm sure she's already trying to figure out what to do next. That girl was never one to let grass grow beneath her feet."

"What if we offered to hire her as the family nanny?" Will suggested.

"The family nanny?" Laurel asked.

"Yes. Between Jessa and Lance's new little one and the rest of the kids in the family, I'm sure we could keep her busy."

"I'm not so sure she wants to hang around here," Laurel pointed out. "She's commented a few times about how she doesn't really like the winters up here."

"And I'm not sure she'd want to be so far away from her parents," Lance said. "They're a very close family."

Will was surprised at the depth of his disappointment at having his idea shot down. "Well, I'll certainly pay her extra for organizing Isabella's party so hopefully that will help her out for a little while."

Not sure that he was the best person to put forth ideas to help Amy, Will held his tongue while the others talked about it. At one point he tried to convince Isabella they should leave, but as usual, she was determined to wait for Amy. He didn't try too hard though. Knowing what he did now, he wanted to make sure that Amy was okay and that she was still up to doing the party for Isabella. He didn't want her to feel overwhelmed by it if she was trying to deal with a bunch of other stuff in her life.

༄༅

Amy gathered up her things and walked to Jessa's car. She had enjoyed her time of quiet and reflection but knew she needed to get back to the manor. Though she still had no answers for what her future held, she felt a little bit more in control of herself. The sadness she'd been dealing with had ebbed a bit. Maybe the future she envisioned was still out there, it would just take a little bit longer to get to it. There would be other teaching jobs. And there would be other men.

Though she could no longer deny she had feelings—both old and new—for Will, she had no intention of acting on them. She just couldn't see them having the type of relationship she wanted. She didn't think it was wrong to want to be a man's only love. Delia had, and most likely always would have, a big part of Will's heart. She was his first real love, the one he'd loved enough to marry. And they had a daughter together—a physical manifestation of their love—and not just a daughter, but one that was the spitting image of her mother. Though Amy adored Isabella, she wasn't sure she could ever be comfortable with the fact that every day Will would see the beauty of his deceased wife in her face.

She started up the car and drove back to the manor. It wasn't a big surprise to see Will's truck was still parked in the driveway. Taking a deep breath, Amy practiced a smile and tried to school her features into a pleasant expression. She gathered up her things and headed for the front door.

Silence greeted her as she walked into the foyer. She figured they were likely in the back yard, and took advantage of that to scoot up the stairs to her bedroom. After changing into something more comfortable, she went back downstairs. It wasn't that she *wanted* to be around people right then, but she knew it would seem strange if she didn't show up at some point.

Lance spotted her first and stood up. As she neared, he grabbed her in a big hug and then held her at arm's length, a concerned expression on his face. "Okay, young lady, why didn't you tell me about the school?"

And just like that, her wall dropped down. Her shoulders slumped as her gaze slipped from his. She shrugged. "I didn't want to worry you."

"Hey. We're family. I'm supposed to worry about you."

Lance chucked her under the chin. "You don't need to shoulder this kind of stuff on your own."

"You already had so much on your plate. I didn't want to add to it." She looked up at him. "How did you find out?"

"Cami called. She's been trying to get hold of you, but apparently you turned your phone off."

"Oh." Amy pulled her phone from the pocket of her shorts and pressed a button. "Oops. I forgot to turn it back on."

"You might want to give her a call. She's worried about you."

"We all are," Laurel said. She stood up and came to give Amy a hug. "You don't need to keep stuff like this from us. We're here for you."

Amy felt tears prick at her eyes. "Thanks. I just didn't want to worry anyone."

"Well, call Cami so you can get her to stop worrying."

With a smile, Amy tapped the screen to call Cami. She saw that her sister-in-law had called six times.

"Amelia Moyer, why aren't you answering your phone?" Cami said in lieu of a greeting.

"I'm sorry, Cam. I needed to think things through. I just needed a little time." Amy sank down into one of the lawn chairs.

"How are you doing?"

"I'm doing okay. Still trying to figure out what to do. They said they can't see any way to run the school year. They made the decision quickly so that parents had time to find alternative schooling for their kids."

"Are you going to be okay financially? You know Josh and I are more than willing to help you out."

"I'd rather not go that route, but thank you for the offer. I'll be fine."

"We'll discuss it more when we come, but now tell me

what's going on with Will?"

"Will?" The word escaped before Amy could stop it. She glanced in his direction and found him watching her, his blue gaze unreadable. She looked away.

"Yes. My sisters were aware that something wasn't right, but for some reason they thought it was Will's fault. Were they right?"

"No, not at all." Amy realized that Cami couldn't know that Will was sitting just feet from her, but she didn't really want to leave and give them the impression that she had something to hide.

"Why don't I believe you?" Cami sighed. "I was worried this might happen. Are you feeling for him the way you did as a teenager?"

"Not really." Amy let her gaze go to the structure where the kids were playing. She hoped that her cheeks weren't flaming red.

"Not really? What's that supposed to mean?"

"Just what I said. Not really. Things change. This is just another one of those things that I have to deal with."

"Ah, sweetie." Cami paused.

"It really doesn't matter. Plans change, but that doesn't mean I have to just settle for less than what I want."

Cami didn't say anything for a few seconds. "Okay, you're being cryptic now. They're all there, aren't they?"

"Yes." *Finally.* "We can talk about my plans more when you come. Maybe by then I'll have a better idea of what's going on."

"Alright, sweetie, but let me know if you need anything."

"I will."

After she had said goodbye to Cami, Amy drew on every bit of her acting skills and pasted a smile on her face as she looked at Will. "I hear you are getting blamed for my change of disposition over the past few days. Sorry about that."

Will's expression was still unreadable as he met her gaze. Nerves fluttered in her stomach when he didn't smile or respond at first.

❧ Chapter Twelve ❧

*F*INALLY, he said, "I've been accused of worse things in my life. And given what did upset you, I almost wish it had been something I did. I'm sorry to hear about the fire."

"It was quite a shock. I never saw anything like this happening. That's for sure."

"What are you going to do now?" Violet asked.

Amy looked away from Will to his sister. "I'm not sure. I'm just trusting that God has a plan because I sure don't."

"We'll be happy to have you stay as long as you want, cuz," Lance said. "I know Jessa would love help with the baby after it's born. Just know that you are more than welcome to stay here until you figure out what to do next. Same salary you're currently getting."

Tears stung the backs of Amy's eyes as she smiled at him. "Thank you. I might just take you up on that offer. I'm going to be putting out some feelers this week regarding subbing positions. If your winters weren't so cold, I'd look into options here."

"Isabella would love that," Will said.

But would you? The thought popped into Amy's head but, as quickly as she could, she shoved it aside. The reality was that part of her emotional upheaval over the past few days *had* been because of Will. Soon the one person who understood more than most her feelings for Will, both past and present, would be there. Amy had to admit she was looking forward to being able to spill everything to her sister-in-law. Though Will was Cami's brother, when it had come to Amy's feelings about him, Cami had always spoken of him as if he was just any guy Amy might have been interested in.

"So is everything going well with the party planning?" Laurel asked.

"My end is going great," Amy said. "I've got plenty still to do this week, but I think everything will be ready in time." She looked over at Will. "Any luck with the tables and chairs?"

"Actually, yes." He straightened in his seat. "I realized today that the church likely had the smaller furniture you wanted. I spoke with the guy in charge of the building maintenance to ask him if we could borrow it for the day. He said that wouldn't be a problem as long as we had it back in place for church the next morning."

This time Amy's smile was genuine as she clapped her hands. "Oh, I'm so glad. And I'll make sure we're done with them in plenty of time."

"Do you know yet if your folks are coming, Will?" Lance asked.

"Last I heard they were still considering it. I wish they'd just make up their minds already. I told them I'd pay for their tickets, so it's not like it's a money issue. And they can stay at Grandma's place."

Laurel poured a glass of lemonade and handed it to Amy. "But Delia's folks are coming for sure?"

"Yes, they're arriving next Friday."

"Same day as Cami and Josh." Amy took a sip from her

glass. "It's going to be a busy few days."

Lance frowned. "And Jessa is not too happy that she can't be part of it."

"I feel so bad for her," Violet said. "I know it's incredibly difficult for her to have to sit out so much of everything going on this summer."

"She knows it's for a good reason, but it's still a challenge for her. Particularly now that she's even more restricted." Lance ran a hand through his hair. "And I miss having her around."

Amy saw the love mixed with sadness on Lance's face. It touched her to see how much her cousin still loved Jessa after nearly a decade together. She hoped it would be that way someday for her.

"And on that note, I think I'm going to go spend some time with my love," Lance said as he stood. "Feel free to come by and see her before you guys leave. She loves it when you visit."

Once he was gone, Violet said, "Do you need our help with anything, Amy? I'm not the most crafty person around, but if you give me some directions, I can probably do a few simple tasks."

"Oh my!" Amy turned to look at Will. "I'm so sorry I forgot. We were supposed to do the piñata today."

Will nodded. "But it's okay. I realize you've had other things on your mind. We can do it another day."

"No, I think now would be a great time," Amy said. "I'll just go get what we need to do it."

Half an hour later as he draped yet another sticky strip of newspaper on the balloon Amy had given him, Will understood what she'd meant about messy. His fingers were coated in the smelly flour paste that she'd made up along with instructions on how to apply the strips to the balloon.

"How's it coming?" Amy leaned over his shoulder, giving him a whiff of her perfume. It was infinitely better than the paste smell.

"I'm getting the hang of it, I think," Will said as he lifted the balloon that now had a coat of strips on it.

Amy reached past him and ran her fingertips along the damp surface. "That's really nice and smooth. You're doing a terrific job."

Will chuckled. "Well, at least I know I could a job making piñatas if Lance ever fires me."

"Yeah, like that's going to happen," Lance said from where he sat on a lounge chair. He'd gone upstairs for a bit but then had reappeared when Laurel and Violet had said they'd go spend some time with their sister.

"How many layers am I doing?" Will asked as he set the balloon back down.

"One on this balloon to start. It needs to dry before we do the next layer." Amy pulled out another balloon and blew it up. "But we can work on this one while we wait."

"How many of these things are we going to make?" Will asked.

"Just the two." Amy tied off the end of the balloon and handed it to him. "Here. How about I get the strips ready, and you can put them on the balloon."

She sat down across the newspaper-covered picnic table and picked up a strip and ran it through the paste. He watched her slender, pink-tipped fingers slide the excess paste off the paper before holding it out to him. As he laid the strip across the balloon, she took another and prepped it for him again. They worked in silence while Lance, Matt and Dean talked. The kids ran over every once in a while to check on the progress. Isabella was particularly curious since she knew they were for her party.

Will fell into a rhythm with Amy, and the process went more quickly except for when they had to wait for the layers to dry a bit before adding another one. In total, they did three layers on each balloon.

"We've got plenty of time for them to dry completely before the party," Amy said. "I'm going to be painting them next week so they won't look like this."

Will held up his paste-coated hands. "This is certainly a first for me."

Amy grinned. "Well, now you can make one for her birthday every year."

"I'm too chicken to tackle this on my own," Will informed her. "I don't know how to make the paste."

"I'll teach you."

"Or you could just make sure you're around to do it yourself." Even as he said the words, Will wondered if he'd crossed a line.

She regarded him for a moment, her expression guarded, but then she smiled. "I might be able to do that. There are worse things than spending summers in Minnesota."

"We'd love to have you come each summer," Lance said. "You've been such a great help."

Amy began to gather up the stuff they'd used. "I'm glad it worked out for me to come. This is the first time I've been in Collingsworth for a summer. The last two times I was here you guys still had snow on the ground. I have to say I like this a whole lot better."

"Are we leaving these out here?" Will gestured to the piñatas.

Amy nodded. "Until they've dried a bit more. I'm just going to clean up the rest of this stuff and get this paste off me before it dries completely."

Will followed Amy into the house. After washing his hands, he said, "Is there a garbage bag I can put all the other stuff into?"

"The garbage bags are under the sink," Amy said as she set down the paste bowl.

"What exactly are those piñatas supposed to be?" Will

asked as he opened the cupboard doors and pulled out a garbage bag.

"I'm still debating a bit on that. I could paint them shades of blue and say they're raindrops."

"Raindrops? Well, there will certainly be showers of candies when they whack them open."

Amy laughed. "True." She scraped the rest of the paste into the garbage can before taking the bowl to the sink and filling it with water. "Probably be the best part of the party. The mad scramble for candy."

"I suppose I need to be at the party, right?" Will leaned back against the counter, hands braced on the edge. "Not that I don't want to be with Isabella on her birthday, but I'm thinking it's going to be mainly mothers at the party with their little girls, right?"

"There will be a few mothers. Not sure that each one will stay. I think there will be a few who hang around." Amy glanced over at him as she cleaned the paste bowl. "But yes, you will most likely be the only male at the party."

"I guess I should just be glad you're not making me dress in a costume," Will said with a grin as he remembered their conversation.

"Well, all I said was you wouldn't have to dress as a fairy. I could still get a costume for you."

Will laughed. "I think I'll stick to human attire, so the other parents there don't feel out of place."

Amy shot him a look, humor in her gaze. "How kind of you."

"I'm nothing if not kind and considerate. My mother would expect nothing less of me."

Though Will was as reluctant as Isabella to leave, when the others all decided it was time to head for home, they got ready to go as well.

"Thanks again for all the effort you're putting into this,"

Will said as Isabella gathered up her things.

"You're welcome. Again." She smiled at him. "I need this to take my mind off...everything else. I know it's not really your thing, so I do appreciate your efforts."

"A few more afternoons like this and it might just become my thing," Will said with a laugh. "You're making me see sides of myself I never knew existed. Who knew I had a crafty bone in my body."

"We still have more to do, so you'll get even more practice." She paused then said, "Do you need your credit card back?"

"No. I have another one if I need to buy something." He paused then said, "And if you need anything for yourself, please feel free to use that card to buy it."

Her brow furrowed at his words. "For myself?"

"I know that money will probably be tight if you don't have a job to go back to in the fall. I have more than I'll ever need, so if you need something, just buy it."

"Thank you, Will. I appreciate your generosity, but I think I'll be okay. Lance and Jessa are paying me well to help out, plus I haven't had many expenses while living here."

"Okay. Just know the offer stands if something should come up. Plus I will be paying you for your help with the party anyway."

Her eyes narrowed briefly. "I believe part of the deal was that you *didn't* pay me, Will. I'm not doing this for the money."

Not wanting to get into a discussion about it right then, he just said, "We'll talk about it after the party is all done."

Isabella joined them with the small bag she'd brought with her. She wrapped her arms around Amy's hips. "Bye, Amy. See you tomorrow."

Amy ran a hand over Isabella's dark hair and bent to press a kiss to her forehead. "Yep. I look forward to it. Bye, sweetie."

Will held his hand out to Isabella. She slid her tiny one into his grasp and skipped along beside him as they went to where the truck was parked. As he climbed behind the steering wheel, he looked over and saw Amy was still standing on the porch watching them, her arms crossed over her waist. He rolled down his window and as he headed down the driveway he lifted a hand to wave goodbye.

৩০৵

Amy watched the shiny vehicle disappear from view. Instead of going back into the manor, she sank down on the top step, drawing her knees close. The sun was still bright in the late afternoon sky, and she loved the feel of its warmth on her skin. As she sat there, the events of the afternoon replayed through her mind.

It was a relief that the others were aware of her situation. She realized now she should have at least told Lance what had happened. Their concern for her was touching and made her glad she was at Collingsworth instead of home in Dallas. Her mother would no doubt have been hovering over her in concern which would have driven her nuts sooner rather than later. Here they had offered their sympathies and, when she had moved onto something else, had not forced her to continue thinking about it. And Will's offer had been touching as well. That care he had for others was one of the things that had always made him attractive to her.

She heard the front door open and looked over her shoulder to see Lance step out.

"You doing okay?" he asked as he sat down beside her.

Amy looked over and smiled at him. "I am, actually. Having the party to focus on is a big help."

"Seems like you have that well in hand."

"I do. Just hope it all comes together."

"I know Jessa would love to help you out. If you have some stuff that she can do, I know she'd appreciate the distraction."

"I was thinking about that as we worked on the piñatas today. I think I have a few different things she and Julia could help me with. And Laurel and Violet said they'd help more too. A girls' day- in might be in order."

"You looking forward to Cami and Josh arriving?"

"Yes. Very much so. How about you?"

"Yeah, I've missed Josh a lot. You know how it is. He isn't just my cousin. I sure wish they could have settled here, but I know that their music ministry is important." They sat in silence for a few minutes before Lance spoke again. "So I know it was kind of a joke thing this afternoon, but was there any truth to you avoiding Will because of something he did?"

Amy glanced over at him. "No, he didn't do anything."

"So maybe the other theory might be worth considering?" Lance asked.

"Other theory? I never heard the other theory."

"When Will insisted he hadn't done anything, he mentioned that he treated you just like he did his sisters."

Amy nodded. "That's true."

"That's when Rose suggested maybe that was the problem."

When she turned to look at him again, Amy found Lance watching her. "I don't have a problem with how Will treats me."

Lance lifted a dark brow. "Are you sure? Rose thought maybe the reason you were avoiding him was because you didn't want to be treated like a sister."

"Are you asking me if I want Will to view me as potential girlfriend material instead of a sister?"

Both of Lance's eyebrows rose at that remark. "I forget that you're not one to beat around the bush too much, are you?"

Amy shrugged. "Sometimes getting right to the point is the best thing."

"And if I *was* asking that?"

"I had a crush on Will when I first met him almost ten years ago. I'm older now and wise enough to know that there's no chance of anything between us." When Lance looked like he was going to question her further, Amy held up a hand. "Just trust me on this. I have my reasons for how I feel. And since I don't think Will is interested in me that way, it's all a moot point anyway."

"Okay. I just don't want your mom mad at me for sending you home with a broken heart."

Amy smiled. "Don't worry about that. I think my mom would be more upset if you hooked me up with someone here, and I didn't go back to Dallas."

Lance laughed. "True."

Their conversation moved away from Will to the week ahead. They had two last sets of guests booked for the week ahead, but because of the family coming in they'd closed the bed & breakfast to any more guests for the following three weeks. Amy was looking forward to a break from guests and to just being able to focus on the family arriving and the party.

Over the next few days, Amy continued to gather what she needed for the party. Slowly but surely the items on her list were getting ticked off. The photographer Jessa had suggested had been available to take pictures at the party. She'd found a caterer who had been willing to work with her on the special food she wanted. The things she'd ordered online were arriving.

All the party preparations had been a nice distraction from constantly thinking about what her future held. Sammi had called her the previous Sunday night, and they'd had a long chat about everything. That had helped Amy as well.

Her friend was always such an encourager and had promised to pray for her. Sometimes, Amy wondered if prayer was the only thing she could do. Everything else she had tried seemed to yield no positive results. She had made several phone calls to schools in Dallas, but no one had any openings. Although she'd left her name and asked to be contacted if something opened up, she had her doubts that anything would. Amy just wasn't sure what else to do and it was getting a bit depressing, so she focused on the party stuff as much as possible.

After the last guests left Sunday morning, Amy breathed a sigh of relief. Not that she hadn't enjoyed meeting the guests who'd come to visit. It had been fun getting to know them and finding out where they were from and why they were in Collingsworth, but now she could focus exclusively on the party and the family who would be arriving at the end of the week.

As usual, everyone gathered at the manor after church for lunch. Knowing the story of their family, Amy was glad to see the closeness that had developed between the siblings. She did wonder about Lily though. Given that Lily had experienced the worry the others had had about Cami when she'd left Collingsworth, Amy was surprised that she would turn around and do basically the same thing. She knew from conversations with Jessa that they heard from her periodically. Enough to know that she was busy travelling around the world.

She wondered if Lily's departure had had anything to do with their mother's death. It was about two years ago that Elizabeth Collingsworth had passed away. Amy remembered when Josh had called with the news that Elizabeth's health was failing and asked them to pray. In the end, it had apparently been God's will to take her instead of heal her. She knew from talking to Cami it had been a difficult time for everyone.

"Ready to eat?" Lance asked, drawing Amy back to the present. Once everyone had gathered together, Lance said grace.

"Is Jessa not coming down?" Violet asked Amy after the prayer was done.

She shook her head as she handed paper plates to the kids. "She said she's been feeling some contractions today, so she's laying low."

"Contractions? Already?"

"Most likely Braxton Hicks as they do go away, but she's not taking any chances."

As they sat down, Amy found herself sitting next to Isabella with Will on the other side. It wasn't hard for her to picture them as a family, but she knew she needed to keep her mind—and emotions—from going in that direction. Heartache was the only likely outcome of such thoughts.

Once the meal had ended, Lance left the group to once again go spend some time with Jessa. After they'd finished clearing up the food and dishes, Laurel said, "Hey, Amy, do you still need some help with stuff for the party?"

"Well, since you're offering..." Amy grinned. "I have a few things you could probably do. Do you want to do some now or wait until later in the week?"

"Now is fine. I'm in no rush to get home."

"Great! I'll go get my stuff, and we can work on a couple of things."

"Should us guys leave?" Matt asked. "I'm not about to get roped into making tutus or crowns."

Amy laughed, feeling better than she had in a few days. "I won't make you do anything. Unless you want to wear tights at the party like Will is going to." She tossed the comment over her shoulder as she headed for the back porch.

"Hey now!" She heard Will call out after her. "I thought we'd decided that wasn't going to happen."

Leaving him to explain her comment, Amy hurried up to her room and went through the bags there to pull out a few things she figured would be easy to do in an afternoon.

❧

"Seriously, I was never going to wear tights," Will insisted.

"Not even for Isabella and Amy?" Violet asked, a grin on her face.

"Not even," Will confirmed. He glanced at Matt and Dean. "Are you telling me you guys would wear tights for your daughters?"

"Not a chance," Matt said.

"Never in a million years," Dean agreed.

"At any rate, it was just a joke. She did get me pretty good though, I have to say."

Laurel laughed. "I wish she'd let the joke play out a little more. I would have liked to have been part of that."

"I think she could hear the absolute panic in my voice as she was telling me all about the costume she had for me to wear. And then she asked if I'd be willing to shave my legs since hairy legs and tights apparently don't go too well together."

Laurel and Violet burst into laughter, joined by their husbands. Will couldn't keep from laughing at the memory as well.

"Oh man," Laurel said through giggles. "I would have paid good money to see the expression on your face."

They were still laughing when Amy came back out. The guys vacated their spots around the picnic table as she began to empty the bag she carried. From his seat in a lawn chair, Will watched her lay out yards of ribbon and some fluffy pink material.

"I'm beginning to rethink my offer," Violet said. "Already this looks complicated."

"It's not," Amy said. "Trust me. We'll start with something easy."

As Will watched her showing his sisters and Rose how to cover shower curtain rings with ribbon, he once again found himself wondering if Amy might agree to go out with him. Now that he'd considered the possibility, he found he couldn't dismiss it. But was he willing to upset the apple cart by talking to her about it?

Suddenly Amy turned around to look at him, and Will realized the other three women at the table were staring at him as well. "What?"

"You have been off in lala land more than once lately," Violet informed him as she got back to work on her project.

"Sorry. Just thinking about something."

Laurel glanced away from the ribbon she was wrapping around a ring. "Care to share?"

"Uh. Nope." Will could only imagine the awkwardness that would ensue should he spill his thoughts. "What were you trying to get my attention for in the first place?"

"I was just saying that these ring things are pretty easy." Violet held up the one she was working on. "And I thought you should give us a hand since it's for your daughter."

Will watched as Amy picked up a ring and a long strand of ribbon. When she headed in his direction, he held up his hands. "I don't think so."

"It's really easy," Amy said. "If you can do a piñata, you can do this. Here I'll show you."

She held out the ring, leaving him no choice but to take it from her. Will tried to keep his attention on her words as she bent down to show him what to do. Unfortunately, the brush of one of her blonde curls on his cheek distracted him almost as much as the soft scent of the perfume she wore.

❧ *Chapter Thirteen* ❧

*H*OLD this part with your thumb like this," Amy said as she placed the ribbon against the ring and moved his thumb to anchor it leaving long strands of it hanging free. "Then you just loop this part through over and over again. Cover just the edge of the ribbon already on the ring each time. When you're done, you'll have two long tails of ribbon. Then we'll knot them. Easey peasey."

As Will began to loop the ribbon like Amy had shown him, he glanced at Matt and Dean. Both men were watching him with smirks on their faces.

"Too bad you guys aren't talented enough to help with such a simple craft," he muttered, which sent both men into guffaws of laughter.

When the laughter suddenly died down, Will looked up to see Violet and Laurel each approaching their husbands with a ring and a length of ribbon. He didn't bother to hide his own snort of laughter.

"Seriously?" groused Matt as he frowned at his wife. "At least make this a little fun." He grabbed Laurel and pulled her into his lap. "Now you can show me what to do."

Violet didn't even wait for Dean to grab her. She settled herself comfortably on her husband's lap and began to give him directions.

One would have thought with several people working it would have gone faster, but both Dean and Matt seemed to need a lot more instruction from their wives than Will had needed. For obvious reasons. He wondered what it would be like to have the right to be that way with Amy.

Shocked by the thought, Will turned his attention back to the ring he held. He stared at it for a minute trying to work through the realization he'd just had. In the past when his siblings had been affectionate with each other, he'd felt a pang of longing for what he'd had with Delia. This was the first time he'd wondered about experiencing that intimacy with someone else. Even though he had been wondering about something with Amy, this was a first.

Guilt rippled through him. He'd never thought that way about anyone but Delia. Without even trying, apparently, Amy had managed to slip past his defenses and turn his thoughts to her. He just wasn't sure how he felt about it. It had been almost seven years since Delia's death. His family had begun hinting a few years ago that he should move on, but he hadn't been ready. Now it seemed maybe he was.

He just wished he could tell if Amy might be interested in him the way he was in her. With Delia, there had never been a doubt. She'd flirted outrageously with him, making it clear, almost from their first meeting, that she was interested in him. Amy, on the other hand, seemed to treat him the same as the rest of the men in the family.

"Are you having a problem?"

Will looked up to see Amy standing beside his chair. "What?"

"You stopped working on your ring. Just wondered if it was giving you problems."

"No, but you are" was what he wanted to say. Instead, he shook his head. "Apparently I can't think and work at the

same time."

She took the ring from his fingers and studied it. "What you've done so far looks great. Keep it up."

Her smile of encouragement did funny things to his gut. "Thanks." He looked back down at the ring and began to loop the ribbon once again. This time he made sure that he continued to work even while dealing with all the thoughts in his head.

If she wasn't Josh's little sister and Cami's sister-in-law, he might not be as hesitant to pursue her, but he didn't want to make things awkward for either of them. And if it didn't work out, would they be able to go back to being friends? Timing would be everything, Will figured. For Isabella's sake, he didn't want to upset things before the party, but once it was over, he would see how things stood and decide whether or not to take the risk. In the meantime, he could put out some subtle feelers with her. See how she responded to him. Or if she started avoiding him. Truth be told, now that he'd thought about it, some of his interactions with her had already bordered on flirting. She made it so easy when she brought out that lighthearted side of him that had been absent for so long.

He looked back at the table and realized that Isabella and a couple of the other girls had abandoned the play structure and were kneeling on the benches of the picnic table.

"Can we help?" Julia asked, reaching out to touch one of the completed rings.

"Sure!" And revealing why she made such a good teacher, Amy patiently showed the girls how to loop the ribbon around the rings.

Once the younger girls were started on rings of their own, Will got up and approached the table.

"I'm done with mine." He held it out to her, keeping the tops of the ribbon tails pinched between his fingers. "Do I pass?"

"Hold it for a second while I finish it off." Amy quickly knotted the two ends of the ribbons then looked up at him and smiled. "Excellent! Ready for another one?"

When she looked at him with those sea- foam green eyes of hers, he couldn't say no. "Sure. How many do we have to make?"

"I'd like to make thirty so each little girl will have two. They'll take them home as part of their goodie bags."

"How is mine, Amy?" Isabella asked.

Will watched as Amy moved to bend over Isabella and inspect her work.

"It's beautiful, sweetie. You're doing a really great job."

His daughter positively beamed at the praise Amy gave her. Will wondered if his expression had been similar when she'd proclaimed his efforts as excellent. He could only hope that if it had been, no one else had noticed.

Eventually, the afternoon wound down as the last of the rings were finished.

"Thank you all so much for your help," Amy said as she gathered up the completed project.

Laurel, Violet, and Rose all offered their services for any other projects before taking off to visit with Jessa. Amy followed with the craft stuff, leaving just the men to ride herd on the kids in the backyard.

"So what did I miss?" Lance asked when he came back outside.

"Did you know Amy was going to rope us into doing crafts?" Matt asked. "Is that why you took off?"

Lance grinned as he settled into a chair. "You guys were doing crafts down here?"

"It was his fault," Dean said with a jerk of his thumb in Will's direction. "He couldn't say no to Amy when she asked him to help with the ring things. The next thing I know, Violet's got me doing it."

"Yeah, and Laurel conscripted me as well." Matt also nodded his head toward Will. "Definitely his fault."

"Not my fault that you guys can't say no to your wives. At least I felt obliged because it was for my daughter."

"Well, I can say that I'm glad that I was upstairs with Jessa," Lance said with a smirk. "Of course, I could have probably said no to Amy if she'd tried to convince me."

When the women came down from visiting Jessa, Amy wasn't with them. Will could think of no reason to hang around once the others began to get ready to go, so he called Isabella to get her things. As usual, she protested leaving without seeing Amy. Julia said she'd take her up to Amy's room to see her.

"Did you get to say goodbye?" Will asked her a few minutes later as they left the manor.

"Yep."

Will had hoped she might give a few more details, but since she didn't continue on, he asked, "What was she doing?"

"She was talking on the phone. To someone named Sam, I think," Isabella said. "When we got to the door she said, 'Just a second, Sam,' and then said goodbye."

Sam? The name was familiar from the text messages he'd seen. He seemed to remember her talking about Sammi being her best friend. Will knew it was none of his business what she did or who she talked to, but, try as he might, he couldn't just shove aside what he was feeling for her. Each time he was around her it got harder and harder to ignore the thoughts in his mind and the feelings in his heart.

☙❧

"I'm sorry I didn't get a chance to take you to the store," Lance said as they cleaned up from supper the following Thursday. "Want to make that grocery run now?"

"Sure," Amy said as she slid the last of the plates into the dishwasher and started it up. "Jessa asked me to add a couple of things to the list."

"I can take you," Will offered. "Unless you really need to go, Lance."

Lance shook his head. "Nope. I was just going to help with the bagging and carrying. We've got quite a list with the family all arriving and getting a few more things for the party."

"Well, in that case, I insist."

Lance turned to Amy. "You okay going with Will?"

She didn't feel she could give any answer except to agree. Saying no would definitely raise questions. Though being around him was difficult at times, having other people there with them had been helpful. This would just be the two of them, and Amy wasn't sure how she felt about that. The key to making it through the summer without total heartbreak was to keep reminding herself of all the reasons it wouldn't work. Unfortunately, going out on a grocery run with him—just like a married couple—wasn't going to help her mindset.

"Sure. It'll be fun to ride in that car again."

Will grinned. "You like my car, eh? I'll give you a ride in it any time you want."

"Would you let me drive it?" Amy asked.

Lance laughed as Will said, "Well, I don't know about that."

"Can I come too, Daddy?" Isabella asked.

"I think it would be better if you stayed here with Julia. It might take a while to get the groceries, and I don't want you to get bored."

"Will you bring me a cookie?" she asked, an innocent smile on her face.

Amy almost laughed out loud when Will sighed and nodded. "Yes, I'll bring you a cookie."

He'd probably get a whole pack of them, Amy figured. She knew she would.

"If you think of anything more, go ahead and pick it up," Lance said as she grabbed her purse and phone from the counter. "Can you cover the bill, Will? I'll settle up with you later."

"Yep. That'll work."

After they said goodbye to Isabella, Will led the way out to his vehicle. He opened the passenger side door for her and with a sweeping motion of his hand, he said, "Your chariot awaits, milady."

Smiling, Amy climbed into the passenger seat and buckled her belt as he shut the door.

I don't want to live where the winters are cold. I don't want to be involved with a man who has loved so deeply before. I don't want to have to compete with a dead woman. She kept running the reminders through her mind as he slid behind the wheel and started the engine.

As they headed for the highway, Amy recognized the song playing as one from Josh and Cami's latest album. She hummed along as Will turned toward Collingsworth.

"I'm looking forward to their concert," Will said. "It's great that they give one every year when they come. I know I'm not the only one who enjoys it."

"I always like it when they give a concert at our church in Dallas. Of course, they have a pretty hard time topping their first concert there."

"The one when Josh proposed?"

"Yep. I was so excited I could hardly keep it to myself. In fact, I avoided Cami most of that day after Josh told us his plan so I wouldn't spill the beans."

"I hear she was quite surprised."

"She told me later that she was beginning to wonder if he'd ever propose. She knew what she wanted, but it seemed to be taking him forever to get to that point."

"Sometimes guys can be a little slow, but we get there eventually."

Though she really didn't want to know, Amy figured that asking about Delia might help break the hold this man still had on her heart. "How did you propose?"

Will's head jerked around, and their gazes met for a moment before he turned his attention back to the road. He didn't say anything right away, and Amy wondered if perhaps he wasn't going to reply, but then he said, "I didn't do anything formal like Josh did. We just both kind of decided we didn't want a long distance relationship, and the only way we could be together was if we got married."

His response surprised Amy. For some reason, she had envisioned a super romantic proposal on the beach at sunset or something. "Not everyone does it up big like Josh did. He's just lucky Cami agreed. I can't imagine anything worse than proposing publically and then having the lady say no."

"I'm sure it's happened a time or two. While it was great to witness Josh's proposal to Cami, I feel it's a more private thing. The wedding is public enough."

"So you wouldn't want your guy to propose to you on the Jumbotron at a football game?"

Amy laughed. "No way. I'd say no and make him do it again privately. But I would hope that any guy that I was that serious with would know me well enough to know how to do it right."

Will didn't say anything more as he pulled the vehicle into the Walmart parking lot and found a spot. Amy opened her car door before he could get around to do it for her. His gentlemanliness was one more attraction she needed less exposure to.

They walked side by side to the entrance of the store.

Once they were inside, she asked, "Do you think we need two carts?" she asked.

"Let's start with one. If we need another one, I'll get it," Will said.

After Will found a cart, Amy directed him to the first aisle. It quickly became apparent that Will didn't know the store any better than Amy did.

"Don't you shop here?" Amy asked.

Will shrugged. "On occasion. Usually I get one of my sisters to pick up what I need. I don't do a whole lot of cooking, to be honest."

"Your mom didn't make sure you knew how to cook before flying the coop?"

"I didn't say I didn't know how to cook. Just that I don't do it a lot." Will grinned. "And yes, my sisters spoil me. Usually they take turns feeding Isabella and me."

"I guess I can't say much since my mom does most the cooking for me, too."

Will leaned on the cart as she picked up two cans of spaghetti sauce. "Do you know how to cook though?"

"Oh yes. My mom made sure all of us, including the boys, knew how to cook all the basics." Amy put the cans into the cart and then added two more and a couple of large packages of spaghetti noodles. "She was determined none of us would ever starve because we didn't know how to cook."

The trip continued slowly as they had to backtrack to pick up items they'd missed. A couple of times they were stopped by people who recognized Will and wanted to chat. Each time he introduced her and then while he chatted, Amy would wander off to get a few more items. It was over two hours later that they finally pushed two carts out to his car.

"I've never bought so much food in my life," Amy said as they began to load the bags into the back of the Escalade. "This is crazy. I almost fainted when the total came up. I'm glad you were the one taking care of it. Not sure my credit card could have handled that."

Will laughed. "My credit card has had more of a workout

the past two weeks than it's had has in a very long time." He put the last bag in and shut the door. "Go on and get in. I'll take the carts back."

Amy nodded and went to the front passenger door and climbed in. She rested her head back against the leather seat and closed her eyes. *I don't want to live where the winters are cold. I don't want to be involved with a man who has loved so deeply before. I don't want to have to compete with a dead woman.*

The two hours they'd just spent together had not been helpful in guarding her heart. Something about both being new at the task had brought about a camaraderie between them. And there had been moments... She'd turn to find him watching her, an unreadable expression on his face. Or he'd tease her about something in a way that made her smile. And then there had been the times he'd laid his hand on the small of her back as he'd moved beside her to reach something on a shelf that was out of her reach. It was all just too much intimacy for her.

The driver side door opened. "You okay?"

Amy opened her eyes but didn't look at Will. "Yep. That was just a bit more taxing than I'd thought it would be."

Will fiddled with the controls on the dash before pulling out of the parking spot and back out onto Main Street.

When he turned right onto the street instead of left, Amy glanced at him. "Are we making another stop?"

"Nope. I'm just going to take the scenic route home. I figured since you like my car so much I'll give you a bit of a longer ride."

The ride would have been great if she wasn't already feeling way too vulnerable to him. And she was starting to wonder if maybe he did feel something for her, too. That would make a difficult situation almost impossible, because how he felt for her didn't change how she felt about the situation. No matter what his feelings for her were, there would always be Delia. Nothing could ever change that.

Thankfully Josh and Cami's voices filled the silence in the vehicle as Will steered it out of Collingsworth onto the highway that headed east out of town instead of north to the manor.

Amy looked out the window, watching as rolling green hills passed by them. Soon he turned off the four lane highway onto a two lane road that went up and down like a rollercoaster. Amy pressed a hand to her stomach as they crested a small hill and started down the other side of it. Will guided the vehicle expertly up and down the hills and around the curves. If it weren't for the tension she was feeling, Amy would actually have enjoyed the ride.

Suddenly, as they came around another curve, he slowed the car and turned onto a road that entered a park. It wasn't the one she'd been to, but it looked similar.

He parked the car and turned to her. "Want to walk to the water?"

"What about the food? We have some cold stuff back there."

"I think it will be okay. I cranked the air in the rear. We won't be long. I just thought you might like to see the sunset here."

Amy nodded and unbuckled her seatbelt. She knew this was a mistake, but she couldn't exactly tell Will that without going into a long explanation. After she got out, he closed her door and locked the car. There were a few small groups of people at picnic tables that they passed on their way to the water's edge.

The sun was just beginning to turn beautiful shades of pink and orange as it dipped behind the trees. It wasn't completely dark yet, but Amy knew it would be before long.

They stood in silence for a moment then Will said, "Hey, would you like to go out on a date?"

❧ Chapter Fourteen ❧

*T*HE breath caught in Amy's lungs as she turned to look at him. "With who?"

Will's eyebrows rose at the question. "With me. Why would I be asking for someone else?"

Amy shrugged. "I just thought maybe you had a friend you were going to fix me up with."

"Nope. Asking on my own behalf."

Amy stared at him, not entirely sure how to respond. "Is this because of Isabella?"

"What do you mean?" Will slid his hands into the front pockets of the black pants he wore.

"Am I the first woman she's become so attached to?" Amy could tell from Will's expression that she was. "I'm not interested in a relationship with someone who's just looking for a mother for their child. Not that I wouldn't want to be Isabella's mother, but that's not a good basis for a relationship."

Will didn't reply at first. "I can't lie and say that's not part of it. But there is more. You're the first woman who has made me laugh like you have. I enjoy being around you and the happiness and joy with which you live your life. It's very attractive. Even when facing struggles, you've continued to be upbeat and haven't let them keep you down."

Amy looked away briefly. Was this God's sign? She sure hoped not, because she still wasn't convinced that Will was the man she wanted to live the rest of her life with, even though her heart seemed to think he was. "I don't date lightly, Will."

"You think I'm asking you to engage in some sort of summer fling?" Will asked.

"I'm not sure what to think. My time here is limited. I hadn't planned on making this a permanent move." She wanted to say more, to reveal to him the real reason she wasn't sure about allowing anything to develop between them.

"I understand that." He shrugged. "I guess I wasn't thinking long term yet. I just really enjoyed this evening with you and would like to do it again. Except without the grocery list. And maybe in a restaurant where food doesn't come in meal deals. I thought maybe you might have felt the same way."

If only he knew. Her heart pounded as she looked at him standing there, everything she'd once dreamed of having, and asking her what she'd longed to be asked eight years ago. She would have jumped on it back then. But now? "I did enjoy being with you tonight."

"But?"

"Is there a way we can do this without Isabella knowing? I don't want her to get her hopes up for something that...well, until we figure out what..." She stopped and took a breath, struggling for words and air.

Will stepped closer and took her hand. "Let's take it one step at a time. How about we go out for dinner once and then decide if we want to try it again."

If her words had been scrambled before, the touch of his hand on hers scattered what few had been left. This wasn't like her. She was usually able to roll with the punches but, right then, a million different thoughts vied for attention in her mind. "Okay. Dinner would be good."

"How about Saturday night? Once all the party stuff is done, and you can relax."

"Sure. That sounds good. But what will you do with Isabella?"

"I'll figure something out," Will said as her hand slid from his. He looked at her more intently. "Are you okay? You look almost...sick."

That was probably a good description for how she felt. Sick with excitement. Sick with fear. "I'm fine. This is all just a bit unexpected."

Will tilted his head. "This can't be the first time you've been asked out."

"No, it's not," Amy admitted.

"So why are you surprised that I asked you out?"

"It's just a very...odd situation with my brother being married to your sister. And honestly, I didn't expect you to see me as potential dating material."

Will's brows drew together. He looked like he was going to say something then stopped. After a brief pause he said, "Well, I guess now you know differently."

"Yes, I do." Amy tucked her hands into the pockets of her capris, trying hard to keep the tumult of emotion from pouring out. "I think we should probably get back to the manor. Don't want the refrigerator items to go bad."

The trip was made in silence but for Josh and Cami singing once again. In the midst of all the emotions, the only feeling Amy could get a real grasp on was anger, but who it was truly directed at was a mystery to her. She felt anger at herself for not knowing her own mind and for being so hung up on Will's past. She wished she could have just said yes without dithering all over the place. And she was a bit angry at God for not making this easier. She didn't like being confused or dealing with such complicated emotions.

After they parked in front of the manor, Amy put her hand on the door handle to open it. When Will touched her arm, she hesitated before turning to look at him.

"I didn't mean to make things awkward between us." His brows were drawn together, his expression tense. "If you'd rather not go out for dinner, I'll understand. We can just forget the past half hour."

Amy shook her head. "Can't forget, but I'll try not to let it affect the things we need to do over the next few days. I'll be honest. I'm really confused. I never expected..." She waved her hand between them. "This."

"I didn't either." A corner of his mouth lifted in a half-smile. "And I certainly didn't know it was going to get so complicated. If I'd had any idea—"

"You never would have brought it up," Amy finished for him.

A smile softened his tense expression. "No. If I'd had any idea, I would have timed our conversation better. Maybe tried a few more subtle hints to give you a clue before springing the invite on you."

Seeing his features relax into a smile and knowing it was because of her, Amy's heart clenched and the breath squeezed from her lungs. Will was offering her everything she'd ever wanted, but fear held her back. There was so much she wanted to say, to share with him. But instead of voicing what was in her heart, she just gave a quick nod and then opened the door. Will didn't try to stop her this time.

He had opened the hatch from inside the vehicle, and they met at the back to begin unloading. After their first trip into the manor, Lance told Amy to stay inside to start unpacking while he helped Will bring in the rest of the stuff. Since she was familiar with the kitchen after working in it for a couple of weeks, Amy was able to quickly put the groceries where they needed to go.

"Here you go."

Amy turned to see Will holding out a bag to her. Without meeting his gaze, she reached for it, but he pulled it back. When she looked at him, he gave her a quick grin and held it out again. She reached for it more slowly this time, her fingers brushing against his. He didn't release it right away so their fingers stayed intertwined. The teasing look in his eyes and the contact with his hand shot Amy's pulse rate up, but when she heard Lance coming, she gave the bag a tug and Will let go.

As she put the contents of the bag into the pantry, Amy prayed that she hadn't made a mistake in agreeing to go out with him. It didn't feel wrong, but it didn't feel quite right either. The way he looked at her, a crazy mix of gentleness and teasing, made her weak in the knees, but there was also a pit in her stomach from anticipation and fear. However, there was no going back now. She just hoped it didn't make things too awkward between them over the next couple of days as they prepared for the party.

"That's the last of it," Will said as he put two more bags on the counter. "I'd offer to help put stuff away but, since I have no idea where anything goes, I'd probably be more of a hindrance than a help."

"No problem." Lance put two jugs of milk into the fridge. "I appreciate you taking Amy to the store for me."

"It was an interesting experience."

Amy didn't look at him, positive that if she did, Lance would read her emotions all over her face. She nodded. "I don't think I've ever needed two carts to get groceries before."

"I'll just go find Isabella and get out of your way. What time are you expecting Josh and Cami?"

"Josh texted earlier to say they were in Minneapolis and hoped to be here shortly after noon tomorrow."

"Sounds good." Will paused then said, "Amy, I'm going to pick up the tables and chairs tomorrow. Do you want to set them up in the afternoon? I don't think they're forecasting rain so they should be okay to sit out overnight."

Amy looked at Will, knowing this was the awkwardness they needed to avoid. "That would be great. Thanks. Will you be able to run a few errands on Saturday morning?"

"Sure. What do you need done?"

"Picking up the cake for one. And anything else I've forgotten."

"I'll be at your disposal." Will smiled. "But I'm sure you've got it all well in hand. Just keep checking things off your list."

Butterflies fluttered in Amy's stomach. Part of her just couldn't believe that Will actually wanted to go out with her. And seeing him smiling made her glad she'd agreed.

"Are the girls outside?" Will asked Lance.

"No, they came in and went up to Julia's room to play, I think."

Will nodded and left the kitchen. Amy took more cans from the bags on the counter and turned to put them in the pantry. She pulled up short when she saw Lance leaning against the fridge, arms crossed, a curious expression on his face. "What's wrong?"

"You tell me."

Amy skirted around him to the pantry. "Tell you what?"

"The tension between the two of you is so thick I could cut it with a knife. Did you have a disagreement or something?"

"Or something," Amy muttered as she put the cans on the correct shelf.

"What was that?"

She came back into the kitchen and continued putting things away in the fridge. "Nothing. Everything is fine."

"Maybe I should ask Will."

"Go right ahead. He'll tell you the same thing." Or at least she hoped he would.

"Or maybe I'll just mention something to Josh."

Amy spun around to see a grin on Lance's face. She pointed a finger at him. "Don't stir up trouble where there is none."

He looked like he was going to say something more but wasn't given a chance because Isabella skipped into the room, Will right behind her.

"Night," she said as she wrapped her arms around Amy's hips. "See you tomorrow."

"You bet." Amy gave the girl a hug and kissed the top of her head. "Be good for your dad."

"Amy, if you need me to do anything else, just give me a call," Will said.

She nodded and smiled, aware of Lance's attention on them. "Don't forget to shave your legs."

Laughing, Will took Isabella's hand. As they left the kitchen, he looked back, winked at her and said, "Never in a million years."

Lance didn't say anything further about Will as they finished putting away the groceries. "Well, I know it's early, but I'm going to close up down here and call it a night. I need to spend some time with Jessa."

"I'll take care of getting Julia to bed if you'd like."

"That would be great." He paused. "I'm a little worried about Jessa and these contractions she keeps having. We're going to the doctor tomorrow though, so hopefully they can tell if it's something we need to be more concerned about."

"I'll be praying that it's nothing more serious than Braxton Hicks."

"Thanks." He gave her a one arm hug around her

shoulders before heading to the hallway to lock up the front.

It took a while, but finally, the little girl had said goodnight to her dad, was satisfied with the number of stories read and was no longer thirsty. Amy let out a sigh when she closed the door of Julia's room behind her. She made her way to her own room, and even though it wasn't super late, she got ready for bed herself. Once she was in her pajamas and comfortable on the bed, she called Sammi.

"I can't believe you agreed to go out with him," Sammi said after Amy had shared the events of the day.

Amy leaned back against her pillows and stared up at the circle of light on the ceiling cast by the bedside lamp. "Tell me about it. Ever since I did, I've gone back and forth a million times on whether it was a smart idea or a dumb one. You probably think it's a dumb one."

"Not at all. I'm just surprised that you agreed. I don't suppose you told him anything about how you really feel about him, did you?"

"I'm not quite sure how I should have broached that conversation." Amy sighed. "Guess I could have just said, 'Oh, by the way, I had a huge crush on you when I was fifteen and believed you were the man God wanted me to marry.' That might have sent him running in the opposite direction."

"You do plan to tell him at some point though, don't you? It certainly is a dynamic in your relationship with him."

"I guess. I haven't had much chance to think about it. He shocked me when he asked me for a date. I didn't have time to think about a response." Amy thought back to that moment and couldn't hold back a smile. "Actually, I think he kinda shocked himself, too."

"Where do you think it's going to go?" Sammi asked.

"No clue. I told him that I don't date lightly and that I hadn't planned to settle permanently here." Amy sighed. "Maybe I should have just said no."

"Too late now," Sammi pointed out. "So don't focus on

the maybe's and what if's. I actually think it's better this way. At least you know he's interested in you. That's not going to be something you have to keep wondering about."

Will is interested in me. Will is interested in me! Amy could hardly believe the words that kept going around in her mind. The sixteen year old inside her was positively dancing with joy. She closed her eyes and curled onto her side. For a moment she was able to forget the past hurt. Forget Delia. Forget everything but the look on his face when he'd told her he wanted to go out with her. Could it really be this easy? Had the hope of her sixteen year old heart just been deferred a few years?

"Are you going to give him a chance?" Sammi asked.

Amy let out a long sigh. It would be stupid not to, but could she keep all the memories and fears at bay? Instead of sharing those weightier concerns, she decided to voice a lesser concern to Sammi.

"Is it weird? The fact that one of his sisters is married to my brother and another to my cousin?"

"Well, it's not the first time I've heard of something like that. At least if you ever did get married to him you know you'd like your in-laws."

"My brother would also be my brother-in-law. That's crazy." Amy twisted a strand of hair around her finger. "Maybe a little too crazy."

"Oh, don't think that way," Sammi admonished her. "If it's what God wants, don't worry about stuff like that. People will think what they want, but if you're certain it's God's will and you're happy and in love, just ignore them."

"It may all be for nothing," Amy said. "It's just one date. He may decide I'm not really who he sees himself with in the long term."

"Then he's not the man for you. But something tells me, from what you said, that there's already something serious enough there for him to ask you out."

She still couldn't get it out of her mind how different she was from Delia, but she didn't say anything about that to Sammi. Her friend would probably think Amy was having self-esteem issues, but that wasn't it. It wasn't that she thought she didn't measure up to Delia, but that if Will had loved Delia who was so different from Amy, how could he love her? Thankfully, the conversation veered in another direction as they began to talk about Sammi's boyfriend, Eli. They'd been dating for ages, and Amy kept waiting for the phone call to let her know that they were engaged.

Once their call ended, Amy curled up on her bed. Sleep was a long way off as her mind still spun with a million different thoughts. The day had certainly taken a few unexpected twists and turns, and something told her that the days ahead would be just as crazy.

§∞§

Will sighed with relief when Isabella finally settled down for the night. He grabbed a can of soda from the fridge and went into the den. After settling on the couch, he turned on the big screen TV and flipped to the channel for the news of the day.

Instead of it capturing his attention like usual, Will found his thoughts drifting to the time with Amy at the lake. He still wasn't entirely sure what had possessed him to ask her out. Was it wrong to want to spend more time with her? To see if that infectious love of life she had would rub off on him? He'd hoped that maybe if they spent time together, she might see that he could bring something to her life, too. And he couldn't lie—to her or himself—that how she and Isabella got along was an important part of the picture. But it certainly hadn't been the main reason he'd asked her out.

Clearly his invitation had taken her off-guard, and he had almost expected her to turn him down. However, she'd surprised him and said yes, though he could see that she had reservations about it—maybe even more than the ones she'd voiced. He understood that. After all, this wasn't her home and dating someone who had roots deeply planted in the town might have put her off. In the meantime, he was going to run with it and show her that considering Collingsworth home wouldn't be the worst thing in the world. And maybe a move to Dallas might be an option, if it came to that.

As he propped his feet up on the coffee table, his glance went to where his phone sat. He half- expected to get a text from Amy saying she was cancelling. Once she had time to think about it, he figured she'd give in to whatever doubts were plaguing her. He didn't know what he'd do then. For the first time since Delia's death, he wanted to spend time with a woman. And not just any woman. He wanted to be with Amy.

Will jumped when his phone chirped an email alert. He lowered his feet to the floor and reached for the phone. Since it was an email and not a text, he didn't hesitate to read it. The email was from Delia's mother detailing their itinerary for the next day. They'd been to Collingsworth several times over the years so had made the decision to rent a car and drive from Minneapolis after they flew in from Seattle where they had been visiting friends. It looked like they were likely to arrive later in the afternoon than Josh and Cami.

As he finished reading the email, his phone rang, and Amy's name appeared on his screen. Will stared at it for a moment, reluctant to answer. Finally, he tapped the screen and pressed the phone to his ear. "If you're calling to cancel our dinner, this is a recording, and I don't check my messages."

There was a beat of silence before Amy laughed. The sound of it brought a smile to Will's face.

"No, I'm not calling to cancel, but I just wondered if postponing it might be a good idea."

Postponing...cancelling...somehow they rang the same in Will's mind. "Why would it be a good idea?"

"I remembered that, uh, Delia's parents are arriving tomorrow. Won't that be awkward?"

"Because I was married to their daughter?"

"Well...yes. Would it upset them?"

"No. If anything, they would be delighted."

Amy didn't reply right away then said, "Delighted?"

"They never expected me to put my life on hold indefinitely after Delia's death. In fact, for the past couple of years Charlotte has suggested with ever increasing forthrightness that I should consider dating again."

"Really?"

"Yes, really. You have nothing to worry about where Charlotte and Henry are concerned."

"Do they have other children?"

"No, Delia was their only child. They could never have children, so they adopted Delia when they were in the Philippines as missionaries. They were already in their forties when they adopted her, so there wasn't much time after that to adopt anymore."

"That must have been awful for them when she passed away."

"It was a very difficult time. Because they were in their sixties, I was afraid it was going to kill them. I know it almost killed me." As soon as he said the words, Will wished he could take them back. He decided it was probably better to just let the moment pass.

There was a long pause before Amy asked, "Does Isabella ask about her?"

"Not often," Will admitted. "I'm still not sure if that's a good thing or not."

"As long as you're willing to talk when she asks, I would guess that she'll ask about the things she needs to know when she wants to know them."

Not comfortable to continue talking about Delia with the woman he was hoping to date, Will said, "So are you still okay with going out for dinner on Saturday?" Suddenly his brain made a connection. Saturday. The day Delia had died.

His first date with Amy.

It was too late to back out now without having to give an explanation. And how did he tell Amy that he didn't want to go out because he needed to remember the day his wife died? Somehow he just knew that wouldn't be a good start to their relationship. He would just have to continue forward with the plans as they stood. It surprised him that he hadn't made the connection earlier, but Saturday had become the day of Isabella's party, not the anniversary of Delia's death.

"As long as you don't think it will cause any issues." Amy's voice drew him back to their conversation.

"Frankly, I'm more worried about issues with Josh than I am with Charlotte and Henry."

Amy laughed. "Yep. Lance asked tonight if something was up."

"Really? Why did he ask that?"

"Guess he sensed a little...tension between us when we got back. And when I wouldn't confirm anything, he threatened to sic Josh on me."

"Are you comfortable with the family knowing we're going out?" Will hadn't really thought too much about how their siblings might react.

"I don't know. Part of me would like to keep it on the down low in case things don't work out."

"Wow. Nothing like starting off with a positive outlook on it."

"You have to admit it would make things a little awkward," Amy said.

"Well, if you want to try to keep it a secret, I suppose we could try, but I doubt we'd be too successful."

"No, we wouldn't be. Cami would know something was up immediately. Better to just put it out there."

"Thank you," Will said.

Another pause. "For what?"

"For giving me—us—a chance. I don't think I'm wrong in feeling that you have some hesitations about going out with me."

"Yes, I do," Amy agreed.

"Aside from the family and your presence in Collingsworth being temporary, you haven't really talked about any of your other reservations."

"I can't just yet. Maybe as we spend time together, those concerns will be resolved."

Will knew in that moment that he would do whatever it took to put her mind at ease. He wanted her in his life. That was the bottom line. "Hopefully Saturday will be the first of many dinners."

"Yes." Though she'd agreed with him, she didn't sound as positive about it as he was. "Well, I'd better go. Busy few days ahead."

Though he would have liked to continue to talk, Will said, "Yep. See you tomorrow."

After the call had ended, Will sat there flipping his phone over and over in his hand. In his mind, he could see the ready smile that lit up Amy's face and made her sea- foam green eyes sparkle. How he wished that those eyes had sparkled with excitement at the prospect of going out with him. But he was going to take what he could get and hope that it would go up from there.

She wasn't going to make this easy for him, but something told him that the end result would be worth all the extra effort it looked like he'd have to expend to keep her in his life.

❧ *Chapter Fifteen* ❧

AMY woke tired the next morning. It had taken forever to fall asleep after her conversation with Will. The constant second-guessing of her decision to accept his invitation was wearying. She knew people would say she was overreacting or overthinking things, but none of them truly knew how deeply she'd been hurt by what had happened eight years ago.

It had been horribly hard to be in the same house as Will and Delia. Jessa had insisted the newlyweds stay at the manor when they'd arrived. Even at sixteen, Amy was aware of the physical intimacies between a married couple. It had crushed her to think of Will and Delia sharing that in a room just a few doors down from her. And his comment during their conversation about Delia's death just about killing him served as a stark reminder of how much he had loved her.

Feeling the negative thoughts begin to pull her down, Amy crawled from her bed and headed to the bathroom to take a shower. As she went through the motions of fixing her hair and makeup afterwards, she kept telling herself to focus forward. The past was never a good place to dwell, but when it came to Will, it seemed to be the place she always ended up.

It took her longer than usual to settle on an outfit for the day. Finally, she pulled on a pair of stonewashed jean capris and a hot pink, short-sleeve t-shirt. She added a necklace and earrings along with the rings she usually wore and slipped her feet into a pair of sandals.

After making her bed, she sank down on the edge of it and began to review everything she still needed to do that day. She wanted to get the majority of it done before noon so that when Cami and Josh arrived, she wouldn't be distracted.

She was surprised to walk into the kitchen and find Will sitting at the table with Lance.

"Good morning," Will said with a smile when he saw her.

Amy returned the greeting, still a little taken off-guard to have found him at the manor so early. "No work today?"

"I took the day off," Will said as he stood up from the table. "Want some coffee?"

"Uh, sure." Amy set her notebook down on the counter. She looked at Lance. "What time is Jessa's appointment?"

"Nine. I'm just waiting for her to text me that she's done getting ready."

"Hoping for good news today," Amy said as she took the mug Will handed her. She dumped some sugar and cream in it before taking a sip. "Where's Isabella?"

"I picked Julia up earlier and dropped both girls at Laurel's. I figured it might be easier if you didn't have them underfoot today."

Lance's phone sounded an alert. "Looks like she's ready to go." He stood and made his way out of the kitchen.

Amy grabbed a container of yogurt and a spoon before sitting down at the table with her coffee and notebook.

Will sat down next to her with a cup of his own. "So what's on the agenda for today?"

Amy opened the yogurt and took a bite. "Mainly finishing up the crafts and the goodies bags for the girls."

"Want to go with me to the church to pick up the table and chairs if you're not too busy?"

"Sure. When were you thinking of going?"

"I planned to do it later, but Charlotte emailed me that they hoped to arrive this afternoon, so I figured maybe it would be good to get it out of the way."

"Yeah, I'm trying to finish up what I can before Josh and Cami arrive too," she said.

"Maybe between the two of us we can do that."

She was just finishing her yogurt when she heard voices from the hallway. Amy got up and went to see Jessa. The woman moved slowly, her hands cupping her stomach. Lance left her with Amy while he went to bring his truck closer to the front door.

"How are you feeling?" Amy asked.

"Nervous," Jessa said with a frown. "Whenever we go to these appointments I'm afraid the doctor is either going to say the baby needs to come, or they're putting me on bed - rest in the hospital."

Amy gave her a hug. "I'll be praying that neither happens." She lightly touched Jessa's swollen stomach. "You stay put, little one. We all want to meet you, but not just yet."

They walked together to the front door and met Lance as he climbed the stairs to slip his arm around Jessa's waist.

As Amy watched them drive away, she said a prayer that God would keep the baby safely inside Jessa for a few more weeks. She touched her own stomach and wondered what it must be like to carry a child and to know that the baby's life hung in the balance. She hoped that one day she'd have the opportunity to have a child—or two—of her own, but without the stress of what Jessa was going through.

"Everything okay?" Will's voice drew her out of her thoughts.

She turned and smiled. "I hope so. Just concerned for Jessa."

Will's gaze went to the now- empty driveway. "It's strange how pregnancies can be so different for women. Laurel and Violet had no troubles with their pregnancies, but then Jessa had so many miscarriages."

Amy noticed he didn't mention Delia's pregnancy, but it would have fit his observation as well. "My mom had two easy pregnancies and then couldn't get pregnant again for several years. After Colin, she had a miscarriage before she had me. And Josh's first wife carried their baby to term, but then she was stillborn. Bringing life into the world is a blessing but never a guarantee."

They stood there in silence for a bit before Will said, "Do you want to get the chairs and tables first or take care of stuff here?"

"I think we should get them first, so we're not away from the manor around the time people might be arriving."

"I brought my truck today so we can load everything in the back."

Amy nodded. "Let me get my purse."

When she returned, Will had brought his truck around and was waiting to open the door for her. "I know you like my other car better, but this one is our workhorse today."

As Amy settled onto the seat of the truck, she just shook her head. Though not as elegant as the Escalade, the truck was still lavish in its own right.

"This is one fancy workhorse," Amy said when he slid behind the wheel.

Will grinned sheepishly. "Sorry. I do like my cars."

The trip into town was filled with small talk about Isabella and the party. When they arrived at the church, Will backed the truck up to the steps. Amy climbed out and followed him up the stairs to the front doors of the large church. He opened the door and motioned for her to precede him into the building.

A large man setting up a ladder turned as they entered, and then headed toward them. "Hey, Will. How's it going?"

"Good, Ken. How about with you?"

"Can't complain." The man's gaze moved from Will to Amy.

"This is Amy Moyer. She's helping plan Isabella's party."

"Moyer?" the man asked her. "Any relation to Josh and Cami?"

Amy nodded. "Josh is my brother."

Ken stuck out his hand. "It's a pleasure to meet you. I sure enjoy your brother and Cami's music. I'm excited for their concert next week."

"And I know they're looking forward to the concert as well," Amy told him with a smile.

"Well, let's get this things you need," Ken said.

It didn't take too long to load the three tables and the fifteen small chairs with Ken's help.

"We'll have these back late tomorrow afternoon," Will told him once the truck was loaded. "Will that be okay?"

"Sounds fine. I'll be here until around six getting things ready for the service."

After they'd left the church, Will said, "Anything else you need in town before we leave?"

Amy quickly consulted her list and shook her head. "Nothing at the moment. We'll need to come in again tomorrow morning though."

Back at the manor, it took a little more time to unload. She helped Will carry the tables from the truck down the path and into the clearing. By the time they were done, she was wiped.

"I'm really out of shape," Amy said as she sank down on one of the small chairs, swiping at a bead of sweat that trickled down the side of her face.

Will looked at her with a glint in his eyes then said, "Your shape looks just fine to me."

Amy felt heat rise in her cheeks. "Well, carrying a couple of tables and a few chairs shouldn't have worn me out like that. I get more exercise riding my bike at home than I do up here."

"I usually end up having to go to the gym a few times a week. My job is rather sedentary, unlike someone like Matt, who is out on the job site."

"To be honest, I'm not a big fan of exercise." Amy pushed up from the seat. "I'd rather just try to stay active in my life than have to work out with a bunch of women in spandex."

Amusement crossed Will's face, but he didn't comment. "Should we head back?"

Amy nodded and followed behind him as he walked down the path to the manor. She kept her gaze on the ground so she didn't trip on anything on the path, but suddenly she found herself plowing into Will. She grabbed his waist to keep from falling over, glad he was solid enough to keep them both upright.

She peered around Will's shoulder to see what had brought him to a halt and spotted a couple of deer standing in the woods a little further down the path. Given the racket she'd created when she'd bumped into him, she was rather surprised they were still there. Heart pounding, Amy inhaled the scent of his cologne and reveled in the firmness of his waist beneath her hands. She wanted to slide her arms around him and rest her head on his back, but that wasn't her right. At least not yet.

Slowly moving her hands, Amy stepped away from Will.

He glanced over his shoulder at her before continuing down the path. The deer scampered away as he moved in their direction. Amy waited until he was a few steps ahead of her before she followed him again, and this time she kept her head up.

Amy hated the feeling of being in limbo with Will. They hadn't gone out on a date yet, and since it was kind of a trial thing, they weren't officially a couple. Yet moments of intimacy kept popping up between them. It actually would have been much easier if he'd just steered clear of her until their date on Saturday. Instead, they were working side by side, and she had to keep her nerves and emotions where he was concerned under control. Especially after moments like that.

"So what do we need to do now?" Will asked when they were back at the manor.

"Let me run up to my room and get the stuff I was going to work on."

Upstairs, Amy sank down on her bed and took a deep breath and let it out. How was it possible to be excited about her dearest dream coming true and yet, at the same time, be terrified that it actually would? Conflicted emotions didn't sit well with her. She liked clarity and direction in her life. This current situation promised neither.

Resolved to push it aside from her mind for the time being, Amy gathered up the bags of supplies she'd bought over the past couple of weeks. It ended up taking her two trips to bring everything to where Will waited in the kitchen.

Grinning, she asked, "Ready to get to work?"

ভ•ঞ

If he'd had any idea of what was entailed in helping Amy, Will probably would have...showed up to help regardless, he admitted ruefully. As he stuffed another piece of plastic jewelry into a bag made out of some sort of see-through fabric, he watched Amy out of the corner of his eye. Once she'd brought all her stuff down, she'd put some music on. As she worked, she bobbed her head and moved her body to the rhythm of the songs. Clearly music moved through her veins much the same way it did her brother's.

He enjoyed watching her work. Preparing for Isabella's party didn't appear to be a task for her. She truly seemed to love what she was doing. Humming as she worked, he couldn't help but wonder what was running through her mind. Was she as excited as he was to see where things might go between them? When she'd run into him on the walk back to the manor, he had been pleasantly surprised that she hadn't immediately moved away. And maybe one day he'd admit to her that he hadn't been watching the deer as much as enjoying her nearness.

They'd been working for about an hour when Amy's phone went. She frowned as she looked at the display before answering it. "Lance? Is everything okay?"

The frown didn't fade as she listened to what he said. A sick feeling took up residence in his stomach as he waited for her to finish the conversation.

"You've talked to her already? Okay. Let us know if there are any more developments."

"What happened?" Will asked when Amy hung up.

She set her phone on the table. "He's taken Jessa to the hospital."

"Is she okay?"

"They want to monitor her." Amy sank down on a chair and propped an elbow on a pile of fluffy fabric. "The decision to admit her hasn't been made yet. I think they're going to hook her up to monitor her blood pressure, any contractions and the baby's heart rate. I know the baby would probably be okay being born now, but it would be so much better for the baby if the pregnancy could continue a bit longer."

When her gaze met his, he could see the green of her eyes was intensified by moisture. He got up and took her hand, pulling her to her feet. As he wrapped his arms around her, he felt her relax into his embrace. "It's going to be okay. They have lots of people praying for them."

He stroked her head, feeling the silkiness of her hair beneath his fingertips. It had been a very long time since he'd held a woman in his arms, and he realized now he'd missed it. But he didn't want to hold just anyone. Amy was the one he wanted to embrace, today and each day afterward. She fit just perfectly, her head tucked under his chin. It felt so right to him. It scared him to think that maybe it wouldn't feel as right to her.

Amy lifted her head. "But sometimes things don't work out even when people are praying."

Will looked down at her and saw sadness in her gaze. He knew she must be struggling with some of that now after what had happened with her school. But was there more? His own personal experience had proven that what she said was true. "Yes, I know, but we need to trust God will work it out for Jessa and Lance."

A tear slid down her cheek. She sighed and leaned her head against his chest once again. "Lance just sounded so worried. He loves her so much."

"Their love is strong," Will agreed.

They stood there for a few minutes before Amy moved back. Will let her go reluctantly. She lifted her hands and wiped her cheeks. "Okay, no more moping around. It won't help Jessa any, and it certainly won't get the rest of this party stuff done."

Before she could turn away, he grabbed her hand. "Want to pray about it?" He saw the surprise on her face and found that he was a little surprised himself. He'd withdrawn from his once very vocal faith over the past several years. He'd struggled so much in the years following Delia's death that he hadn't been vocal about his faith because it felt hypocritical. The emotions that had been slowly coming to life over the past few weeks though had included a desire to share that faith with those around him once again.

"Yes," Amy said. She took his other hand, so they stood facing each other, hands clasped.

Will stared at her bent head for a moment before he closed his eyes. He paused, gathering his thoughts as he prepared to pray with this woman who was growing more and more important to him with each passing day.

"Father, Amy and I come to You today, thanking You for the many blessings You've given us even as we ask for Your protection for Jessa and her little one. You gave them the blessing of this child after so many years of losses. We believe that You can, and will, allow this pregnancy to proceed to a point that is safe for both Jessa and the baby. Please give Jessa and Lance peace as they deal with the uncertainty of today and the days ahead. We love them very much and know that You do, too. We also pray for safe travels for all the family members journeying here today. Thank you for the blessing of being able to be together once again. In Jesus' name. Amen."

When Amy looked up after his prayer and met his gaze, Will could see that the tumult of emotion had eased a bit.

"Thank you," she said, a gentle smile curving her lips. She gave his hands a brief squeeze before releasing them. Her shoulders lifted as she took a deep breath and then let it out before turning back to the task at hand.

In that instant, Will knew, even without having gone on a single date with her, that he loved Amy Moyer. Savoring the thought for a moment, he wondered how long he was going to have to keep that revelation to himself. Something told him that Amy wasn't quite prepared to hear it from him just yet.

Amy took the time to change the music to some upbeat worship songs. She turned it up and sang along as they continued to work. Her voice could no doubt have launched a singing career if she'd been so inclined, especially with a brother already in the business. And yet she'd chosen to teach children instead...because that was what she loved. It was one more thing that endeared her to him.

"Here, I'm going to need your help to tie these," Amy said.

"What do you need me to do?" Will eyed the pile of bags that now contained an assortment of items that were sure to delight the hearts of all the young girls at the party the next day.

"Just hold them so I can tie the ribbons."

"Sounds easy enough," Will said. "I shouldn't be able to mess that up too much."

"You won't mess it up at all." Amy grinned as she handed him the first bag. "You haven't messed up yet."

True to her word, all he needed to do was hold the bag while she tightened the ribbon and tied it into a bow. They were standing close, Amy's head bent over the bag, Will's gaze on her, when he heard someone clear their throat loudly.

Will jerked around. The contents of the bag he'd been holding spilled out on the floor as he took in the sight of his sister and Josh standing in the entrance to the kitchen. Cami's gaze went from him to Amy, an expression that he could only peg as concern on her face.

Josh lifted an eyebrow and said, "Are we interrupting?"

"Josh! Cami!" With obvious delight, Amy hurried past him and flung her arms around first Josh and then Cami. "I am so glad to see you guys!" She moved on to hug the two little girls who stood with them. "I didn't expect to see you here so soon. Lance said you wouldn't be here until after noon."

Cami looked at Will, and her eyes narrowed briefly. "We were all up earlier than planned so we decided to just head on out. And then Lance phoned with the news about Jessa. I'm glad we are here sooner rather than later."

"Me, too," Amy said as she hugged Cami again.

Will moved to give his sister a hug, trying to figure out what was going on with her. He shook hands with Josh. "Glad you made it safe and sound."

Josh grinned. "Safe anyway. If sound means sane, that's debatable."

"Do you need help bringing your luggage in?" Will asked. "I'm sure your rooms are ready upstairs."

"Sounds good."

Will turned to Cami. "You can take over my job of holding bags for Amy."

Again, no response, just an odd expression on her face. Something was definitely up with her, but he had no idea what it was.

When they brought the first of the luggage into the foyer, Amy told them which rooms to put it in. It didn't take too long to empty their big bus. After they were done, Josh got behind the wheel to drive it around to the side of the manor.

Back in the kitchen, Will found Cami helping Amy straighten up the birthday stuff. It appeared the last of the bags had been tied, and sadly, his time alone with Amy had come to an end.

"Do you want all this up in your room?" he asked. "I'm assuming you want it put away before the girls come back."

Amy nodded. "But I think I'm going to sneak it all into the library and try to keep the girls out of there. Maybe we can just pile it in a corner and cover it with a sheet or something." She put the last of the bags into a box. "Let me go see what I can find."

As soon as Amy left the room, Cami turned to him. "Is there something going on between you and Amy?"

Will's eyes widened in shock. Had Amy mentioned something about their upcoming date? Since they'd only talked about it the night before, he would have been surprised if that had been the case. "What do you mean?"

"You're my brother, and I love you, but if she gets hurt again by you, I will be very angry." Emotion flashed in Cami's eyes.

Feeling more confused by her response, Will asked, "Hurt again by me? What are you talking about? What is going on?"

"Just don't take advantage of her feelings for you." Cami lifted a finger and pointed it at him. "She deserves better than that."

Will stared at his sister. Were they having the same conversation? Amy had feelings for him that Cami knew about?

❧ *Chapter Sixteen* ❧

I think this will work." Amy's voice ended the conversation, but not the questions in Will's mind. She seemed totally oblivious to what had just transpired between him and Cami as she gave each of Cami's girls a small bag to carry and led the way to the library.

Once she was out of the kitchen, Will turned to his sister, sure that some temper was showing in his own eyes. Keeping his voice low, he said, "I have no idea what you're talking about, but I have no intention of hurting Amy."

He had no time to elaborate before she came back in. "Are you two planning to help?"

Will took the bags she held out to him and left the kitchen, Cami's words still ringing in his head. She made it sound like he'd hurt Amy before. How was that even possible since they hadn't really known each other until she'd arrived at the manor at the beginning of summer?

He wasn't able to ask Cami any more questions because just as they finished putting the last of the party stuff in the library, Laurel, Rose and Violet arrived with all the children. It didn't take long for the kids to welcome their cousins and take them out to the backyard. Left alone with Josh and the women, Will sat down on one of the stools at the counter.

"I'd like to go see Jessa," Cami said. "Will they let us in while they're monitoring her?"

"Why don't we just take a chance and go?" Josh suggested. "I'd like to see Lance, too."

Laurel held out her keys. "Go ahead and use my van. Just let me take the food out. We brought stuff for supper."

"How could we possibly need more food?" Will asked. "Amy and I must have emptied the store last night. We've got tons here."

Cami's gaze came his way again, but it was Laurel who responded. "I'm sure there will be plenty of opportunities to use that up. We'll eat what we brought for tonight."

"We can use what we bought for lunch," Amy suggested. "Since all of you are here."

Josh and Cami decided not to wait for lunch, but once they were gone, Laurel and Violet worked with Amy to get food on the table for the rest of them. Wanting to be where Amy was, Will offered his help, but they turned him down.

After they'd finished eating, Will helped clean up. He was still thinking about Cami and wondering just what he had missed. He would have liked to ask Amy about it, but she and the ladies were too busy discussing the plans for the party the next day.

"If you guys have all this under control, I'm going to pop into the office for a bit," Will said. "Delia's parents are supposed to arrive later this afternoon. They said they'd text me when they got close to town, so I'll be back before they arrive."

Surprisingly, Amy walked with him to the front door. "Thanks for all your help. I'm glad to have it all done now, so I don't have to think about it again until tomorrow morning."

"I enjoyed spending time with you," Will told her.

She stared at him for a minute, her green eyes serious. "I enjoyed spending time with you, too."

His heart lifted at her response. He reached out and touched her cheek. "I'll be back in a bit."

She nodded and stood in the doorway as he walked down the steps to his truck. As he drove out of the drive, he glanced over and saw her still standing there watching him. It warmed him to see her there. Having acknowledged to himself how deeply he felt for her, it was encouraging to see that she seemed to be opening up to him as well.

࿐

Amy breathed a sigh of relief when she stepped into her room. She shut the door and leaned against it, head tilted back and eyes closed.

The day had been a whirlwind of activity with the party preparations and all the arrivals. Will had come back to the manor shortly before Delia's parents arrived. Isabella had been over the moon with excitement at seeing her grandparents and had eagerly introduced Amy as her best friend.

Right away Amy could see that Charlotte and Henry were warm and friendly people as they greeted each of the family members. She still wasn't sure they would be as welcoming of her if they knew of Will's interest in her, but only time would tell.

Without question, the best part of the day had been when Lance and Jessa had arrived just before dinner. Jessa had been released to continue her bed -rest at home which was a definite answer to prayer. The contractions had been sporadic and hadn't gotten any worse through the time they'd monitored her. And it seemed she wasn't dilating either, so she had been sent home.

Dinner had been a loud and fun experience with so many children and adults all talking at once. Amy, however, was glad when things began to settle down. And now she relished the peace and quiet of her room.

A knock on the door jerked Amy from her relaxed state. She turned and opened it, not too surprised to see Cami in the hallway. "Were you standing right there?" Cami asked as she quirked an eyebrow.

"Yeah, actually, I was." Amy stepped back so her sister-in-law could come into the room. She wasn't too sure how she felt about having a talk with Cami given the latest developments with Will.

"Up for a chat?" Cami asked as she sat down on Amy's bed and tucked her legs under her.

"Sure." Amy dropped down on the other side of the mattress and settled back against her pillows. "It's been forever since we've talked like this."

"How's it been going here?"

Amy filled her in on how it had been, helping with the bed and breakfast side of things, as well as how Jessa had done. "And, of course, there are the preparations for Isabella's party."

"She seems to have mellowed a bit since we were last here," Cami said. "And, for that matter, so has Will. Is that your doing?"

"Me?" Amy shrugged. "I don't know. I just loved her, like I do all the kids I come in contact with."

"And Will? Did you love him, too?"

Amy willed herself to keep her gaze on Cami. "He's undergone some changes, but Jessa is more responsible for that than I am. She had a long chat with him, apparently, about being a better parent to Isabella."

"I saw the way he was watching you when we arrived."

"Watching me? We were tying the bags for the party."

"That may have been what you were doing, but he was watching you."

No matter how she tried, Amy couldn't keep the heat from rising in her cheeks. "I wasn't paying attention."

"I thought you said you were over your feelings for him from back then."

Amy shrugged. "Guess I was wrong. And even if I was, it doesn't mean new ones can't grow in their place."

"Is that what's happened?" Cami asked.

This time Amy dropped her gaze to where her hands fidgeted in her lap. "I don't know."

"I told him not to hurt you."

Amy jerked her gaze back up to meet Cami's. "Why would you do that?"

"Because I saw what happened the last time and if this time around he actually showed interest in you before ending things, it would be even worse."

"I don't know what's going to happen, but believe me, I'm not rushing into anything. I know you still see me as a teenager, but I do have a little more common sense now, and my emotions aren't controlling me like they did back then."

"Do you still believe he's the man God wants you to marry?"

Amy shook her head. "I haven't believed that in a very long time. Not saying it couldn't happen, but I'm not clinging to that belief like I did last time. In fact, God will have to make it pretty clear to me this is what He wants. I have my own reservations about things with Will."

"Like what?"

"Like having seen his previous relationship with Delia, and knowing how different I am from her. Not just in looks, but it seemed in personality, too. If he loved her, why would he love me?"

"You'll have to figure that out if you do want anything to work between you two."

"I know. Right now, for me, that would be the biggest hurdle."

Cami reached out and laid a hand on hers. "Just don't rush into anything. If you aren't one hundred percent at peace about that, it will undermine everything."

Amy nodded. "I know."

"I love you both." Cami squeezed her hand. "I want each of you to be happy. And if that's together, that's great, but if not, I don't want to see you hurt. Either of you."

"Thank you." Amy sat forward to hug Cami. "I love you, too. And I'm so glad you're here."

"I did have an ulterior motive when I suggested you come here for the summer," Cami said as she sat back from the hug. "I knew I'd get to see you."

They chatted a bit more about the family in Dallas before Cami slid off the bed and stood up. "It's been a long day. I'm going to go round up my hubby and head for bed."

Amy got up and gave her another hug. "See you guys in the morning."

This time after the door closed, Amy scooted into the bathroom to get ready for bed. Tomorrow was going to be her long day, and she didn't want to start it off tired.

She woke well before her alarm went off the next morning and decided to go ahead and get up. Because she still had to get into her costume later on, Amy decided that an early start to the day might be a good thing. She pulled on a pair of jeans and a t-shirt and gathered her hair into a ponytail to keep it out of the way. Figuring she'd sweat it off anyway, she skipped the makeup and headed downstairs.

The manor was quiet since it was barely past six-thirty, but she wasn't the only one up. She found Lance sitting in the kitchen, Bible open in front of him, coffee mug cupped in his hands.

"Hey!" he said as he spotted her. "You're up early."

"Woke up and figured I might as well get things underway." She took in his bare feet, shorts and tank top and asked, "Everything okay?"

"I was awake early, too. I didn't want to wake Jessa with my tossing and turning so just got up."

"Well, I won't keep you from your devotions. I'm going to get all the stuff to the clearing and start the decorations."

Lance pushed himself up from his seat. "Let me get some shoes, and I'll help you."

"You don't have to do that," Amy protested.

"I know I don't have to," Lance said with a smile. "But I can't let you do it all by yourself."

Amy watched her cousin leave the kitchen and then grabbed a banana and poured some coffee into a travel mug. She went into the library and pulled the sheet off the decorations. Thankfully, it was only the decorations that had to be taken out. The men had carried out a ladder and the tables she needed for the food and other things the night before.

"I figure we'll use the wagon to cart the stuff out," Lance said as he joined her.

"Sounds good."

With Lance's help, it didn't take long to take the stuff to the clearing. After their last load, Lance stood looking around. "You certainly have some lofty plans. Are you sure you don't need my help?"

"I'll be fine. I know how I'm going to make it work, so it's all good."

"You have your phone?" When Amy nodded, he said, "Call if you need anything."

After she had assured him once again that she'd be fine, Lance left her alone in the clearing. She turned on her favorite playlist on her phone and set to work.

ঙ৹৶

"Where's Amy?" Will asked as he looked around the kitchen. Charlotte and Henry were seated at the table with Josh while Lance and Cami were dealing with an assortment of children and their breakfast requests.

"She's out at the party location." Lance handed Julia a cup of milk. "Go sit at the table."

"Already?"

"Yep," Lance said. "She's been out there for a couple of hours. She was down here around 6:30. I helped her get the stuff out there and then left her to it."

Will looked at Charlotte. "Will you keep an eye on Isabella for me? I'm going to see if Amy needs help."

"Certainly," Charlotte said with a wide smile. "Never a hardship to watch her."

He heard Lance say something about Laurel and Violet coming over, but he was already headed out the back door. As he neared the party location, he heard music and smiled.

He stepped into the clearing and looked in surprise at the transformation it had undergone. Even though Amy had explained it all to him, he hadn't quite pictured it this way. She had done a beautiful job creating this fairy party for his daughter. He was pretty sure that if someone asked Isabella what her idea of heaven was, it would look like this.

Amy was standing on a ladder draping some gauzy- type material from a tree branch. Apparently the music had masked the sound of his arrival because she didn't turn around as he moved toward her.

"Good morning," he said as he stood a few feet from the ladder.

She jerked around and stared down at him. "You just about gave me a heart attack."

"Guess I should have been louder. You could have fallen off that ladder, too," Will pointed out. "But I would have caught you."

"And probably injured yourself in the process." Amy climbed down, and when she stood on the ground, she faced him with a smile and sparkling eyes. "So? What do you think?"

Even though he'd already looked at it, Will looked at all the decorations and then back at Amy. "You are going to make my daughter one very happy little girl."

"I'm so glad. Let me show you everything," Amy said. She paused then held out her hand to him.

Surprised, Will took it and allowed her to lead him around the clearing.

"This is where the photographer will take some posed shots of the girls. Otherwise, the rest will be candid." She pointed to another table. "We're going to have the girls decorate their own wings before putting them on. And Rose will do the fairy art on their face as they arrive."

Will found his throat tightening as they moved to the last area. He couldn't believe she had done all this for his daughter.

"Thank you." The words came out rough with emotion.

Amy turned to look at him, her expression wary, as if unsure how to respond to his reaction. "You're welcome. I have really enjoyed doing this. I'm almost sad it's going to be over soon."

"I never realized just how much Isabella has missed by not having a mom. My sisters have done their best, but you've shown so much love to her since the day you arrived." He slid his free hand behind her neck, feeling the weight of her hair on the backs of his fingers. "You just exude love and light. You're beautiful."

Her eyes widened at his words. Her hand slipped from his, and he felt a tentative touch on his waist. He slid his other hand behind her neck and ran his thumb along her soft jawline. Though he knew what he wanted, he paused, giving her a chance to move away. When she lifted herself up on her tiptoes, Will closed the last few inches and covered her lips with his.

The rush of emotion caught him off-guard, and he poured it into the kiss, wanting so badly for her to know how much she meant to him. Her hands tightened briefly on his waist and then slid around him. He moved his hands to the small of her back, relishing once again the feel of her in his arms. He had been right. She fit perfectly there. As if she'd been made just for him.

Knowing things could get out of hand fast with the two of them alone in the clearing, Will broke off the kiss and buried his face in the silkiness of her hair, inhaling the soft floral scent.

"Oh. My. Word."

The exclamation had Will jerking back because it hadn't been Amy who had uttered the shocked words. He turned to see three of his sisters and his brother-in-law standing there staring at them. Violet and Laurel looked surprised but also somewhat amused. Cami's expression was more concerned and Josh's...well, Josh looked ready to kill him.

Will glanced down at Amy and winked. "Busted."

As he released her and stepped away, Will saw a myriad of emotions cross her face. He understood the chagrin and even the regret, but the fear mystified him.

"I didn't know you guys were coming out here," Amy said as she turned to face the group gathered at the edge of the clearing, her arms wrapped across her waist.

"Obviously," Violet said drolly, a mischievous smile on her face. "Sorry to have interrupted."

"I'm not," Josh said, crossing his arms over his chest. "Something I should know? That was my sister you were sucking face with."

Will glanced at Amy, but she was still staring at the group. Or maybe at Cami, in particular. "I think this is between Amy and me."

Josh took a step toward them but stopped when Cami laid a hand on his arm. "Not the time, nor the place, babe."

Will could see the frustration in Josh's gaze as he looked back and forth between him and Amy. Something was just...off with the reactions of Cami, Josh and Amy. Sure he and Amy had been caught kissing, but they'd been fully clothed and with no intention of going any further. Their reactions seemed more in line with having caught the two of them doing something far more scandalous. Something about Amy and him being together was causing concern, and he just couldn't figure out what it might be. Clearly he needed to get to the bottom of this before things went much further.

"So what do you think of the decorations?" Amy asked as she walked toward the group. "Think this looks like a fairy party?"

Josh slid his arm around her shoulders. "To be honest, it looks a bit like a craft store threw up all over the forest."

Will saw Amy jab Josh in the ribs with her elbow. "You're just jealous because you don't get a fun party for your birthday."

"Yeah, that's right," Josh said as he rubbed his knuckles on her head. "Seriously though, it looks fabulous. I had no idea you had this kind of creativity in you."

"To be honest, I didn't really know either. But once I started gathering ideas, I just couldn't stop."

"The girls are absolutely going to love it," Laurel said. "You've done a spectacular job. You may have missed your calling."

"Well, now that I don't have a job, I may have to consider other options," Amy said ruefully.

"I bet you'd drum up some business once the other mothers see what you did for Isabella," Violet commented. "I'm sure I could even come up with a reason to hire you."

Will liked the idea of Amy setting up a business in Collingsworth. It would certainly make it easier to have a relationship with her, but he wasn't going to let something like a little distance deter him at this point.

"Did you need any more help?" Cami asked. "We didn't just come to admire your handiwork."

"I think it's all good for now. I'll come back out once the caterer arrives with the food. In the meantime, we have some little girls to get ready."

"And some big girls, too," Laurel added. "Rose was super excited about her fairy costume."

"Are you dressing up?" Cami asked.

Amy grinned. "You bet. After all the work, I want some of the fun, too."

"But it's a definite no to me in tights," Will reminded her.

Josh laughed. "Now *that* I would have paid good money to see."

"Keep your wallet in your pocket, brother," Will said. "That ain't ever happening."

Amy lifted her hands and shrugged. "I did try."

Will was grateful that the situation had been diffused by Amy. For the time being anyway.

As they made their way back to the manor, Will found himself wondering once again about Amy's reaction to their kiss. After finally getting to the point where he actually wanted a relationship with someone again, he was anxious to get moving on it.

He stopped to chat with Charlotte and Henry, who were seated in lawn chairs in the backyard watching the kids play. One of the things he loved about the couple was their capacity to just embrace everyone. He'd seen their love for people firsthand during his mission trip to the Philippines. He didn't think he'd ever met a more selfless couple.

When he looked around, Will realized that Amy had disappeared. Excusing himself, he went into the house to find her.

"I think she went up to her room," Laurel said when he asked about her. "How did we not know there was something that serious going on between you two?"

"Because there wasn't until just recently." Will sat down on a stool at the counter. "Like two days ago."

"That kiss didn't look like it belonged to a relationship that is only two days old."

Will lifted an eyebrow at his sister. "Were you just standing there watching the whole thing?"

"Well, I think we were all shocked speechless. Violet was just the first to recover." Laurel leaned a hip against the counter and crossed her arms. "Josh and Cami don't appear to be too happy about this latest turn of events. Not sure why."

"Where are they?" Will asked, glancing around the kitchen. "And Vi?"

"Violet's upstairs with Jessa." She paused. "I think Josh and Cami are with Amy."

Will tried to tamp down his irritation. Would they try to convince her to steer clear of him? If so, he wasn't sure why. He didn't think there was any reason for that. Given the reservation he'd sensed in Amy when he'd first asked her out, he was worried that she'd be swayed by Josh and Cami's concerns. If they'd only let him in on the issues, it would be much easier.

～ Chapter Seventeen ～

*W*HAT were you thinking?"

Amy stared at Cami and let out a long sigh. What *had* she been thinking? That being held in Will's arms had been the most wonderful thing in the world. That the closeness she'd dreamed of having with him so long ago was even more than she could have imagined.

Instead, she said, "I don't know."

"I had no idea when we talked that you were already this involved with him."

Amy plopped down on the bed across from Cami. Josh, thankfully, had gone on to their room. Amy didn't think she could have handled both of them right then. "We really aren't that involved. That kiss came out of the blue. Neither of us planned it."

She thought Cami was going to continue on about it, but when her sister-in-law spoke, all she said was, "Be careful."

"I'm trying to be. It's hard though. One minute I feel like it's great then the next I'm filled with doubt." Amy fidgeted with the bedspread. "Right now I wish I had never known him before. It's left too much stuff is going around in my head."

"Maybe it's time to tell him everything. Just get it out there."

Amy flopped back on the bed and stared up at the ceiling. "He'll probably think I'm nuts and drop me like a hot potato."

"I think his emotions are a little too mixed up in this for him to do that." Cami ran her fingers over Amy's cheek. "I can see how he looks at you. I know it took forever for Josh and me to get our act together, but that doesn't mean things can't happen much more quickly for others."

"How do I keep Delia out of my head?" Amy turned to look at Cami. "Do you ever think of Emma?"

"No. But that's a bit different. I never saw her and Josh together. I don't know how I'd feel in your situation." Cami laid down on her side, propping her head in her hand. "Have you prayed about it?"

"I've tried, but honestly, I wasn't sure what to pray." She frowned. "I've had some issues with God regarding this whole situation with Will."

"Maybe it's time to settle those and seek His will for what's happening now. I know it's hard to not dwell on the past, but it needs to stay there. Delia, your feelings back then, the heartache. It all needs to stay in the past."

Amy nodded. "I know. Easier said than done, however."

"We'll be praying for you. And just so you know, I reminded Josh that no one was really all that keen when he showed an interest in me. He will cut you guys some slack, but if Will hurts you...all bets are off."

"Thanks."

Cami pushed herself up. "I'm going to go and let you get ready. Come show me your outfit when you're dressed."

"I will. Did you find the outfits I bought for Grace and

Jojo? I left them in your room."

"Yes, I did. They were thrilled with them."

"I've asked Matt if he, and maybe Josh, could take the boys into town or something so they don't feel too left out."

"I'm sure Josh will be happy to tag along with them. Is Will hanging around for the party?"

"Oh yes, I told him he had to. Even without tights."

Cami tilted her head and smiled a gentle smile. "You've changed him. And Isabella, too. As his sister, I thank you."

Amy gave her a hug and then, after Cami left the room, began to get ready for the party.

ॐ

Will tried to stay out of the way of the large group of fairies that were flitting around the clearing. He was more than a little amazed at how organized Amy managed to keep it. The mothers who had stayed were seated around a table with food and drinks of their own while their daughters had their faces painted, decorated wings, blew bubbles, pinned wings on a fairy, and took a whack at the piñata. And in the midst of that they had eaten butterfly-shaped sandwiches and drank sparkling fruit punch out of tiny plastic cups.

Isabella was in her element. The lavender-colored fairy outfit she wore complimented her dark coloring, and she beamed from ear to ear. He didn't think she'd stopped smiling since arriving in fairyland. And he was equally pleased with the smile on Charlotte's face as she watched her only grandchild's delight in the party that had been thrown in her honor. He thought maybe it was good for her to have a wonderful memory to replace the one that had overshadowed this day for seven years.

For the first time since Delia's death, his first thought that morning—the anniversary of her death—had not been of sadness and grief. Instead it had been the anticipation of the wonderful memories that lay ahead for his daughter. Today they were celebrating life and love instead of mourning loss.

It was about celebrating the parts of Delia that continued on in their daughter. Will knew that today would forever change how he felt about this day.

His gaze settled on Amy, and he had to work to keep a smile off his face. She wore a light green outfit that matched the color of her eyes. Though the top was fitted like a leotard, the skirt was made of what looked like long gauzy handkerchiefs. She may have let him off the hook, but the green tights had still made an appearance. Only she wore them along with ballet flats. Her blonde hair hung in long ringlets over her wings, and she wore a crown of dainty flowers. She definitely looked the part of fairy princess. His fairy princess.

A couple of the women who had stayed for the party were single moms, and they'd been quite friendly with him at first. However, when he'd stuck close to Amy, they'd eventually gotten the lay of the land and had given up. For now, he was leaning against a tree watching the girls line up for pictures with the photographer. Each little girl was more than happy to preen and smile for the camera.

Finally, after the presents were opened, and the cake was eaten, the party began to wind down. Mothers took their reluctant fairies off down the path, the girls clutching the bags he'd helped Amy fill the day before.

Soon it was just him, Amy, and his sisters left. He'd had Charlotte take Isabella back to the manor to say goodbye to her friends as they left, and Rose had tagged along. Will thought Amy might take a break, but she started right in on the clean-up. She'd obviously prepared for it as she pulled out garbage bags and began to clear off the tables.

Violet, Cami and Laurel took back the first load of stuff. When it was just him and Amy in the clearing, Will approached her.

"Hey."

Amy glanced over her shoulder as she reached to grab the plastic cups and paper plates on the kids' table and dropped them in the garbage bag. She straightened and turned toward him, a smile on her face. "Hey."

"Are you happy with how it turned out?" he asked.

"That's the question I should be asking you," she replied.

He reached out and touched her cheek. "I'm beyond happy. You did a wonderful thing here for my little girl. I don't think I could ever thank you."

"No thanks necessary. I was happy to do it for her. And for you."

Will stepped closer to her and took her face into his hands. "Still. Thank you." He lowered his head and pressed a lingering kiss on her lips. "You look very beautiful today, too. And definitely much better in those tights than I would have looked."

She laughed, her eyes sparkling. "Well, thank you. It was fun dressing up like the girls."

Aware that his sisters would be returning soon, Will ran his thumb along her cheek before releasing her. "They're never going to forget this party. And you've probably just made life very difficult for the mothers of those girls who are going to be wanting a party like this one."

Amy picked up the garbage bag and dropped more things into it. "Well, it's a bit time-consuming, but they could do it if they put their minds to it."

"Or they could hire you to do it."

She gave him a small smile. "Maybe."

Before he could say anything more, he heard the sound of the women returning. He bent to help Amy clean off the table. By the time the clearing was empty of decorations, Matt and Josh had returned, and they came to help load the tables and chairs for the church into the back of Will's truck.

It was after five by the time they returned to the manor. Laurel and Violet had food out for everyone since what had been at the party, while filling for little girls, hadn't been exactly hardy fare for the adults. Will still hoped to take Amy out for dinner, but when he looked around the kitchen, she wasn't there. Hoping she was upstairs changing, he bided his time. When fifteen minutes had passed with no sign of her, he turned to Rose, who was standing next to him at the island, to ask if she'd seen her.

"I think she went upstairs. Want me to go check on her?" Rose offered.

"If you don't mind."

Rose flashed him a smile before heading out of the kitchen, still wearing her fairy attire.

"You going to eat?" Josh asked him as he approached the counter where the food had been spread out.

Taking the risk of telling him the truth, Will shook his head. "I had planned to take Amy out for dinner. To thank her for all her hard work on Isabella's party."

Josh lifted an eyebrow. "I hear it was quite the success."

That hadn't been what Will had expected to come out of Josh's mouth, but he was happy to have avoided any sort of lecture. "It was wonderful. She did a fantastic job."

"She loves children, so I'm sure it was a pleasure for her to do this for Isabella."

"Will?"

Hearing Rose's voice, he turned from Josh to where his niece stood. "Is she okay?"

"Um...she's sound asleep."

"What?"

"I found her on her bed, still dressed as a fairy, sound asleep," Rose said.

"I'm not surprised," Lance commented. "She was up before seven this morning and worked hard all day. She's probably exhausted."

While Will felt a shaft of disappointment, he knew that if

she needed the rest, it was best to just let her be. They could have their dinner another night.

"Well, guess I'm eating supper here after all," he said as he grabbed a plate.

ళ్లలు

Amy woke slowly, groaning as she rolled to her back. Her body ached in places it hadn't in a very long time. She lay there for a moment before she turned onto her side and pushed into a sitting position. Thankfully the nap she'd taken had refreshed her, but she hoped she wasn't too late in getting ready for dinner with Will. She'd only planned to rest for a few minutes after finishing the clean-up.

Sitting on the edge of her bed, she pushed back the mass of curls that slid over her shoulder as she reached for her phone. She flipped it over to see the time. Six o'clock. Well, it looked like it might be a late dinner, but hopefully Will would understand and forgive her tardiness. She pulled off the fairy costume and dropped it on the floor on her way to the bathroom. After removing the painting Rose had applied on her face, she redid her makeup and left her hair loose.

Not sure where they would be going, she decided on a jean skirt that ended just above her knees and a sleeveless button-up shirt in soft pink. She slipped on a pair of white sandals and grabbed her purse before heading out of her room.

As she reached the top of the stairs, she realized that the house seemed way quieter than she would have expected. Maybe everyone was outside. She walked down the stairs and found the kitchen clean and empty of people. When she grabbed the handle of the back door, she found it locked.

Dread filled her as she pulled her phone out again and looked at the time. Now it said six thirty...AM. She'd not only slept through her date with Will, but she'd slept all night. Shoulders slumped, she sat down at the table. How could she have done something so dumb? She'd only planned to lie down for a few minutes. Her feet and back had been aching, so she'd taken some pain pills before lying down. Clearly her body had decided it wanted more than just a nap, and apparently the adrenalin let-down had guaranteed she slept the whole night.

What did Will think? Their first date and she'd missed it.

"Well, if it isn't Sleeping Beauty."

Amy turned to face her brother, a scowl on her face. "Really?"

Josh grinned. "You look very nice. Going somewhere?"

"Shut up." Amy pushed her phone to the center of the table and got up to make herself some coffee.

Dressed in a pair of athletic shorts and a t-shirt, Josh leaned against the counter. "You know, he understood. He was disappointed, sure, but he knew you were tired. Lance said you'd been up since before seven."

Amy shot him a wary look as she started the coffee pot. "He told you about us going out for dinner?"

Josh nodded. "He sent Rose up to check on you after we got back from dropping off the stuff at the church. Apparently you were one passed out fairy."

She pulled a mug out of the cupboard. "You want coffee, too?"

"Sure."

After putting two mugs on the counter, she stood watching the coffee drip into the carafe. She felt an arm around her shoulders and looked over to see Josh watching her, his expression serious.

"You really feel something for Will?"

Amy turned her gaze back to the coffee. She wasn't sure she was ready to have this discussion with her brother without at least one cup of coffee under her belt. Thankfully she was spared from having to respond when Lance joined them.

"Hey, you're up early," he commented when he saw Amy.

"Funny. I actually thought it was six o'clock PM. As in, last night. Imagine my surprise when I realized I'd just slept twelve straight hours. So yeah, I'm up early. Or late. Depending on how you look at it."

Lance chuckled. "I think that's a first."

"And hopefully the last," Amy commented as she pulled another mug from the cupboard. Once the coffee was done she poured it into the three cups. "At least I'm ready for church in plenty of time."

It wasn't long before others began to join them in the kitchen. Since she was up and ready, Amy tackled making breakfast for the group. Charlotte showed up and insisted on helping out with the pancakes while Henry set out plates and cups and then cut up some fruit.

"Are you staying with Jessa?" Cami asked Lance. "I'd be happy to hang with her if you'd like to go to the service."

Lance's brow furrowed. "I usually stay with her, and we watch the live feed together."

"Why don't you go this time? I'll watch with her."

"If you're sure," Lance said, not sounding one hundred percent convinced.

"I'm positive. You'll just have to help Josh with the kids."

"Oh, well, in that case..." Lance grinned. "Just kidding. I'll talk to Jessa about it when I take her breakfast up."

Amy handed him a plate with a couple of pancakes on it. "There's fruit there, too."

Once breakfast was done and cleaned up, people scattered to get ready for church. Amy settled down at the table and enjoyed another cup of coffee. Before leaving, she went back up to her bedroom to grab her Bible and then joined Lance in his truck with Julia. She'd debated texting or phoning Will to apologize but figured she'd wait to do it in person.

She was talking with Charlotte and Henry in the foyer of the church when she felt small arms grasp her hips in a tight hug. The familiar embrace brought a smile to her face. "Hey, sweetheart. How are you?"

"I'm great! Daddy said I had to remember to thank you for my party. Since you were asleep last night."

Amy dropped down on one knee, so she was at eye level with Isabella. "Did you have a good time?"

"It was wonderful. The best day ever." The little girl's voice cracked as she flung her arms around Amy's neck. "Thank you."

Amy closed her eyes as she hugged her close. "You are very welcome. I had fun, too."

Isabella released her and stepped back. "I loved being a fairy. I wanted to wear it again today, but Daddy said no."

Amy glanced up to see Will standing behind Isabella. He looked so handsome in his pleated black slacks and white button up shirt with the sleeves rolled up to his elbows. Her heart skipped a beat as their gazes met. He held out his hand, and she slipped her hand into his and allowed him to help her back to her feet.

He smiled, not releasing her right away. "Good morning."

"I am so sorry about last night," Amy said. She described her morning, glad to see Will didn't seem upset at all about what had happened.

He reached out and ran his fingers along her cheek. "It's all good. I know you were tired. Maybe we can try again soon."

Amy nodded. "Definitely."

She glanced at Charlotte and Henry, suddenly remembering their presence. Even though Will had told her that they wouldn't have a problem with him moving on, it still surprised her to see wide smiles on their faces.

"Why don't we go in and find seats?" Will said.

They found an empty pew, and Will stepped back to allow Charlotte and Henry to go in first. Amy followed Isabella in as she wanted to sit between her grandmother and her "best friend." As Will settled on the pew next to her, his leg bumped her and nerves fluttered to life in her stomach. Their choice to sit together was pretty much an all-out declaration that they were together, and she wasn't oblivious to the glances that were sent their way.

The rest of the family found seats in the pews in front of them, and once again the Collingsworth clan took up a large section of the left-hand side of the church. Amy felt bad that Jessa and Cami couldn't have been there, too, but she knew it wasn't worth the risk to Jessa.

As they stood to sing, Amy gripped the pew in front of her to keep from swaying into Will. She had dreamed of moments like this. Being in church with him. Singing and worshipping together.

They sang familiar songs, some going back to her childhood, but as they began one in particular, a memory hit her like a wrecking ball. The pain it brought took her breath away and made her stomach heave. She swallowed hard, but when her hands started to tremble, Amy knew she needed to leave.

Keeping her head bent, she said, "Excuse me."

"What's wrong?" Will asked in a low voice as he moved to let her past.

Without saying anything, Amy hurried as fast as she could to the back of the church and out into the foyer. She headed to the bathrooms and straight into an empty stall. Thankful the toilet had a lid, she shut it and sank down. How could a memory shake her up so badly? Had it been because her emotions were already so near the surface that this particular memory had pushed through so easily? Every pain she'd felt back then had flooded her with scalding hot hurt.

She hadn't wanted to come to church that day. The pain of seeing Will and Delia together had been still so fresh that she hadn't wanted to be anywhere near them. Especially in a place where she'd dreamed of being with him in just the way Delia was. But her parents had insisted, so she'd gone and tried to look anywhere but where they were, just two pews ahead, seated with his family.

As they'd stood for the closing song, Amy's gaze had gone to them as if drawn by a magnet. Will had bent down to say something to Delia, his arm around her slender waist. She'd lifted her head and smiled at him. The look of love blazing between them had stabbed at her like a knife. And when Delia had turned to slip her arm around Will's back, her head pressed against his chest, it had taken all Amy's strength to look away and to keep the pain from her face. A truly difficult task for a girl who was used to sharing what she felt with the world. The depth of the hurt she felt had become an anguished secret she'd hid from everyone around her.

Amy braced a hand against the wall of the bathroom stall. She took several deep breaths and let them out. *The past must stay in the past. The past must stay in the past.* How was she supposed to keep it there when these memories kept sneaking up and taking her unaware? What did she need to do to get beyond these memories and the hurt?

He was with *her* now.

He wanted to be with *her* now.

But did he really? Delia had been his first choice, his first wife. If she hadn't died, he would still be with her. He hadn't had a choice in having her taken from him. Could he say that if he'd been able to go back and do things differently, he wouldn't make the choices that would mean Delia would live?

Amy knew she had to go back to the sanctuary. Will must be wondering what had happened to her. But she needed to pull herself together in order to be able to brush aside his concern. She closed her eyes and took several more breaths, willing herself to calm down. If she could hide her emotional upheaval as a teenager, she could do it now.

Finally feeling the emotions ebb away and the pained memory fade, Amy left the stall. She looked at herself in the mirror and realized that at some point she'd been crying. Ripping a paper towel from the dispenser on the wall, she dabbed at the wetness on her cheeks. Because she didn't have her purse, she couldn't fix up her makeup, but since it hadn't been a full-on crying jag, there wasn't too much damage. Once satisfied that she didn't look too worse for wear, Amy left the safe confines of the women's bathroom and headed back to the sanctuary. She half expected to find Will waiting for her somewhere along the way, but she made it to the door without running into him.

She opened the door and slipped inside. The singing was done, and now the pastor was praying, so she stood at the back, head bowed, until he was finished. Moving quickly, she walked down the aisle and laid a hand on Will's shoulder to alert him to her presence. He glanced up and then turned his legs to the side to allow her into the pew. She felt his hand briefly on her hip as she scooted past him and settled down once again between him and Isabella.

"Everything okay?" he asked as he leaned close to her, concern evident in the softly spoken words.

"Yep." She gave him what she hoped was a reassuring smile. "Just a bathroom emergency."

It looked like he didn't completely believe her, but obviously the middle of a church service wasn't the appropriate place to have any sort of conversation. She gave him another quick smile before turning her attention to the front of the church. The pastor had called all the children forward for a prayer before dismissing them for their own service. As Isabella moved past Amy, she gave her a quick kiss and then gave one to Will as well.

Amy smiled at the sight of the dark haired girl skipping down to the front of the church. She knew that skipping wasn't exactly appropriate in a church, but Amy liked the joy it exuded, and she thought it would make God happy, too. As she watched the children gathered at the front, Amy wondered if this thing with Will might lead to the day when it would be a child of theirs joining Isabella and the others at the front.

She glanced at Will and found him watching the children at the front of the church as well, a small smile on his face. A memory came to her again, but this one was more recent as she recalled seeing him again for the first time when he'd showed up at the manor with Isabella just after she'd arrived in Collingsworth. Then she'd thought he'd look hardened and tense, but today he was anything but. The emotion on his face for Isabella revealed just how much he'd changed in the past few weeks.

Was she really responsible for it like some seemed to think? Or had his changes been more for his daughter than anything else?

Once the prayer was done, the congregation stood for one more song as the children left the sanctuary. This time Amy kept a tight rein on her thoughts and focused on the words of the song, desperate to keep any more memories at bay.

∾ Chapter Eighteen ❦

WANT to ride back with us?" Will asked Amy as they stood in the sanctuary with the rest of his family. "I brought the Escalade."

Amy smiled at him. "Well, I certainly can't refuse a ride in that."

He was happy to see her smile. Her rapid exit from the sanctuary still played in his mind. He wasn't entirely convinced it had been the bathroom emergency she'd claimed. For one thing, she hadn't looked at him and had, in fact, looked like she was keeping her head purposefully down. But he wasn't going to press her about it. They weren't yet at that point in their relationship where they were sharing everything, so he'd bide his time.

Though he'd been disappointed that they hadn't made their date the night before, it had been hard not to laugh at the events that had transpired for Amy that morning. If she hadn't seemed so distressed about having missed their date, he might have chuckled about it. He hoped that one day they could look back on their first date and the events that followed and laugh about it together.

Once Isabella joined them, they stepped out of the church into the bright summer sunshine. It was a beautiful day, and Will looked forward to spending a relaxing afternoon at the manor with the rest of the family.

"I can get that file for you," Will said as he sat with Matt and Lance at the picnic table after they'd finished eating. "I meant to bring it over yesterday but forgot."

"Would you mind?" Lance asked. "Matt's heading out early to the job site tomorrow. I hate to do business on Sunday, but I want to run the numbers with you two once more before the job starts."

"I'll go get it now. It's at my apartment." Will stood and extricated himself from the picnic bench. He glanced around and saw Amy sitting with Cami and Josh. He hesitated then walked over to where they were. He touched her shoulder. "Interested in going for a ride?"

She looked up at him. "A ride?"

"Yes. I have to go to the apartment to get a folder for Lance and wondered if you wanted to go along for the ride. We won't be gone long."

"Sure." She stood and turned toward her brother and Cami. "See you in a bit."

They both nodded, but Will didn't miss the ever-present concern that was on their faces once again.

It didn't take long to get to the apartment block even though he hadn't even been going the speed limit.

"This is a nice place," Amy said as he pulled into his parking spot.

"Yep. I own the building, actually. It was a bit run-down when I bought it, but I had Lance's team gut it." He got out of the car and met her on the sidewalk. "There used to be four apartments per floor, but they were small, so I combined some of them. The main and second floors still have the four apartments, but the third and fourth each have two and the top floor just has one. Which is mine."

He unlocked the door then held it open for her. She glanced around the foyer as he found the elevator key. There were two elevators at the far end of the entrance. One was for the first four floors, but the other one was strictly access to his apartment and was locked at all times. He placed his hand on Amy's back to guide her into the elevator when the doors slid open.

Though he had initially planned for the elevator to open right into his apartment, he'd decided that as an added measure of security he'd still have a small entry with a locked door to his place. As they stepped into the apartment, he glanced at her to gauge her reaction.

"It's beautiful," Amy said as she looked around.

"I'm afraid I can't take any credit for it. Interior decorating is definitely not my thing." His phone rang, and Will glanced down at it. He frowned when he saw his mom's number, but tapped the screen to answer it. "Hey, Mom. What's up?"

Amy stood beside him as he listened to his mom ask him if he had a few minutes to talk. He didn't, really, but at the same time, she was his mother, and he respected and loved her enough to give her what she needed. "Hang on just a second, Mom."

Muting the call, Will turned to Amy. "It's my mom. This might take a few minutes. I'm going to go into my office to get the file. Make yourself at home. The kitchen is through there if you want something to drink."

"Okay."

"Hopefully, it won't take too long," he said and then unmuted the call and put the phone to his ear as he headed for his office.

৯৵৻৶

Amy watched as Will disappeared through a doorway leading off the living-room. She still stood rooted in place, almost afraid to look around. But finally, she just couldn't help herself.

She let her gaze skim the surfaces in the room looking for the pictures she figured would be there. There were pictures in frames, but all of them were of Isabella at varying ages. There were none of Will or Delia. She turned to look down the hallway. Did she dare? There was a burning need to know, even though she knew that the knowledge could bring great hurt.

She glanced back toward the office door, hearing the muffled sounds of Will's conversation with his mother. Though the voice in her head screamed not to do it, she hurried down the hallway and immediately found the door to his bedroom. It stood open, and the curtains were pulled back, so she didn't even have to touch anything as she moved to the entrance. One side of the large bed was unmade, but her gaze skimmed over that to the nightstand. And there she found it. The picture she'd thought she'd see in the other part of the apartment. The one of him and Delia.

Feeling sick to her stomach for the second time that day, Amy turned away and found another open door. This time it led to the bathroom. Numbly, she stepped onto the tile floor and closed the door behind her. Why had she looked? *Why?* She had known what she'd find. Had been almost certain of it. But she'd had no right to go looking, snooping into his room. The one he'd shared with Delia. Now this pain was the price she had to pay.

Knowing she wouldn't have long to compose herself, Amy pushed aside the pain. She had to. She would deal with it another time. Later when she could completely fall apart at the knowledge that the man who had expressed such interest in her, the man her heart longed for, still had a picture of his first wife next to his bed. The first thing he saw in the morning. The last thing he saw at night. How could she bear this pain she'd brought on herself?

Forcing herself to think about other things as she drew in several deep breaths, Amy looked into the mirror and stared at herself until she'd managed to erase the torment from her expression. Never had she been so glad that she had learned to hide her emotions when necessary. She had decided early in her teaching career that she wouldn't bring her outside emotions into her classroom if she could help it. No matter how bad her day was, the kids in the classroom wouldn't bear the brunt of that. So she'd taught herself how to keep a positive expression on her face even when she was upset.

She moved to flush the toilet and wash her hands as if that was her sole purpose in wandering down the hallway. Back in the living room, she could still hear Will's voice coming from the office. She went in the direction he had indicated the kitchen was in and got a bottle of water from the fridge.

She was standing in front of the large glass window looking out over the neighborhood when she felt Will come up behind her. Pasting a smile on her face, Amy turned and said, "You've got a nice view here."

"Yep. Nothing like the sprawling metropolis of Collingsworth," Will said drolly. "Are you a city girl? Do you enjoy the cityscape more than the country?"

Amy looked back out the window as she shook her head. "Not really. I love the manor and would kill for a place like Dean and Violet have. She gave me a tour the other day. That place is gorgeous."

"Yes, it is."

"Everything okay with your mom?" Amy asked, taking her gaze from the view.

"Yes. She was just upset about something one of my younger siblings had done. And then had to give me a rundown on everything else that was going on."

"That's nice she keeps you up-to-date on family things," Amy said as she uncapped her water bottle and took a drink. She could hardly believe she was pulling this off, but an eerie numbness had begun to spread through her body.

"Well, guess we'd better head back to the manor," Will said. "Don't want anyone sending out a search party."

Amy glanced at his hands which held only his phone. "Did you get what you needed for Lance?"

Will gave a shake of his head. "Good thing you're here looking out for me." He grinned at her and then once again disappeared into the office. This time he returned more quickly with the file in hand. "Okay. Now we can go."

Back at the manor, they walked around to where the family was gathered.

Will touched her arm. "I need to meet with Lance and Matt for a bit. Don't fall asleep on me again. I'd like to talk with you before I leave tonight."

Amy's stomach clenched at the thought of talking with him in her current state of mind. "Okay. I'll be around."

Once Will disappeared into the house with Lance and Matt, Amy knew she needed some time alone. Retreating to her bedroom was somewhat appealing, but in the end, Amy headed toward the lake.

"Hey, Amy!"

She turned to see Cami coming toward her. As her sister-in-law got closer, Amy felt tears flood her eyes. She looked away, but obviously not before Cami had seen. Immediately she felt an arm around her shoulders, and Cami propelled her in the direction of the path she'd already been walking toward.

It wasn't long until they came out of the forest at the beach and the heavy, weathered, wooden swing that sat there. Cami led her to the swing and sat down, pulling Amy with her. "What happened?"

"I can't do this." Amy stared out at the water. "I want to, but I just can't."

"Delia again?" Cami asked. At Amy's nod, she said, "I wondered if it was a good idea going to his place."

"I shouldn't have done it. I know I shouldn't have, but I went to his room while he was on the phone with his mom. He still has a picture of her beside his bed. His side of the bed."

"Ah, sweetie." Cami slipped an arm around her shoulders again and leaned her head against Amy's.

"And it wasn't just that." Amy recounted what had happened in the service earlier in the day. "Out of nowhere that memory hit me. I'm just not strong enough to deal with it all. Just when I think I've got a handle on it, something else happens to pull me back to where I don't want to be."

"I wish I knew what to tell you. I understand being trapped by the past. I've been there, and it's not as easy as just saying it's not going to bother you anymore. I understand that completely." Cami fell silent for a moment. "Satan preys on those weaknesses in us. Even now out of the blue I'll see someone the age my baby would have been, and the thought will hit me. *That's the age your child would have been if you hadn't killed it.* I only get through moments like that with God's strength. Have you prayed about this?"

"Every day. Every hour. Honestly, I feel like it's a prayer constantly running in the back of my mind. But maybe this is God's way of telling me once again that Will is not meant for me."

"Don't be so sure of that, sweetheart. Just because something isn't easily obtained doesn't mean that it still isn't God's will for us. However, only you can figure that out for yourself. None of the rest of us can live your life. None of us understands the pain you felt all those years ago."

"I just want it gone. I want to love and be loved without the shadow of another woman hanging over that love. And Will deserves a relationship with someone who isn't dealing with stuff like this. I can't undo the past. I can't unmeet Delia. I can't unsee everything that happened back then. I think it's just too much to overcome." Amy stared out at the water, feeling hot tears course down her cheeks. "I feel like I'm right back there again. That teenager feeling so hurt and not being able to do anything about it."

"But she was strong enough to move past the hurt and get on with her life," Cami reminded her. "You've dated other men. You've been moving ahead with your life. You've been living life and embracing it."

"Yeah, but with everything that's transpired over the past couple of weeks I kind of feel like the chair's been kicked out from beneath me. No job. No relationship. I feel like I embraced life, and it turned around and slapped me." She kicked at the sand with the toe of her sandal.

"You can't let this get you so down, sweetie. The blessings you have in your life far outweigh the struggles you're facing now. This is not like you."

Amy sighed. "I know. I just don't know what to do. I need to end this thing with Will because letting it go on will only make things worse for both of us."

"You really think ending it is necessary?" Cami asked. "Maybe you just need to explain to him. Let him know what you're struggling with. He may be able to help you."

Amy glanced at Cami. "I don't know if I can do that. Not without becoming an emotional mess."

They sat in silence for several minutes before Cami reached over and took her hand. "Let me pray with you."

Amy nodded and bent her head. Tears dripped onto their joined hands, and though she longed for it with all her heart, there was no peace that flooded her at the end of Cami's prayer. Still just turmoil and hurt.

♥

Will was glad that Lance didn't take too long going over the file. Once the other two men began discussing specifics of the job that didn't involve him, he excused himself. Out in the backyard, he glanced around for Amy but didn't see her. He did see Cami and Josh standing close to each other, apparently deep in discussion about something. Josh pulled Cami into a tight embrace, resting his cheek on her hair.

Something about the action was unsettling, but he wasn't sure why.

Laurel and Violet were sitting nearby on lounge chairs, so he approached them. "Do you guys know where Amy is?"

"I think I saw her go down to the lake," Laurel said. "Cami went with her, but she came back alone, so I assume she's still down there."

Will nodded, an uneasy feeling growing in the pit of his stomach. He was pretty sure his sister had seen him head that way, and he half expected Cami to stop him as he walked toward the path leading to the lake. But she didn't. His steps slowed as he saw the beach ahead.

As he stepped onto the sand, he immediately spotted Amy sitting on the swing. Sitting with her hands under her thighs, shoulders hunched and head bent did not bode well in Will's mind.

Not walking any closer, he shoved his hands into his pockets. "Amy?"

Her head jerked around, and the emotion on her face was like a kick in the gut. She stared at him for a moment before lowering her head once again.

No, this was not good.

Slowly, Will approached the swing and settled onto it, careful not to crowd her. He was afraid that she was just skittish enough she might bolt if he got too close.

"Have I done something to upset you?" He figured that was a good place to start, giving her the opportunity to get it out if he had, in fact, done something.

Her head lifted, but she didn't look at him. Instead, she stared out at the lake, and he could see there was dampness on her cheeks. Something told him that whatever had concerned Cami and Josh about him and Amy had come to fruition.

﹋ Chapter Nineteen ﹌

WHAT'S wrong?" he prodded again, desperate to know what was going on.

He saw her take a deep breath before she turned to face him.

"I can't do this with you," she said, her voice hoarse. Fresh tears spilled down her cheeks. "I'm sorry."

Will swallowed hard. How was it that the end of a relationship that hadn't even really gotten off the ground could cause so much hurt. "Why?"

She took so long to answer Will wondered if she was going to. But finally she said, "I don't know how to be in a relationship when there's another woman involved."

"What?" Will stared at her, certain he hadn't heard her right. "Another woman? I'm not involved with another woman."

She looked away from him. "It's Delia." He heard her voice crack on Delia's name.

"Delia? This is about Delia?" Will wished the fog of

confusion would clear from his head. "I don't understand."

"I saw you with Delia, Will. I was here the night you arrived with her as your new bride. I saw the love and adoration you had for her. It was hard to miss. I'm the opposite of Delia in pretty much every way, and I just can't get past feeling like I would be second best. That I would never have all your love." Amy rubbed a hand just below her left collar bone. "And maybe I'm just being naïve, but I don't want to be someone's second choice. I don't want to have to share someone's heart with another woman."

"You've put some thought into this," was Will's only response as he stared at her.

Amy's head dropped before she looked at him again. "Yes." As she stared at him, Will sensed that she was trying to decide if she should go on. "You don't know this, but you've already broken my heart once."

"What?" The fog of confusion suddenly got even denser. "I have no idea what you're talking about."

"I know." She paused before continuing. "When I was here that Christmas for Lance and Jessa's wedding and I met you for the first time, I was positive that you were the man God wanted me to marry."

Of all the things he'd thought she'd say, that hadn't even been on the radar. "Uh, you were how old?"

"I was fifteen, but I felt it strongly. I wanted to say something, to ask you to wait for me, but figured you'd just think I was crazy, so I didn't. When I came for Cami and Josh's wedding, I talked to Cami about it. I was so excited to see you again and had made the decision to talk to you. During that year or so since I'd last seen you, I'd prayed that if it wasn't meant to be that God would take what I felt away. I prayed for you every night."

"You did?" Will was more than a little baffled at the direction of the conversation.

"Yes. Every night I prayed that God would keep you safe

and guard your heart for me. Then that night at the wedding..."

"I showed up with Delia as my wife."

"Yes. I was devastated. I couldn't figure out what had happened. I was angry at God for not taking away the feelings I had for you. I was angry at you for falling in love with someone else. It was a very rough time for me. And I couldn't talk to anyone but Cami about it. And even she didn't know how deeply I hurt."

He had no idea how to respond. "I'm...sorry?"

"No need to be sorry. How could you have known?" Amy sighed. "I spent a lot of time moving on from my feelings for you since then. I had even convinced myself it was just some teenage crush that had lasted too long. When Cami asked me to come here, I was sure it wouldn't be an issue. I was even more convinced when you didn't even recognize me that first morning at the manor."

"I don't even know what to say to all this," Will said. "I had no idea."

"I know you didn't. What I'm struggling with now isn't your fault. When I started feeling things for you again, and then you seemed to reciprocate, I thought I could do it. But it seems that I can't." Amy's shoulders slumped. "The memories keep cropping up and sucker punching me. I feel like I'm on a rollercoaster. I just can't do it. I'm sorry."

"This morning?" Will asked.

Amy looked at him, her head tilted to the side. "What about it?"

"When you left the service. Was it one of those sucker punch memories?"

She stared at him for a long moment before nodding.

"What was it?"

Her brows drew together. "I don't know if it was the song or what, but suddenly I was sixteen again watching you and

Delia stand together two rows in front of me. You had your arm around her, and when you looked at each other, all I could see was the love you had for her. The love I thought you would one day have for me."

Will remembered that day. Their first service as a married couple in his hometown. It was odd to think that something that had been so special to him had brought such pain to Amy. But he hadn't known. And even if he had, he wasn't sure he would have done anything differently. He had loved Delia, and they'd already been married.

"Was there more today?" he asked, curious if the trip to the apartment had triggered something.

Her gaze dropped from his, and she hunched forward. "The apartment."

"I never lived there with Delia. I had all that done after she passed away."

"Not that. When I went to the bathroom, I looked into your bedroom."

Will closed his eyes, well aware of what she would have seen.

"I'm sorry. I shouldn't have snooped." Her voice cracked, and she took a deep breath. "But I think it was for the best because, picture aside, I can't seem to get past all of the rest of this."

"So that's it?" Will asked, anger flaring inside him. "A few memories and a picture on my nightstand are enough for you to end this without even trying?"

"No. This is about pain and heartache. And the fact that I feel it deeply each and every time a memory surfaces. You kiss me, and I remember seeing you kiss her and how much it hurt me back then. You lay your hand on my back to guide me somewhere, and I remember how you did that with Delia. I remember seeing how you cherished her and how I had wished that was me." She paused as tears spilled down her cheeks. "I know it must sound ridiculous to you since I was only sixteen, but it was so very real to me. I truly believed that you were going to be my husband. You can't imagine the pain my teenage heart endured. This was more than just a crush. So much more."

"You're right, I don't understand. I'm sorry about what happened back then, but I didn't know. And at that point, even if I had known, there was nothing I could do."

"And you wouldn't have wanted to do anything about it anyway. You had your love, your wife."

Will couldn't deny what she said. "What can I do to get you to give us a chance?"

"I *did* give us a chance. That's why I accepted your date invitation. It's why I kissed you. It's why I sat with you this morning." She lifted her head and stared at him, her green gaze intense. "You tell me what to do. You tell me how to make it not matter to my heart that I'm your second choice. That if you had a chance to do it all over again, you'd probably do what you could to keep Delia from dying. That she, now and forever, will have a large part of your heart. That the things I imagined us learning together, you've already done with her." Her voice again cracked with emotion. "Tell me how to make none of that matter. Tell me!"

Confusion and hurt pushed away the anger, leaving Will feeling helpless and desperate. "I don't know what to tell you. All I know is that I'm a different man now than I was eight years ago. And the man I am today is choosing you."

Amy's expression crumpled into tears as she lifted a clenched hand and pressed it to her heart. "But you chose her first."

And there was absolutely nothing Will could do to change that. He looked at Amy, his heart aching as he realized that, for the second time in his life, he was losing the woman he loved.

She wrapped her arms across her waist and seemed to curl into herself as if to ward off any more pain. Knowing that there was nothing left to say, no words that could give soothing for her pain or freedom from his past's effects on her, Will swallowed hard and got up from the swing.

His steps leaving her were as slow as the ones that had taken him to her earlier. He had known it wasn't going to be good, and his intuition had been correct. Clearly it wasn't in God's plan for him to have a love that lasted.

As he walked from the trees to the backyard, he realized the family was all still gathered there. Not interested in any conversation, he went to the person he figured would give him the least grief at this point.

He moved towards where Cami still stood with Josh. Her gaze, full of sadness, was on him as he approached her.

"Would you guys be willing to keep Isabella here for the night? She doesn't have anything to wear, but I'm sure Julia has a few things she could loan her."

Cami nodded. "Of course." Her gaze went past his shoulder toward the lake. "Is she okay?"

"No. And there's nothing I can do about it. Someone should have told me about her feelings sooner. I had no idea."

Josh clapped a hand on his shoulder. "I'm sorry, bro. I didn't know anything about it until Cami told me the other day."

"I'm going to go now. I don't think she'll come back as long as she thinks I'm still here."

Will turned and walked toward the side of the house, his head bent.

"Will?" He heard Laurel call out to him, but he kept on going. Let Cami and Josh fill them all in on the details. He didn't think he could do it right then.

Once at the apartment, he went to his office. He slumped down in his chair and stared at the framed picture that sat on the corner of his desk. It wasn't the same picture that was on his nightstand. That one had been taken on their honeymoon. This one had been at their wedding. He reached out and snagged it, staring intently, not at Delia, but at himself. That guy seemed so young now. But he had loved Delia deeply and would have moved the world for her.

Weathering that first storm during her pregnancy had been a major hurdle, but Will realized now that all the concessions to make her happy had come from him. Her argument had been that he was getting the child he wanted, so she should get everything *she* wanted. And he'd been young enough to agree to her demands. He would like to hope that had she lived they both would have matured and learned how to make decisions together, and how to deal with the rough patches in their marriage in a healthier way. But it was possible that they wouldn't have.

The small part of him that was still that Will from eight years ago would always love Delia. But what he'd told Amy had been absolutely true. The man he was now had chosen her. Too bad it hadn't made any difference at all.

His breath caught in his lungs as he laid the framed picture face down on his desk.

〜∞〜

Amy hadn't wanted to return to the manor and face the people there. No doubt they would be angry at her for leading Will on and hurting their brother. If they could only understand how much she hurt, too.

When she'd felt the swing move and realized he'd left, the shaft of pain through her heart had taken her breath away. She hadn't even known it was possible, but the pain she felt right then was even worse than her teenage heartache. Back then, her pain had been from unrequited love. This time around, it was from the knowledge that if she could have just overcome his past, she could have realized her dreams. If only she had been stronger.

It wasn't long before Cami came to her once again. They sat in silence for a while. Amy had no more words to share the maelstrom of emotions within her heart. Finally, Cami slipped her arm around her shoulders. "If only this swing could talk. The stories it could tell. I think all of us have had a crisis of relationship here on the edge of the lake." She fell silent again for a few minutes then said, "Let's go back to the manor. It's getting late."

Though she didn't want to, Amy nodded. Dusk was beginning to settle around the lake. Slowly she stood. "Have the others left?"

"Yes. They were getting their things together to leave when I came here."

Grateful for that much, Amy followed behind Cami along the path among the trees. As they walked side by side across the back yard, Cami slipped her arm around her waist, and Amy returned the gesture. She was so thankful for Cami's presence in her life. Amy was sure it was difficult to see her and Will upset since she loved them both.

No one questioned her when she got to the manor. Cami ushered her up the stairs to her room. "Isabella's here, and I'm sure she's going to want to say goodnight in a little while."

"That's fine. I'll just take a shower and get ready for bed. Bring her in when it's time for her to go to sleep."

Feeling marginally better after her shower, she was able to say goodnight to Isabella without her asking any questions. And though she'd worried she wouldn't be able to sleep, by the time Amy crawled into bed, exhaustion brought on by her emotional turmoil pulled at her, and she slipped into the blissful oblivion of sleep.

She woke the next morning hoping it had all been a nightmare, but that thought was quickly pushed aside by reality. As she sat on the edge of the bed trying to find the strength to face the day, her phone rang. Her heart pounded as she reached for it. Looking at the display, she saw it was Sammi. Though she wanted to share everything that had happened with her best friend, Amy didn't think she had the ability to do it right then. She contemplated not answering, but she figured Sammi would just keep calling back.

"Hello?"

"Amy! Can you make it here by Wednesday?" Sammi asked without any preamble.

"What? Why?"

"They've decided to do interviews for substitute teachers at my school. Apparently they lost a couple over the summer to other schools. We just found out today. They're doing interviews over the next couple of days. I put your name down for an interview on Wednesday. I vouched for you, so they were willing to include you without your resume. Just bring it with you when you come."

Amy let out a long breath. *Home.* Suddenly she knew it was where she wanted—needed—to be right then. She didn't care what it took, she would make it to that interview. "I will make sure I'm there."

"Excellent! I can't wait to see you!"

"Me either. We need to have a serious talk, but right now I need to get off the phone and make arrangements to fly tomorrow. It's probably going to cost me a fortune, but I need that job."

"I can't guarantee you'll get hired, but I know for sure you won't be if you're not here. So get your butt home."

Amy knew that it would be okay for her to leave now that Cami and Josh were there to help Jessa and Lance. And maybe focusing on her future was what she needed right now. That and the sanctuary of her home.

She quickly got dressed, once again forgoing the makeup, and then headed downstairs. Cami, Josh and Lance were in the kitchen when they got there and looked at her expectantly as she rushed into the room.

"What's up?" Josh asked.

"Sammi just called. She said she's arranged an interview

for me at her school for a substitute teaching position. The interviews are on Wednesday. Is there any way I could get a flight there tomorrow, do you think?" She glanced at Cami and then Lance. "I figured that with Cami and Josh here, you could spare me to do this interview."

"Well, you're in luck. I have to drive to Fargo tomorrow to meet with a supplier and can take you to the airport there if you're okay with not flying out of Minneapolis." When Amy nodded, Lance said, "Let me go talk to Jessa to see about flights and if they'll work with when I have to be there." He stood up and walked toward the door then turned back around. "Roundtrip?"

Amy paused. "I guess." She looked at Cami and Josh. She really did want to spend more time with them. "Yes. Roundtrip."

Lance nodded and disappeared.

As she sank down in the chair next to Josh, Cami asked, "How are you doing this morning?"

"Trying to move forward. This interview is an answer to prayer. I need a job."

"It's just an interview though, right?" Josh asked. "Not a job offer."

"No, not a job offer, but I'm trying to think positive. I need something. I can't just stay here indefinitely." She swallowed. "Especially now."

Cami nodded. "I understand."

Any further conversation was stopped by the arrival of Julia, Isabella, and Cami and Josh's two kids. Cami and Amy stood up and began to prepare breakfast. They were just getting ready to serve it when Charlotte and Henry walked in the back door.

"What a beautiful morning for a walk," Charlotte exclaimed.

"Did you go down by the lake?" Josh asked. "On still mornings like today the water is like glass."

"We actually walked on the path through the woods past the greenhouse," Henry said as he sat down at the table next to his granddaughter.

Lance appeared in the door of the kitchen. "Amy, what day did you want to come back?"

She stood for a minute trying to think. With Josh and Cami's concert on Sunday, she wanted to be back before then. "Would someone be able to pick me up on Friday?"

"Yep, we can arrange that," Josh assured her.

"Okay then, Friday."

Again Lance disappeared.

"You're leaving?" Charlotte asked as she placed slices of apple on a plate.

Amy glanced at the older woman, wondering what she thought about everything that had transpired the previous evening. "Just for a couple of days. I have a job interview on Wednesday for a substitute teaching position."

"You don't live here?"

Amy shook her head. "No, I live in Dallas with my folks. I'm just here to help Jessa and Lance while Jessa is on bed - rest."

"You're a teacher?"

"Yes. I teach first grade. Unfortunately, the school I've taught at the last couple of years burned down the other week. That put me out of a job, so I'm on the hunt for a new one."

"Maybe you should consider staying here in Collingsworth. From what I hear, Isabella would be delighted if you did."

Amy let her gaze go to the little girl sitting beside Henry. "Yes, I know she would. Unfortunately, right now my life is in Dallas."

"Is it? How about your heart?"

Tears pricked at Amy's eyes at the question. She looked down at the platter of pancakes in front of her. She felt a touch on her arm and saw Charlotte's hand resting there. Wrinkled with age spots, but oh so gentle in its touch.

Charlotte's hand slid down to cover Amy's, and she said, "I would very much like to spend a few minutes talking with you."

Amy glanced over at the woman and saw a soft smile on her face. "Okay." The word came out as barely a whisper but when Charlotte moved her hand, Amy knew she'd heard.

She picked up the platter and moved around the counter to set it on the table. In Lance's absence, Josh prayed for the food. With all the chatter from the children, Amy found it easy to avoid conversation. She was trying hard not to think about what had happened the night before. She needed to get through the next few days without crying and, if possible, thinking about Will.

Lance arrived halfway through breakfast to inform her that the ticket was booked, and everything was a go for her to fly out of Fargo the next afternoon.

"I didn't mean for you to pay for the ticket," Amy protested. "I will pay you back."

Lance laughed. "You'll do no such thing. Consider it a bonus."

Amy got up and gave her cousin a hug. "You spoil me."

She felt a rush of affection as he tweaked her nose and said, "I don't have a sister of my own, so you'll have to do."

Once breakfast was done and cleaned up, Amy texted her flight plans to Sammi, who had offered to pick her up from the airport. She figured she'd surprise her parents with her arrival. It would also give her some time with Sammi to spill everything.

"Come walk with me?"

Amy glanced up from her phone to see Charlotte standing there. "Walk?"

"Yes. Just around that lovely big back yard."

☙ Chapter Twenty ❧

NOT wanting to disappoint Charlotte after agreeing to talk with her, Amy slid her phone into her pocket and followed her out the back door. As they began to walk, Charlotte grasped Amy's elbow.

"I loved my darling Delia," Charlotte said without preamble. "She was God's miracle gift to us when we couldn't have children of our own."

Not sure what to say, Amy nodded. She had heard that much already.

"When she and Will wanted to get married, Henry and I were not sure it was the best idea. Don't get me wrong, we loved Will, but they seemed so young. Especially Delia." Charlotte had set a slow pace as they walked the perimeter of the yard. "But we could see their determination, so we agreed."

Amy's resolution to keep her focus on her future was being sorely tried by Charlotte's words.

"I am not unaware that Delia was a willful young woman. Will was so good to her, but she demanded a lot from him. I think his love for her blinded him to many of her shortcomings. As it should be, I suppose. Goodness knows Henry overlooks many of mine because of our love." Charlotte chuckled. "But I was concerned that if she didn't mature and outgrow her selfishness, there would be trouble for them. Will would never share how bad it got for them during those months of her pregnancy, but I knew. She called me every day to complain, and I know that if she did that with me, she must have been doing it with Will, too. We were responsible for that. We spoiled her, giving her everything we could because we loved her so much. Will did much the same.

"I would like to believe that had she lived, she would have realized she needed to set aside her own wants for the needs of her child and husband."

"Why are you telling me this?" Amy asked.

Charlotte stopped walking, bringing Amy to a halt as well. "I see how Will looks at you. I see how you look at him. Maybe it's not full-blown love yet, but there is something there between you. And I see your giving spirit. What you did for Bella was incredible. Already there is love flowing out of your heart in their direction. And when I saw Will the other day when we arrived, I praised God. For the first time in a long time, he looked happy. Happy, relaxed and content. He was showing affection to Bella like I'd never seen before. It was everything Henry and I had been praying for him. We didn't know why, but we were grateful."

"I know Jessa spoke with him about his relationship with Isabella," Amy told her.

"I'm sure she did, but probably only after she saw the beginning of change in him." Charlotte gave her a gentle smile. "You see, I was watching him when you walked into the room for the first time after we arrived. He lit up with joy like I hadn't seen on his face in far too long. You did that for him."

Amy bent her head, not able to stand the intensity of Charlotte's bright blue gaze.

"So what went wrong? What happened yesterday to cause him to walk away looking as if his world had just ended?"

"Let's sit there," Amy gestured to the steps of the chapel not far from where they stood.

Once they were seated, at the older woman's bidding, Amy told her everything. She rubbed the tears from her cheeks as she recounted the events of the previous day.

Charlotte leaned toward her. "I haven't experienced what you have, so I have no advice on how to help you deal with these memories that are tormenting you. I do know from personal experience, however, that not everything that is God's will for us comes easily. But where there are two people determined to work through the difficult times, there is joy." Charlotte reached out and gripped her hand again. "Please give him a chance. I see in you the opportunity for him to experience that giving love that he never really truly had with Delia. I know that she loved him in her way, but the man he is now deserves so much more."

"I don't know. What if I can't get past it? Then it just prolongs the hurt."

"Or maybe you will get past it and experience the love you have always wanted with Will."

"It's a risk. And the longer I let it go on, the greater the hurt will be if it doesn't work out."

"Anything worth having is worth taking the risk. Pray about it. While you're gone, pray about it." When the woman's voice cracked, Amy looked over to see tears in her eyes. "Will is the son we never had. He has treated us just like his parents ever since marrying Delia, and that didn't change with her death. We want to see him happy again, and both Henry and I believe that God brought you into his life for a reason. Pray about it?"

Amy nodded. "I will."

She didn't add that she'd already been praying about it for weeks, and nothing had changed, but it was an easy promise to make, and it made Charlotte happy.

As they continued their walk around the yard, Charlotte asked her more questions about Dallas and the job she'd had there. She didn't mention Will again, but she didn't have to. Amy's thoughts were filled with him once more.

Back at the house, Charlotte went in search of Henry, and Amy went upstairs to her room. She spent part of the morning phoning the people she had hired to help with Isabella's party to thank them. The photographer informed her that she was already working on the pictures and would have them ready in a couple of days. Amy asked her to drop the disc off at Will's office in town. She knew that Isabella would be anxious to see them and wouldn't want to wait until Amy was back.

After lunch, she went back to her room to pack a few things for her trip. She spent some time out in the yard with the kids while Cami and Josh went into town to the church to connect with the pastor about their concert.

As she sat watching the kids play, Amy wondered if Will was going to come to the manor that evening for dinner. No one had said anything about him, and he hadn't shown up yet. Around four -thirty, Henry came to watch the kids while she went inside to help Charlotte get supper ready.

Josh and Cami came home, and Lance arrived shortly after that. When it was time to eat, Will was still absent, and Amy wasn't sure if she was disappointed or relieved. After the meal was done, it became apparent that Isabella was spending the night again.

After everyone else had gone to their rooms later that evening, Amy shut off the lights in her room and sat on the window seat, staring at the nearly full moon that hung low in the sky. She thought over Charlotte's words from earlier that day. She had made it seem so easy. *Just pray about it.* Well, she *had* been praying about it, and it hadn't made a lick of difference. All along she'd said that God would have to make it blatantly clear if He wanted them together. Unfortunately, she'd allowed herself to get involved before seeing that sign, and now she'd hurt Will.

Finally accepting that no answers were going to come as she sat there, Amy crawled into bed, half excited about the next day, half dreading it.

Will knew he couldn't avoid the manor—and Amy—forever. It had been two days. Surely his emotions were well enough in hand that he could see her without the hurt overwhelming him. He'd prayed and thought a lot over the past couple of days but to no avail. He had no answers. He had no way to help Amy get past her fears and hurt. This was something she needed to work through herself before they could go any further.

Unfortunately, he had the feeling that she'd been trying already with no success. Which left them exactly where they were, unable to cross the chasm of the past that stretched between them.

Shoring up his defenses, Will drove out to the manor. Lance had called on his way back from his meeting in Fargo to ask him to come for supper, but he hadn't committed until right before he'd left the office.

His heart lightened when Isabella darted to greet him as soon as he walked into the manor.

"Daddy!" She flung herself into his arms.

He caught her and lifted her for a tight hug and a kiss. "How are you, sweetheart?"

"I've missed you." Her words were a balm for his hurting heart.

"I've missed you, too, but have you been having fun here?"

Her head bobbed enthusiastically. "But I was kinda sad today when Amy left."

Will felt his heart drop. "Amy left?"

Isabella nodded then squirmed, so he set her back down.

Cami was standing next to the table, so he shot her a questioning look. "She's gone?"

"Yes, Lance took her to Fargo today to fly home to Dallas."

A sick feeling flooded Will. In that instant he realized that in spite of all evidence to the contrary, there had been a part of him that had been so sure they'd work things out. But they couldn't do that if she wasn't here.

❧ Chapter Twenty-One ❧

I thought she was here for the summer. The summer isn't over yet."

"She'll be back," Cami told him. "Her friend arranged an interview for her, so she flew home for that."

Though it was great to hear she was coming back, the fact that she was looking for a job in Dallas didn't make the sick feeling go away. She seemed to be moving on from whatever short-lived relationship they'd had. If only he could do the same.

He swallowed hard, hoping it wasn't obvious how the news upset him. "I know she was worried about getting a job." He paused. "I hope the interview goes well for her."

Cami tilted her head to the side then reached out and rested her hand on his cheek. "No, you don't, and neither do I, but I guess we'll just have to wait to see what unfolds over the next few days."

Easier said than done, Will thought.

❧❧

After Sammi had picked her up at the airport, they had gone back to her folks' place. As expected, her mother and father had been thrilled with her surprise visit. And even happier about the reason for the trip. Amy had hoped she'd be able to chat with Sammi, but her friend had promised to call later and then they'd arranged to meet at Sammi's apartment after the interview the next day.

Though she was happy to see her parents, she found it hard to keep up her end of the conversation. Her thoughts were split between Will and the interview the next day. She knew there was no sense in talking with them—particularly her mother—about Will. Her mom would no doubt say it was for the best since Will lived so far away. That was not really what Amy wanted to hear right then.

After her parents retired for the night, Amy crawled into bed and sent Cami a few texts. Though Cami had commented in her reply that Isabella missed her, there had been no mention of Will. Amy supposed it wasn't her right to know anything about how he was doing.

"So tell me what's going on?" Sammi said when Amy answered her call

That was all Amy needed to spill everything out. It wasn't easy since the emotion of it all was still so fresh. Thankfully, Sammi patiently waited through her bouts of crying for her to finish.

"You thought something like this might happen," Sammi commented. "I'm sorry that's is the way it's worked out."

Amy sighed. "I suppose your advice is the same as everyone else's."

"What's that? To pray?"

"Yes. No one seems to understand that I *have* been praying about it."

"What exactly have you been praying for?" Sammi asked.

"That God would help me deal with the memories. That they wouldn't hurt so much when they come."

"And that's all you've done? Pray?"

"Well, it's been pretty hard to do anything else when I'm trying to keep from falling apart when a memory hits."

"All I'm saying that sometimes—often—God requires more than just us praying for His help." "

"What more can I do? I don't know how else to get this stuff out of my head."

"I don't know either. I'm sorry," Sammi said, her voice gentle. "I am *so* sorry you're hurting like this."

After their conversation had ended, Amy curled up in her bed. It had felt good to be home. To talk with her parents. To chat with Sammi. To lie down in her bed. But now as she lay in the darkness, her thoughts went to those in Collingsworth.

She wondered if Isabella had had a good day. The little girl hadn't been happy to hear she was leaving, even when Amy had assured her that she would be back. What was going to happen when she had to leave for good? How would Isabella handle that? Oh, she'd go back to visit, most likely. Or maybe she wouldn't. Could she handle seeing Will move on with someone else? She'd watched him find love with someone once already, she wasn't sure she could survive that again.

A band tightened around her heart, and she found it hard to breathe. The thought of him loving some unknown woman in the future hurt more than the memory of his love for Delia. The realization caught her by surprise. Amy struggled to sit up and catch her breath.

Head bent as she sat in the darkness, she tried to imagine her future without Will, but all she got was pain at the thought. Would the pain over the future lessen as time went on? Or would she be left with never-ending regret and wondering what if? Yet maybe with time, she could get past the pain of Will's past.

She stood up and began to pace her room, able to avoid bumping into furniture because of her familiarity with the placement of everything. All she knew was that if it weren't for this struggle over Will's past with Delia, she'd gladly move to Collingsworth to be with him and Isabella. Even with its frigid winters.

As she paced, the words of both Cami and Charlotte came to mind. Not everything in God's will would necessarily come easily. She realized now that she had just assumed if it was God's will for her and Will to be together, He'd make it easy for that to happen. That His clear sign to her would involve her not dealing with this emotional upheaval over every memory that cropped up. Maybe God expected her to take that step of faith, believing that she and Will could work through her struggles together.

Amy returned to her bed and laid down. She closed her eyes and this time when she prayed, it was a different prayer than the others.

Please give me the strength, God, to take this step of faith. I don't know if Will will even give me a chance now, but if he does, I'm going to trust that You will work in both of us and that this relationship will bring You honor and glory. And if it's not meant to be for Will and me, I will trust You to bring healing from this for both of us.

Amy had always figured that it would take knowing with certainty that things would work out between her and Will to bring her peace. Surprisingly enough, it was this prayer of faith that brought her the first measure of peace she'd had since all of this had started.

She would go to the interview the next day, but something told her she wouldn't be taking this job. Something deep inside told her she needed to turn it down if they offered it to her. It would be yet another step of faith. She was going to go back to Collingsworth trusting that she and Will would be able to get through this.

If he'd give her another chance even after she hadn't given him one.

The next few days were torture for Will. Cami had told him that she'd gone to her interview but that there had been no official job offer yet. From what Cami said, it sounded like it was just a matter of time though. It was disheartening, but not surprising.

Needing some direction in his life since everything had fallen apart with Amy, Will decided to tackle the house that sat empty. He approached Lance to see if he'd have room in the next few months to finish up the interior so he could put it on the market. There was no doubt he would take a loss on it, but at this point he just needed it gone.

Even if Amy did, by some miracle, decide to give them another chance, knowing what he did about how she felt regarding his past with Delia, he couldn't ask her to live in a house that he'd initially started building for his family with her. He didn't think it would make any difference to her that Delia had told him she didn't want to live out in the forest and that, after their decision to move, they never would have lived there as a family.

"You're sure you want to do this?" Lance asked him as they sat in his office Friday morning. "I know you had big dreams for that place."

Will shrugged. "Seems my plans don't count for much these days."

"You do need to get out of that apartment though."

"Yes, I agree, but I think I'll just try to find a house here in town with enough yard for Isabella. The two of us don't need that much room."

"It might not always be just the two of you."

"I don't think I'm destined to find lasting love," Will said without emotion. It was the conclusion he'd come to over the past couple of days. "Right now I just need to focus on my daughter and doing what I can to make up for the way things have been between us."

Lance looked like he was going to say something but

instead just nodded. "How about we go by there tonight? We can figure out what you want done and then see when we can fit it onto the calendar."

"Thanks." Will stood.

"Listen, Will." Lance also stood up and came come around his desk. He clapped his hand on Will's shoulder. "Do you want to talk about what happened with you and Amy?"

Will could see the concern in his brother-in-law's face, but he just didn't have it in him to spill his guts. "Not really. But thanks for offering to listen."

"Well, if you need a listening ear, I'm here for you. We love you both, and it's difficult to see you hurting."

Will nodded, not trusting himself to speak. Returning to his office, he shut the door before going to sit behind his desk. He had hoped that getting the ball rolling on the house would give him a sense of purpose, but if anything, it had just been a reminder of what he'd lost. First Delia and now Amy. The home he'd hoped to provide for his family was a joke. Maybe just getting it done and sold would bring about the peace he wanted.

In the meantime, he'd try to keep busy with the things in his life that he could count on. His job and his daughter.

❧

"Is Will coming over tonight?" Amy asked Cami when she arrived back at the manor shortly after five Friday afternoon. Isabella had been there to warmly and enthusiastically welcome her home, but there'd been no sign of Will.

"I don't know." Cami glanced to where Laurel and Violet stood. "You guys know?"

"I think Matt said he was going to meet Lance at the house."

"Is he going to finish it?" Violet asked.

"Matt said Will talked to Lance this morning about finishing it, but not to live in. He's planning to sell it."

"A house?" Amy asked, looking back and forth between them. "What house?"

"Will has a house that he was building when Delia died. Since then it's been unfinished and empty. I guess he figured now was a good time to finish it up and get rid of it."

A sudden rush of panic engulfed Amy. She had returned with the intention of seeing if Will would give her a second chance, but it sounded like he was moving forward, cutting off any idea of having a family in that house he'd built.

She picked up her phone then looked at the women standing there. "Will you guys pray for me? I need to talk to Will."

"Are you going to try and work things out?" Cami asked, a hopeful expression on her face.

"Yes. If I haven't burned that bridge already."

The three sisters exchanged looks that made Amy uneasy.

"We'll definitely pray for you," Laurel assured her. "Just cut him a little slack. He's reverted back to the old Will in some ways. It might take some effort to get through to him."

Amy nodded. "I understand." She lifted her phone. "I'm going to phone Lance and see if he's with Will."

"I'd say good luck," Violet said, "but I don't believe in luck. I will say that I hope you can work this out with him."

"Thank you."

⁓∾⁓

Will stood in the center of the big open room. Even after all these years he could still picture in his mind what he'd planned for the space. The memory didn't bring him any of the joy it used to.

"Sorry about that," Lance said as he walked in. "Got hung up on a phone call at the office."

Will swung around. "No problem."

Before he could say anything more, Lance's phone rang again. He plucked it from his belt and stared at the display. Frowning, he said, "I've got to take this."

Will watched as Lance walked back out of the house. From his vantage point, he could see through the large glass windows at the front of the house. Lance had walked out onto the sidewalk and stood with the phone pressed to his ear, one hand on his hip. As he talked, he glanced toward the house. After he had lowered the phone to his belt, Lance stood for a moment, his fingers pressed to his forehead.

"Everything okay?" Will asked when Lance walked back into the house.

"Yeah, I hope so." Standing with his hands on his hips, Lance surveyed the room. "Are you just going to stick with the original plans you had drawn up for the place?"

"I think that would be easiest. I don't really want to spend any more time on this than I have to."

Lance stared at him for a moment. "Are you sure about selling it?"

"Yes," Will said without hesitation.

They walked around for the next ten minutes discussing materials and timeframes. After finishing up on the main floor, Will led the way upstairs. While up there, he heard the sound of an engine.

"Were you expecting someone?" he asked Lance as he walked to one of the front windows to look out at the driveway.

"Maybe we should go down and check it out," Lance suggested.

Without waiting for him to respond, Lance headed for the stairs and began to descend. Abandoning the window, Will strode to the stairs and followed him.

By the time he reached the last step, Lance was standing with his back to him talking to someone. Will started in his direction, but froze as Lance leaned forward to hug the person then stepped around them and left the house.

Amy.

Wearing a flowing sundress in a soft pink and her hair down in long curls, she had never looked more beautiful. She fidgeted with her purse strap as she watched him.

For a moment, Will wondered if this was another of the dreams he'd been having ever since she left. The ones where she came back to him, and they were able to live happily ever after.

"Hi, Will," she said, her voice soft.

Will stood with his hands on his hips, squashing down any flicker of hope. Nothing short of a miracle could have changed things for her. "What are you doing here?"

∼ Chapter Twenty-Two ∾

AMY didn't flinch at his words or his tone. "I needed to talk to you."

"I thought we said everything there was to say at the lake." If she'd come to get closure from him, he wasn't going to make it easy. She was just going to have to find that on her own.

She looked around the room. "I didn't know you had this place. It looks so beautiful from the outside."

"It won't be mine for much longer."

"Why?" Her gaze was as direct as her question.

"Well, since it's going to be just me and Isabella, this place is far too big." He glanced around. "I had foolishly assumed I'd have a larger family one day. Since that's not happening, I'm finishing and selling it. I'll find a place in town for me and Isabella that is more suited to our needs than this."

Amy stared at him, her eyes wide. Even though they stood several feet apart, he saw a single tear slip down her cheek.

Afraid it would be his undoing, Will cleared his throat and asked once again, "Why are you here?"

No longer fidgeting with her purse strap but gripping it with both hands, Amy said, "I asked the school in Dallas to not consider me for the job."

That hadn't been what he'd expected her to say. "Why?"

"A step of faith."

"A step of faith?"

"Several people challenged my idea of how things should have worked out for us."

Will lifted an eyebrow. "What does that mean exactly? You made it pretty clear to me that it wasn't going to work."

Amy nodded. "I told everyone who asked that yes, I had prayed about things with you. I had prayed that God would take away the memories or lessen their impact on me. I prayed that I wouldn't remember the pain from that time eight years ago. When I realized I still had feelings for you, I told God He was going to have to make it blatantly clear that we were supposed to be together before I'd consider risking my heart again. In my mind, that meant that everything would work out smoothly."

Will still wouldn't allow himself to find any hope in her words. He had a hard time believing that so much had changed in the past five days that she was able to put his— their—past behind her. And he still didn't trust himself to say anything, so he remained quiet, waiting to see where this was going.

Amy paused as if expecting him to say something. Her brows drew together a bit when he didn't respond. She caught her lower lip between her teeth for a moment then continued. "I wanted Him to take it all away, but Cami and Charlotte both told me that sometimes the things God wills for us don't come easily. I wanted things to be easy for us, but over the past few days I've realized that maybe that isn't God's will for us."

"So you're not here to tell me that you've gotten over your issues with Delia and the hurt from your past?"

Amy shook her head. "No, it's all still there."

"Then I don't understand. What more do we have to say to each other?"

Slowly Amy walked toward him, stopping when she was within arm's reach. She looked up at him, her green eyes luminous with emotion. "Lots, I hope. I'm here to ask you to help me."

"Help you? There's nothing I can say to change what's happened in my past. I can't will what I had with Delia out of your mind. I thought we settled that already."

"I know you can't do that. But over these past few days I got a glimpse—a really big one—of what life would be like without you and Isabella. I didn't like it very much. In fact, the pain of not having you in my life hurt far worse than the pain I've endured because of the memories I have of you and Delia."

Will felt his throat tighten and for the first time allowed hope to flicker in his heart.

"What I need from you..." Amy paused and took a quick breath. "What I need from you is understanding. I know that we're still in the early stages of this relationship, and that your feelings for me aren't what mine are for you yet, but I'm hoping that by understanding what I struggle with, you might be willing to help me."

"How can I do that?"

"Just by accepting that I will have moments when these memories will take me off-guard. Maybe I'll get emotional. Maybe I'll get angry. But I'm committed to working through them. Getting to the other side of them without messing things up between us."

"You want another chance? Just to see if things work out or not?"

Her face paled a little at his words, and she blinked

rapidly. "I love you, Will."

The words, though softly spoken, hit him with the force of a sledgehammer.

"I know what I want." This chance will be for you. If you decide it's not working for you, you can walk away. I wouldn't expect you to stay with me if that made you unhappy."

Now Will wanted to speak, but the words wouldn't come past his tight throat.

"With God's help, I'm going to learn to accept these memories instead of wishing them away. I'm willing to take whatever part of your heart and your love you're willing to give me, because I've realized that part is better than nothing at all. You make me feel things that no other man has. Please give me a chance to prove that I can do this. That I can love you and Isabella the way you deserve."

"Oh, Amy." Her name came out as a ragged whisper as he reached for her. He didn't kiss her, he just pulled her tight against him, tucking her head beneath his chin, over his pounding heart and held on. He pressed his cheek against the soft silkiness of her hair and closed his eyes. If this was a dream, he never wanted to wake up.

He felt her arms wrap around his waist, and they stood like that for several minutes. When the tightness in his chest and throat eased enough for him to speak, Will loosened his hold so he could look at her. He took her face in his hands.

"You don't get part of anything, sweetheart. Not my heart, nor my love. You get it all." Will used his thumbs to wipe away the tears that spilled from her eyes. "I know you don't get it, and I can't explain it very well. I *remember* the love I had for Delia, and I always will, but I *feel* the love I have for you. And yes, I do love you. My time with Delia is kind of like a dried rose—still beautiful but in a different way. I can remember how it was when it was alive, but I don't experience it in the same way I did then. This between us now is as vibrant and alive as what I had with Delia years ago, but this is now. It doesn't replace what I had back then because this is beautiful and wonderful in its own right. I choose you. On this day and every day to come, I choose you."

A sob escaped Amy's lips, and more tears flowed. This time it was she who had no words.

He bent down and pressed a kiss to her lips. "And I will do all I can to love you the way you deserve to be loved."

Amy's hands came up then to slide behind his neck. She rose up on her tiptoes as she drew his head to hers. Their lips met again in gentleness. Will found himself awash in emotion as he held her in his arms again. His perfect fit.

When the kiss ended, she looked up at him, her gaze still bright with tears. "So you'll be understanding when I still struggle."

"Yes," Will said without hesitation. "Here's what we're going to do. When one of those memories comes along and sucker punches you, I want you to reach for my hand and look into my eyes. And I'm going to remind you that I have chosen you. That I love you. And if we're not together when it happens, I want you to phone me so I can still remind you of that. Deal?"

Amy nodded.

"And in time, I hope that you will get to the point where when one of the memories comes along, you'll be able to say to yourself *he chose me. He loves me.* And no longer need me to reassure you because you'll know in your heart that it's true."

Amy smiled at him then. "Can I ask one more thing from you?"

"Anything."

"Please don't sell this house. I want to make it our home. I want this to be where our love grows and blossoms. I want to have that large family with you."

Will tilted his head as he looked down at her. "Are you

proposing to me, Miss Amelia?"

Her eyes widened briefly. "I guess it kind of sounds like I was, but no, that's your job. I trust you'll know when it is the perfect time to pop the question since we're still kind of new at this."

"But do I have to ask the question if I already know the answer?"

"Oh, you most certainly do," Amy said with a grin. "Or you'll definitely be wearing green tights at the next birthday party I plan."

Will laughed but then sobered as he looked down at her, his heart swelling with the love he felt for this beautiful woman. "You will get everything you ask for. We'll make this house our home. You'll get the proposal you want. And...if you're really good...I might let you drive my car."

"Now I know you really do love me." Amy was smiling when she pressed her lips to his again, and Will knew that his heart had finally found the home it had longed for all these years.

❧ The End ☙

OTHER TITLES AVAILABLE BY

Kimberly Rae Jordan
(Christian Romances)

Marrying Kate

Faith, Hope & Love

Waiting for Rachel (*Those Karlsson Boys: 1*)
Worth the Wait (*Those Karlsson Boys: 2*)
The Waiting Heart (*Those Karlsson Boys: 3*)

Home Is Where the Heart Is (*Home to Collingsworth: 1*)
Home Away From Home (*Home to Collingsworth: 2*)
Love Makes a House a Home (*Home to Collingsworth: 3*)
The Long Road Home (*Home to Collingsworth: 4*)
Her Heart, His Home (*Home to Collingsworth: 5*)
Coming Home (*Home to Collingsworth: 6*)

A Little Bit of Love:
A Collection of Christian Romance Short Stories

For more details on the availability of these titles,
please go to

www.KimberlyRaeJordan.com

Contact

Please visit Kimberly Rae Jordan on the web!
Website: www.kimberlyraejordan.com
Facebook: www.facebook.com/AuthorKimberlyRaeJordan
Twitter: twitter.com/Kimberly Jordan

Made in the USA
Middletown, DE
04 March 2016